THE CURSE OF SHIPWRECK BOTTOM

Book Three

THE CURSE OF SHIPWRECK BOTTOM

The Misadventures Of Inspector Moustachio

by Wayne Madsen

illustrated by Lisa Falzon

PUBLISHED BY

Community PRESS

Published By

COMMUNITY PRESS

239 Windbrooke Lane

Virginia Beach, VA 23462

© 2008 by Wayne Madsen

Illustrations ©2008 Lisa Falzon

Library Of Congress Control Number: 2008934577

ISBN 9780979757228

Printed In The United States Of America

12 11 10 09 08   10 9 8 7 6 5 4 3 2 1

2008 First Edition

Visit our website at www.communitypresshome.com

The universe is filled with endless possibilities just waiting to be discovered!

TABLE OF CONTENTS

How The Misadventures Began...

On Jake Moustachio's eleventh birthday his grandmother gave him a very special, magical magnifying glass that had once belonged to his beloved grandfather, the great Inspector Buck Moustachio. Being a would-be detective himself, Jake, accompanied by his eight-year-old sister, Alexa (a.k.a. Inspector Girl), immediately took the magnifying glass and combed their house for clues in an attempt to solve their first mystery: the whereabouts of their missing cat, Rex. When the two sleuths finally ended their search in the Moustachio's attic, they found their pesky pet and a whole lot more than they bargained for!

To their amazement, they were unexpectedly contacted through the magnifying glass by Delbert, The Keeper of Time, and the children and their cat soon realized that their grandpa's seemingly ordinary magnifying glass was the portal to worlds of fantastic misadventures and mysteries to be solved.

Delbert, it seemed, was in desperate need of their help to solve a perplexing case. A mystical Egyptian stone that controls all time had been stolen!

With a little help from their new mentor, Jake and Alexa were able to figure out how to travel through the magnifying glass and were quickly transported to the Museum of Time, a strange and spooky castle once owned by the famous archaeologist Lord Grimthorpe.

To find out who snatched the Egyptian artifact, Jake, Alexa, and their crazy cat, Rex, were able to use their keen detective skills to gather clues, while encountering a collection of the most dangerous suspects and curious talking animals.

After successfully solving the case, Jake discovered that he is the descendant of a long line of famous detectives and that he is next in line to control that magnifying glass and all its mystical powers. The one that is purest of heart and of thought who comes to possess a magnifying glass of good will be able to unlock all the mysteries of the universe! And that, Jake had been told, is him!

But the Moustachio children must be very careful because they also learned that there is an evil baron who will stop at nothing to get his maniacal hands on the purest of all magnifying glasses in order to rule the universe.

Jake, Alexa, Rex, and an unforeseen member of the Moustachio family, who had stowed away for the journey, cautiously took a new case to solve, aware that the Baron Von Snodgrass lurked beyond the glass, craving his revenge on their family.

They were drawn into a western world of deception and intrigue when they were called upon by Big Daddy, the biggest cow rancher there was and will ever be, to find a kidnapped cow with an ancient map painted on its hide that revealed the truth to a baffling, historical mystery.

But the Baron Von Snodgrass had set a trap for the young sleuths that led to a wild western showdown, which ended up with Jake coming into possession of a mysterious journal that Snodgrass had stolen from Jake's grandfather. With Grandpa Buck's secret book in hand, the Moustachio children returned home with the mission of decoding the Pig Latin-encrypted book in order to find out the hidden mysteries to the glass, who is sending them on all these misadventures, and, most important all, what fate has in store for them on the other side of Grandpa Moustachio's mystical magnifying glass.

And now, get ready to read the next swashbuckling installment in

The Misadventures of Inspector Moustachio:
THE CURSE OF SHIPWRECK BOTTOM!

CHAPTER ONE
Grandma's Cottage

"Help! Help!" cried out Alexa as she and Rex frantically ran down the beach chasing after her runaway kite with the ever-so-pink ribbons dangling from its tail.

The unexpected stormy sky over her head turned a deep, dark, ominous grey as the wind howled off the surf. The white, salty foam flew from the huge, breaking waves of the ocean as they came crashing down onto the sandy beach.

Jake, with his magnifying glass in hand, was lying all snuggled into the sand dunes off of Grandma Moustachio's deck, trying to unravel the secret code of Grandpa Buck's mysterious, brown, leather book. Jake and Alexa were spending the weekend at Grandma's beach cottage down the shore.

Jake had an annoyed look on his face as he looked up at the spectacle of his furry cat, Rex, scampering shamelessly after his sister's kite. "Rex," he shouted, "grab the string, you fur ball, not the ribbons. You're going to get all tangled up!"

"Jake, come help us!" begged Alexa, running in and out of the surf.

Jake sprang up from the sand and bolted down the dunes to Alexa's side, and they both raced after their crazy cat, who was still chasing after the renegade kite.

"How are you doing decoding Grandpa's journal?" Alexa asked Jake as they made foot prints sprinting in the sand. "Have you figured out any new commands to work the magnifying glass yet?"

"Well, it's definitely written in some kind of Pig Latin," he answered. "And I have figured out a couple of the phrases to work the magnifying glass better! But there is something else encoded in there that I can't quite figure out yet."

"Oooh, that's mysterious!" she exclaimed.

"We'll definitely be ready the next time Baron Von Snodgrass comes out of hiding looking for us. He's never going to get his boney hands on my magnifying glass or on this book as long as I'm around!"

"Well, I hope you're going to be around for a while," Alexa proclaimed with a worrisome tone while slushing in the tide.

"During my battle with Snodgrass at Comanche Canyon," recalled Jake, "I wasn't too sure about that. Snodgrass is very powerful, and he's had years to figure out how to work his own magnifying glass."

"But remember what our friend, Delbert, The Keeper of Time, said," Alexa shouted with complete confidence. "'You're the Great Inspector Moustachio, the one with the purest of heart and thought. It is your destiny to defeat the evil Snodgrass and gain control of his magnifying glass. Once you have that...'"

"I know," uttered Jake. " '...With both magnifying glasses in your possession, the mysteries of the universe will await you!' But for now," he continued as he saw Rex all tangled up into a knotted fuzzy ball, "we need to figure out a way to get that pesky pet untangled from all that kite string and ribbon."

"And we better do that fast!" announced Alexa. "It looks like a terrible storm is about to come blasting in from the ocean."

3

"Yeah," added Jake, "I heard on the news this storm is going to have a name starting with the letter *J*."

"Why do they name tropical storms and hurricanes, anyway?" his sister asked.

"I think it's so meteorologists can track them as they move across the ocean. Remember, there can be more than one storm at a time. So by naming each one, it's less confusing keeping them all straight," he meticulously explained.

"So because this new storm's name starts with the letter *J*, the tenth letter in the alphabet, it means that this is the tenth storm that formed out in the sea this year—right?" Alexa asked.

"Right you are, Inspector Girl!" he declared.

Jake and Alexa darted down the beach, finally reaching Rex. "Well, was it really necessary to jump on the tail and drag the kite down?" scolded Jake with an annoyed wrinkle in his brow.

"*Meow*," snapped Rex, "yes," as he rolled enjoyably around in the sand.

The children proceeded to untangle the matted mess, pulling the kite string ever-so-carefully out from the ribbon tangled up in Rex's rusty, golden, furry paws and tail.

"Hold still, Rexy Cat!" scolded Alexa, tugging and pulling away.

"Jake! Alexa!" shouted Grandma from the top of the dunes. The wind started to blow furiously, kicking up swirls of sand funnels across the tan-speckled, colored beach. Grandma looked very nervously at the tumultuous ocean as she held tightly onto Alexa's guinea pig, Sandy, caressing her trembling, light–brown, short fur gently. Grandma's crazy, salt and pepper-colored hair blew wildly in the wind as her hairpins shot out spontaneously into the sand beneath her toes. "Come quickly, you three! There's a horrible tropical storm coming in from the sea. The news just said it might turn into a hurricane any minute!"

The children quickly scooped up Rex and what was left of Alexa's kite and ran as fast as they could back to Grandma. "Coming!" they shouted against the wind.

Jake grabbed his magnifying glass and the brown, leather book from atop the dune and headed for the house. They all ran for their lives down the cedar deck to the back door of the cottage. The navy-blue shutters banged violently against the crisp, white, linen house from the force of the ocean breeze. Grandma's favorite lilac bush danced back and forth, trying to stay firmly planted in the sand. One by one the petals flew off of the purple, fragrant flowers, shooting straight into the blustery wind.

"Wow!" exclaimed Grandma. "That is quite a storm brewing out there. Someone must be very angry in the sea!" she kidded. "Why, I can't recall ever seeing a storm come across the ocean that fast in all the years your grandpa and I have lived down here."

"And that's been a long time, huh Grandma?" asked Alexa.

"Longer than you can imagine, sweetheart," she replied with a warm smile, remembering the past. "Your grandpa and I met a few miles just down the road, many, many years ago. I was just a young girl. My friends and I used to spend the summers down here working at the Krenville Inn waiting tables. It was so much fun. Grandpa Buck spent his summers working on a fishing boat, so he said. I never was quite sure what he was actually up to. Anyway, one day I was strolling along the boardwalk, taking in the beautiful view of the ocean, and there he was unloading a crate of the most unusual seashells I had ever seen."

"Tell us more, Grandma," begged Alexa with anticipation.

"Well—he handed me, of course, the largest and most beautiful shell of them all," she explained, pointing to it on the mantel of the fireplace. "Oh, how I just love that shell. It holds the sweetest of memories. Your grandpa used to say that 'inside each and every seashell lies a secret, mysterious world of the sea, filled with creatures and sorts, just waiting to be discovered.' "

Grandma then took the seashell off the mantel and raised it up to the children's ears for a listen and said, "See, you can hear the ocean echoing inside the shell."

Jake and Alexa each gave a listen. The ocean waves vibrated and sang from each chamber of the magnificent, pink and white, pearly conch shell.

Jake's eyes lit up with excitement. "Maybe this shell holds the lost city of Atlantis or a trapped sea monster!"

"*Meow!*" bellowed Rex, wanting to find what was inside.

Alexa's nose crinkled as she closed one eye, trying to look deep inside the shell. "I can't see anything!" she exclaimed. "How would all the people, houses, and seahorses fit in there, anyway?"

With a look of exasperation showing on his face, Jake snapped, "Lexy, I was kidding! There are no lost cities or sea monsters in there! It's just a shell! The only thing that ever lived in there was probably a big, old, nasty crab!"

"*Meow!*" added Rex as he stuck his paw into the shell, trying to find a little, crabby snack to eat.

"Well, how do you know there's not a city or monster in

there?" she argued.

"Because there's not!" he replied.

"Says who?"

"Says me!"

"Then how do you explain the ocean sounds every time you listen to a shell?" Alexa asked in an accusatory tone. "Hmmmm—Jake?"

"The ocean sounds come from background noise bouncing off of the configuration of the seashell structure!" he declared. "Everybody knows that! It's not really the ocean you hear in there."

"**Really!**" she protested with strong determination in her voice. "Do you want to bet your magnifying glass on that one? Need I remind you, Inspector, that I was right about strawberry milk coming from pink cows!"

"*MEOW!*" shouted out Rex, reminding Jake that they did, after all, find pink cows on their last misadventure.

"Traitor!" snapped Jake, glaring in disapproval at Rex for taking Alexa's side. "Grandma, help me out here!" begged Jake.

"Oh, no," she said as she put the shell back up onto the mantel. "I know when not to get in the middle of an argument with you two. You each can believe in whatever you want to."

"What do you believe, Grandma?" Alexa asked.

"Well, my darlings, I like to think there are endless possibilities in the universe just waiting for us!" As Grandma's right dimple grew into a suspicious half-grin she made with her orangey-red lips, she gave Jake a wink, fluttering the long, flowing eyelashes of her right eye. Her beautiful, crystal clear, green eyes sparkled as she asked in a mysterious tone, "Wouldn't you agree, Inspector Moustachio?"

As he fiddled with the handle of his grandpa's mystical magnifying glass, which was sticking out of his back pocket, Jake smiled, remembering all the strange places, crazy characters, and cases he solved traveling through it. He remembered Mrs. Smythe, the crazy, poisoning cook from the museum who stole The Bell of Time, and wondered where the evil Baron Von Snodgrass had hidden her. And he would never forget Big Daddy's missing cow with the treasure map painted on its hide at Comanche Canyon and the treasure that awaited them. "Well, I guess you guys are right. Maybe there are endless possibilities in the universe just waiting for us! After all, we've seen stranger things than an undiscovered, mysterious, undersea world living inside a conch shell. Now, haven't we?"

"**You have?**" questioned Grandma, startled, as her thick glasses slipped further down her nose.

The children's faces turned a beet-red color as they tried to figure out what to say to dampen Grandma's suspicions of their mysterious misadventures.

"Oh—he means we've thought of stranger things than that when we are making up stories!" exclaimed Alexa, giving her brother the evil eye. "**Don't you, Jake?**"

"Y–Yeah," he stuttered, "when we're making up—uh—stories!"

"Well, that makes more sense," said Grandma. "You had me worried there for a second! Your grandpa had a wild imagination of his own."

Suddenly, a roar of thunder exploded over the cottage as they all trembled in fear.

"Oh, dear," uttered Grandma. "The storm is really kicking up out there. I don't think we'll be going back outside any time soon." She thought for a minute about what they could do to have fun inside. "Now, let me see...how about a game of cards?"

Alexa started to jump up and down in a frenzy of excitement. She loved playing cards with Grandma Moustachio. Grandma was the state bridge champion seven years in a row. "I'll get the cards. They're in my Inspector Girl backpack," she screamed, dashing down the hallway.

"I'll get the fishy crackers!" Jake exclaimed excitedly as he headed for the kitchen with Rex trailing closely behind. "We can use them to bet with. Besides, you can't play cards on an empty stomach."

"*Meow!*" Rex agreed.

"Don't get the pizza ones, Jake. They give Rex gas," echoed Alexa from the other side of the house.

"Oh, dear!" professed Grandma. "We wouldn't want that." Grandma started to toddle over to her favorite, white, beaded-board cabinet and started searching for some candles to light just in case the storm blew out the electricity. She placed her favorite sea ship with the three blue candles in the center right in the middle of the knotty, pine dining room table and then lit them. The glow from the candles made the room look warm and toasty on such a grey, stormy day. She placed Sandy to her right as she sat down at the head of the table, adjusting the hairpins in her hair just so.

Alexa came bolting into the room with her backpack in hand, rummaging for her favorite Inspector Girl Go Fish cards.

Jake followed with two bags of their favorite, cheddar

fishy crackers, which he spread all over the table, dividing them equally among the players. "Where's Rex?"

"Rexy Cat, where are you?" called out Alexa. "We're about to start the game!"

Rex came happily running into the room with a big bag of pizza fishy crackers dangling from his mouth.

Jake looked down at him with disapproval. "What do you think you're doing, you crazy cat. You know you can't eat those."

"*Meow!*" Rex growled, jumping up to take his place at the table, reluctantly dropping the bag of pizza fishy crackers.

Grandma got a competitive smile across her face as she started to deal the cards out. "Why, sometimes I think that cat actually understands everything we're saying!"

"*Meow!*" he shouted in a Rexy Cat "yes."

CHAPTER TWO
Go Fish

They all broke out laughing themselves silly at Rex as they each viewed their seven cards filled with lobsters, crabs, dolphins, whales, and numerous other creatures of the sea.

Jake started the game as he glared at Alexa like a world-class card shark. "Alexa," he asked, "do you have any dolphins?"

Alexa ever-so-carefully scanned her cards, reluctantly searching for a match for her brother. She had a lobster, a sea turtle, a walrus, two goldfish, and two octopuses, but no dolphin. "**GO FISH!**" she squealed with delight, having not given Jake any matches.

Jake slowly pulled a new card from the top of the deck, which was lying next to the sea ship glowing from the warm candles. He slid the card towards himself face down across the table so no one would see the card. As he raised the card, a smile grew across his face. "**YES!**" he exclaimed.

"Is it a dolphin?" Alexa inquisitively asked.

"I'm not telling," he uttered in satisfaction, having made a match with two sword fishes.

"You have to tell if it's a dolphin."

"Do not!"

"Do too!" cried out Alexa. "Grandma!"

"Oh, alright!" snapped Jake. "It's not a dolphin. Your turn."

"Well, that means you must have another match," Alexa explained as she crinkled her nose in disappointment.

"Maybe I do, and maybe I don't!" he smirked back.

Alexa then turned to Grandma and asked her if she had any octopuses. Grandma's eyes pierced through the thick glasses still dangling from the tip of her nose for any signs of octopuses in her hand.

"Why, yes, I do!" she exclaimed as she handed Alexa the card.

Knowing she now had three octopuses and only needed one more for a full house, Alexa held on to that card for dear life.

Jake could see a small start of a smile out of the right corner of her face. "You have three octopuses, don't ya' Lexy?" he asked.

"Maybe I do, and maybe I don't!" she answered with a very secretive tone in her voice.

"My goodness!" giggled Grandma. "You two are quite the card sharks. You play a mean game of Go Fish!"

Alexa looked up at the painting of the majestic ship that had always hung on the wall next to the dining room table. "Grandma," she asked, "whose ship is that in the painting?"

"Well, sweetie, I actually don't know."

"How come, Grandma?" asked Jake.

"The day your grandpa and I bought this house the painting mysteriously arrived at the front door."

"Who sent it?" Alexa questioned.

"I have no idea. There was an unsigned card attached to it, as I recall." Grandma scooted over to the buffet table and started rummaging through the top draws. "Now, where did I put that? Oh yes, here it is!"

Jake, always enjoying a good mystery, asked, "What does it say?"

Grandma pushed her glasses up from her nose and said, *"Earth's End!"*

Suddenly, a crack of lightning exploded over the house as a rumble of thunder shook everything around them.

"How spooky is that?" Alexa whispered from behind the three octopus cards she was clutching ever-so-tightly.

Jake grabbed his magnifying glass to examine the strange card. "Well, that makes no sense. Earth is a round mass. Wherever you start, you will eventually wind up at the same point. There is no *Earth's End!"*

Another flash of lightning and thunderous roar rattled through the house, blowing out all the lights except for the three glowing candles in the middle of the sea ship on the dining room table.

O.K., that is just too weird, thought Jake. "Every time you read what's on this card, lightning strikes and thunder roars."

"Stop scaring your sister," scolded Grandma. "Just look at poor Rex and Sandy. They're huddled in a ball together with their fur all puffed up, shaking like two entangled leaves. And they don't even like each other."

"Jake, stop!" cried Alexa. **"YOU'RE SCARING ME!"**

"No—really, just listen!" Jake read the card again out loud. *"Earth's End!"*

All of a sudden, a massive ray of lightning flew across the ocean sky, followed by a tumultuous boom of thunder. An eerie wind blasted through the cottage, blowing out the candles on the table, leaving them in complete darkness. Alexa screamed out in fright as Sandy leaped into her lap, quivering in fear. Rex high-tailed it over to Jake, plopping right on top of his head.

"Get off of me, you crazy hair ball!" he yelled, swooshing Rex off his head. Rex then jumped over to Alexa's lap, clinging on to Sandy for dear life.

"I'm scared, Grandma," cried out Alexa. "What are we going to do?"

"It's just the storm, my darling. There is nothing to be afraid of. This is just a coincidence. It has nothing to do with that card your brother just read. **Does it, Jake?**" she asked in a scolding tone.

Jake giggled in the darkness.

"Jake!" Grandma exclaimed. "Tell your sister it was just a coincidence."

Jake giggled again. "O.K., O.K.! It has to be just a coincidence."

"Alright, then," announced Grandma. "I'll go to the kitchen and find some matches, and we'll have those candles lit in no time!"

"Arrrrr—that be a fine thing to do, me lady!" echoed in the darkness.

Rex let out a piercing meow, which was followed by another shrieking scream from Alexa.

"Jake Moustachio, stop scaring your sister with that pirate voice!" warned Grandma firmly. "It's not funny. Why, sometimes you remind me so much of your grandfather with all those practical jokes of yours."

"Sorry, Grandma!" Jake said somewhat insincerely.

Alexa rummaged through her Inspector Girl backpack searching for her favorite, pink flashlight. "Here, Grandma," she said as she turned it on. "Use my Inspector Girl flashlight to see on your way to the kitchen."

A beam of light poured out of the flowery head of the

flashlight as Grandma started to make her way from the dining room table. "Thank you, sweetie," she said as she stumbled through the darkness. "I'll be right back. And Jake, no more scary pirate voices, though it was pretty good. If I didn't know any better, you would think it was a real pirate talking. "

"O.K. Grandma!"

The children and their trembling pets just sat there in the darkness.

"That wasn't very funny, Jake," grumbled Alexa.

"*Meow!*" agreed Rex.

"Blimey, I thought me lady would never leave!" exclaimed a voice.

"Jake, I'm telling Grandma," Alexa protested.

"It wasn't me!"

"What do you mean, it wasn't you?"

"It's coming from the magnifying glass!"

Alexa's eyes flew open wide as she was about to let out another piercing scream. Jake leaped up from his chair, knocking it down as he bolted over to his terrified sister. He quickly spread his hand across her mouth and whispered into her ear not to speak. "Shhh! We don't want to scare Grandma."

Suddenly, another gust of wind blew across the room, lighting the candles in the center of the table once again. They all scanned the room as fog started drifting in from the chimney of the fireplace. The flames from the candles cast a strange glow through the fog, which sent a chill up their spines.

The magnifying glass started bopping and bouncing on the table as the voice mumbled from within.

"Is that Delbert needing our help to solve another mystery?" whispered Alexa.

"I don't think so," answered Jake anxiously.

"Maybe it's someone else needing our help," she said. "After all, we are the world's greatest detectives."

"*MEOW!*" added Rex, followed by a "chut, chut, chut" from Sandy.

"There's only one way to find out!" Jake slowly made his way through the fog to the magnifying glass and picked it up. His hand trembled as he tried to hold it steady. The faint glow from the candles mixed with the foggy air made it impossible for him to clearly see the figure in the glass.

"Ahoy there, laddie!" squelched the raspy voice. "I be needin' to find Inspector Moustachio. He be you?"

Jake squinted his eyes as he tried to rub the fog away from the magnifying glass with his sleeve. He had no luck in the darkness seeing the stranger with the deep, throaty voice. "I'm Inspector Moustachio!" he exclaimed.

With Sandy and Rex clutched in her arms, Alexa jumped out of her chair. The fear that ran through her bones was now filled with excitement at the prospect of a new mysterious case to solve. "And I'm Alexa Moustachio, the one and only Inspector Girl. Oh, and this is our Critter Detective, Rex, and our Junior Pet Detective *in training*, Sandy!"

"*MEOW! MEOW!*" hissed Rex with objection.

"I'm with him!" snapped Jake in objection, too. "Since when did the guinea pig get a detective name? This is a trio, not a foursome!"

"*MEOW!*" hissed Rex in agreement.

"Come on, you guys!" she pleaded. "Sandy was a big help on our last case. If it wasn't for her, Rex would have been cooked alive in that popcorn kettle. And don't forget when the evil Baron Von Snodgrass sent his henchman after us, she did allow us to shoot her over in Grandpa's slingshot to stop him. And she did help me find the treasure map on the back of that pink cow!"

"Yeah, but I remember her forgetting to tell us that Mrs. Smythe escaped from prison with Snodgrass's help. Why, he and that crazy, cake-poisoning cook from The Museum of Time could be just waiting for us on the other side of the magnifying glass for a chance to steal it and snatch back Grandpa Buck's secret book. And I haven't even finished decoding it all yet."

"*Meow*," bellowed Rex as he sniffed around the golden frame of the magnifying glass.

"Please? Please, Jake?" begged Alexa. "Let Sandy come. I promise she'll be better this time. I've been working with her on her short-term memory loss. She's getting much, much better."

Jake looked down at Rex, who was adamantly shaking his head no. "She did save your furry butt!" reminded Jake.

Rex gave up and collapsed on the floor in exasperation, knowing the decision.

"O.K.," Jake grumbled. "Sandy can come this time! But that doesn't mean she's officially part of the team. She's still in training, and she has to prove she's a good pet detective."

"Avaunt, Inspector!" shouted the angry voice. "We be runnin' out of time!"

"Oh, sorry!" exclaimed Jake, almost forgetting about the mysterious stranger. "Who are you anyway?"

"Why, I be Cap'n Snappy," answered the gravelly voice. "I

have a fierce fire in me belly for ye help!"

"Help with what?" questioned Alexa as she stuck her nose tightly up against the magnifying glass, trying to get a good look at the captain without any luck.

"**We be—cursed, lassie!**" he exclaimed as the wind howled once again through the cottage.

"Cursed!" uttered Jake in fear as he tried to hold the magnifying glass still in his shaking hand.

"That's what I be sayin'—cursed," grunted the dry, crackling voice.

"Who's cursed?" questioned Alexa.

"Me crew and me ship, that's who!" groaned Captain Snappy. "Come closer, me buckos—**Closer!**" he urged.

The children moved in really closely so they could hear his tale. Rex and Sandy clung on to them, shaking from the sound of his voice and the roar of the ocean's storm. They could smell the stench of fish coming from his breath through the glass.

"*MEOWWOWOW!*" purred Rex in utter delight.

"Long ago a wicked sea witch by the name of Jezebel be takin' over the waters. Arrrrr! The storms she sends, they be swellin' in the ocean, destroyin' everything in thar path. With each ship and crew she be swallowin' up into the sea, her powers, they be growin' stronger and stronger. She become so powerful she be wantin' to rule King Neptune's very own kingdom, Atlantis. King Neptune would never be lettin' Jezebel have his kingdom or the seas without a fight, and a great battle to control the waters of the world began. They be battlin' for seven days and seven nights on the Seven Seas, till Jezebel be scoopin' up the great island of Atlantis and banishin' it and its people into a mystical seashell she dredged up from the bottom of the ocean. She cast the shell into the depths of the water, never to be seen or heard from again. King Neptune's kingdom was lost forever. He become enraged, callin' upon all the Seven Sea Gods to be givin' him more powers to defeat Jezebel. With the help of the gods, Neptune be gatherin' greater powers so he could banish the evil witch into another mystical conch shell given to him by the gods. Tis be the largest of the conch shells with a pink and white, zebra pattern spread across it. Upon capturing her, he threw that shell into the deepest depths of the sea to be gone forevermore—so we thought!"

"Greedy pirates...the likes no one has ever seen before, been searchin' for the lost shell of Jezebel forever. Some ruthless scoundrels stumbled upon her shell and released her back into the sea. But they be deadly wrong if they be thinkin' she be grateful and reward them."

"Who were they?" Alexa questioned, shivering in the fog.

"And why would they release such an evil force back into the sea?" pondered Jake.

"Those foolish scalawags, their whereabouts, and thar reasonin' to be awakenin' such an evil witch be a mystery— to us all," confessed Snappy. "The ocean swells from her anger. She be cursin' all the ships that sail the Seven Seas and their crews to be swallowed up and dumped where all ships go to die...Shipwreck Bottom."

"What happened to the shell that Jezebel was in?" Jake asked.

"It be told it had vanished to where it come from," Captain Snappy explained.

"Where's that?" questioned Alexa.

"Shiver me timbers, lassie, it be somewhere at—*Earth's End!*"

Suddenly, an explosion of lightning lit up the sky as the cottage shook from the tumultuous roar of thunder.

"That be where the mystical conch shells come from. Anyone who has enough power can capture anythin' or anyone and trap 'em in thar shell. Me be thinkin' that be you, Inspector!"

Shocked, Jake uttered, "**Me...?**"

"Aye! That's what I be sayin' matey—*you!*" exclaimed Captain Snappy in a tirade. "Jezebel, she be not swallowin' up me ship ever! I'll be stoppin' her. That's why I be callin' ye. We need to find the shell and get her back in it before all the ships end up at the bottom of the sea. When the last ship ends up buried at Shipwreck Bottom, Jezebel will be havin' enough power to rule the world, and there will be not a pirate soul left on the high seas to stop her."

"How will she do that?" asked Jake.

"She be sendin' more of her storms out to the sea. Tidal waves, they be huge like no one has seen before. They will be takin' over the land, drownin' everything and everyone in thar path—arrrrr!"

"They'll be nothing left but a world of water," cried out Alexa in fear for her friends and family.

"You be right thar, lassie!" mumbled the captain.

"We have to stop her!" declared Jake. "We can't let the world end this way."

"But how?" Alexa shouted out through the foggy air.

"Arrrrr, me hearty crew and I be swashbucklin' on the high seas, engaging in some sweet trade, when me buccaneers came upon an ancient sea scroll with a riddle to the whereabouts of the first of seven secret sandstones marked by each of the Seven Sea Gods. At the bottom of each stone is a riddle needed to be findin' the next one. Me parrot and I unraveled four of the riddles. And we be findin' four of the seven sandstones. But we be needin' your help to unravel the fifth riddle to find the fifth stone. Once we solve all the riddles, find all seven of the sandstones, and put the pieces of the puzzle together, we'll be knowin' where to find Jezebel's shell. And then you can trap her in it and throw her back into the sea—arrrrr!"

"**Me—?**" Jake questioned again, trembling in fear.

"Arrrr, that's what I be sayin', boy! Are ye hard of hearin' laddie—*you?*" he yelled out.

"**Jake!**" declared Alexa, worrying about her brother taking on such a dangerous case.

"*Meow!*" agreed Rex with Sandy, adding a chut, chut, chut of concern.

Captain Snappy exhaled a long deep breath. The fog blew through the room like a ghost floating through time. "Arrrrr," he grunted. "I be needin' ye all on my side of this here magnifying glass. Me ship, the Krusty Katfish, is docked at Pirate's Point. Hurry. The world, she be in grave danger. Me crew and I be waitin'!"

The children and their sleuthing pets quickly prepared for their new misadventure. Alexa plunged her head deep into her backpack, searching for a misplaced item.

"What are you doing?" questioned Jake in an annoyed voice.

"I lost something!" she exclaimed.

"Lexy, you didn't lose the gift certificates Rupert gave us to stop time, did you? I think we're going to need them."

"No, no," echoed from the inside the backpack. "I have the four that are left. If we get into any trouble, we'll be able to stop time a minute for each certificate."

"Then, what did you lose?"

Alexa feverously searched and searched. "Got it!" she exploded as she held up her find to examine it in the candlelight.

The dim light flicking from the center of the table revealed an uneasy smirk spreading across Jake's face. **"What is—*that*?"**

A burst of excitement exploded from Alexa's cheeks as she explained. "It's a backpack for Sandy. It's her very own teeny-tiny Inspector Girl backpack. Isn't it cute? Grandma helped me make it." She then proceeded to strap it on to Sandy's light brown, short-haired, slightly quivering back.

"Oh, brother," sighed Jake. "You made a backpack for a guinea pig. That's crazy!"

"Of course," declared Alexa. "Well, how do you expect her to carry a crayon and notepad around?"

"Why would she need that?" he asked in exasperation.

"For the clues," she explained. "The clues! While you've been decoding Grandpa's secret book, I've been teaching Sandy shorthand writing. This way, whenever she discovers a clue or something important to the case, she can jot it down. She'll never forget anything again. It's not easy having short-term memory loss, ya know!"

"Alright, but be quick. We need to get going," Jake ordered. He ran over to the huge glass doors looking out to sea and saw the waves getting bigger and bigger as they crashed against the windswept beach. "The storm is getting out of control," he warned. **"We have to go!"**

Alexa quickly fastened the last clip on Sandy's backpack as Rex snatched up the bag of pizza fishy crackers and snuck them into Alexa's Inspector Girl backpack.

Jake tucked Grandpa's secret, brown, leather book safely into his front pocket and grabbed the magnifying glass from the dining room table. "**Moustachios ready!**"

Alexa screamed out, "***Ready,***" placing Sandy safely into her own backpack.

"***Meow!***" hollered Rex, sniffing the musty fish smell emanating from the magnifying glass.

"O.K., Grandma will never know we're gone!" he exclaimed, holding up the magnifying glass like a sword of honor. Suddenly, a small flicker of light glimmered across the cherry wood handle as the words to activate the glass appeared one by one.

Through the magnifying glass you will see, the many misadventures that can be.

Jake proceeded to read the words as he had done before. But this time he stopped. He thought about Grandpa's secret, brown book filled with all the Pig Latin commands to the magnifying glass sitting securely in his pocket. An impish grin spread across his face as he whispered to himself, "***What if?***"

Alexa glared at him with disapproval. "Jake, don't do it!" she warned. "We don't know what will happen."

"***Meow! Meow!***" Rex muttered in objection as his fur puffed up, quivering in anticipation of the doom that was to come.

24

"There's a first time for everything," he yelled. **"Stand Back!"** As he threw the magnifying glass into the foggy air, he blurted out the phrase in Pig Latin.

"Oughthray ethay agnifyingmay assglay ouyay illway eesay, ethay anymay isadventuresmay atthay ancay ebay."

He smiled with pride, knowing only a true detective could activate the magnifying glass, and that, of course, was he! A flash of light exploded from the glass more powerful than the children had ever seen before. An enormous vortex of wind shot in and out of the center of the magnifying glass, blowing cards and fishy crackers everywhere. Lobsters, sea turtles, walruses, goldfish, octopuses, and dolphins danced among the crackers in the air as they swirled around and around the room.

They were used to traveling through the magnifying glass, but with Jake's new command, it looked much more treacherous than ever before.

Alexa crawled under the table, wrapping her arms around the leg. Her long, flowing, strawberry-blonde hair blew wildly about her head as she gripped a tight hold on her backpack. "That doesn't look the same as last time!" she shuddered through the relentless force of the wind.

Rex was clinging for his life on to Jake's leg, trying not to get sucked into the vortex just yet. His feet and tail dangled in mid air. "I think we'll be O.K.!" Jake shouted, holding himself steady on the mantel of the fireplace. "Let's all let go on three."

"I'm too scared, Jake!" Alexa confessed.

"It'll be alright! I'll never let anything happen to you!"

"One, Two...Three!"

And with that said, the crime-stopping, mystery-solving foursome let go as the powers of the magnifying glass sucked them right into the ominous vortex. They shot tumultuously through the gigantic flow of air, endlessly twisting and turning inside the magnifying glass. Their screams echoed through time as they slid faster and faster with every bend and turn. They body-surfed the tidal wave of sparkly stars that flew past their amazed eyes until the magnifying glass violently spit them out one by one to the unknown, mysterious world that awaited them.

CHAPTER THREE
All In Good Time!

Tumbling over each other, they slid across a red and black, checkerboard-square floor, crashing into a mile-high pile of tiny cuckoo clocks that toppled over, burying them all underneath.

"Hey, what's the big idea using a different command to activate that darn thing!" snarled Rex as he popped his head out of the pile. *"We could have been killed. And I'm not even sure how many lives I've got left!"*

"Oh—stop your belly aching, you crazy cat. I only said the phrase in Pig Latin, and I'm sure you have a few more lives left, anyway!" Jake muttered, pushing the clocks off him. Dazed and confused, they all crawled out from under the cuckoo clocks. The sounds of endless **"cuckoos"** echoed through the room as various colored, little, wooden birds came flying out of their clock houses.

"Where are we?" asked Alexa as she rummaged through her backpack looking for Sandy.

"I'm not sure!" Jake replied curiously. The magnifying glass was hovering way up high in the vaulted ceiling. Jake raised his hand up towards the most delightfully-colored stained glass windows. He commanded to his magnifying glass, **"Omecay otay emay!"** It obeyed his order, shrinking back to its original size, flying into the palm of his hand. "I don't see any signs of Captain Snappy or the Krusty Katfish."

"Catfish!" Rex squealed uncontrollably. *"That reminds*

me, I'm starving!" He then dove headfirst into Alexa's backpack, searching for a morsel of food. "*Hey,*" he growled, "*where's the leftover grilled 'kraut and flounder sandwich from lunch I was saving?*" He then popped his fuzzy, golden, red head out from under, looking furiously for Sandy, and cried out, "*Where is she? Let me at her. If pig breath ate any of my grilled 'kraut and flounder sandwich, I'm gonna turn her into bacon bites and feed her to that stupid dog next door!*"

Sandy shot her teeny-tiny head out of the secret side compartment of Alexa's Inspector Girl backpack. She quickly hid the last morsel of food she had been nibbling on in her own tiny backpack. Chuttering away, she declared, "I'm nnn—n—not a pig- pig, you hairy clod. I'm a guinea pig from **Peru!** You can't turn me into bbb—b—bacon bites because, for the last time, I'm not an oinking—**PIG!** Therefore, I'm not made of bacon, you stupid clod. You make absolutely no sense what-so-ever! It's amazing what comes out of that foolish feline mmm—m—mouth of yours! Are you a lion just because you have whiskers and that dumb look on your face?"

Rex bent down and faced Sandy nose to nose. He could smell the sauerkraut on her breath as he sniffed her backpack using his keen, cat-like detective skills. "*You know,*" he whispered, "*if I eat you right now, it will be like having two meals at the same time. I'll get my grilled 'kraut and flounder sandwich and a little guinea pig dessert all in one bite!*"

"You wouldn't want to ddd—d—do that!" she warned.

"*Why not?*" he snarled.

"Because I ate some of your pizza fishy crackers as my

appetizer, and you know how they give you gas—big time!"

Rex's fur puffed up in attack mode. His tail stuck straight up towards the high ceiling as he shook in anger. Alexa quickly scooped up Sandy, protecting her while Jake stood between them.

"Listen, you two annoying animals," he warned. "Stop your squabbling. We have to figure out where we are, find Captain Snappy, and we're running out of *Time!*"

"If *Time* is what you need, my dear Inspector, then I am at you humble service."

"*Delbert!*" they all gasped in disbelief.

"Welcome, everyone!" he greeted. "Welcome back to The Museum of Time!"

Jake had a puzzled look spreading across his face.

"What's the matter, Inspector? You don't look very happy to see me," Delbert questioned as he fumbled with the array of tiny, gold clocks dangling from his short, red suspenders.

"Oh no—Delbert," Jake said, stumbling over his own words, "It's great to see you. It's just—ahhhh…"

"What, Inspector?" Delbert asked with a quirky grin.

"Well…it's just that we were on our way to solve a case," explained Jake, "and ended up here. Did you send for us?"

"Why, no, Inspector, I did not!"

"Then why did we end up here?" asked Alexa as she grabbed a pink scrunchy from her pants pocket and rearranged her hair just so.

"I'm not sure," Jake whispered suspiciously under his breath. "I'm not sure!"

"Sometimes unexpected detours can pop up during life's journeys. Wouldn't you say so, Inspector Moustachio?"

questioned Delbert in a lecturing tone.

Rex sniffed his way around the room, searching for a familiar sight or smell. *"I don't remember this room the last time we were here."*

"MMM—M—Me either!" Sandy exclaimed as she anxiously grabbed her notepad and favorite, gigantic, purple crayon from her backpack, ready to jot down some clues to solve the case.

Rex stopped dead in his tracks and turned around with a devilish grin under his whiskers. He shrank down very low, looking Sandy in the eye, and sneakily said, *"You mean you don't remember Delbert, The Keeper of Time, and searching for the missing bell? You do know you almost destroyed the universe, don't ya?"*

Sandy became all nervous, turning bright red with embarrassment having thought she almost destroyed the universe. **"I DDD—D—DID!"** she blurted out. Flipping through her notepad, shaking frantically, she searched and searched for any mention of her part in destroying the universe. She moaned, "NNN—N—Now, why can't I remember that?"

"Rexy Cat, bad boy! Bad! Bad! Bad!" scolded Alexa. "Stop messing around with Sandy. You know she was never here and had nothing to do with almost destroying the universe."

Alexa scooped up Sandy and calmly stroked her frazzled fur. "Sandy, you were never here. Don't pay any attention to Rex; he is just playing around with you. Aren't you—Rex?"

"You mmm—m—mean I didn't destroy the universe?" Sandy asked, dazed and confused.

"Not yet!" Rex snarled. *"But the day is just getting started!"*

"Knock it off, you pesky cat!" Jake yelled. "No one is destroying the universe. At least I hope **not!**" He then grabbed his magnifying glass from his back pocket and started combing the room, examining all the crazy clocks hanging from the walls. "So, Delbert," he asked, "what room is this anyway?"

"This, my dear Inspector, is the new, grand hall of von Sachsen, named in honor of the owner of the very first known cuckoo clock, Prince Elector August von Sachsen. Isn't it magnificent! I've spent years collecting them all. This museum now has the largest collection of cuckoo clocks in all the worlds...I mmm...mean world," stuttered Delbert, correcting himself.

"I'm getting a little cuckoo myself listening to all those crazy birds cuckooing," snapped Rex, trying to swat a little, orange–beaked, yellow canary with his paw as it kept popping out of the doors of its dark brown, wooden clock chalet house. *"Can't you shut them up?"*

"It's the top of the hour, my good pussycat," Delbert explained, snapping his clock-filled suspenders. "They'll stop eventually."

"What do we do in the meantime?" yelled out Alexa over the annoying and never-ending "**cuckoos.**"

"Why don't we go into the kitchen and have a spot of tea?" suggested Delbert.

"That sounds great! I'm starving!" purred Rex, licking his lips in anticipation. *"Does Mrs. Panosh know how to make a grilled 'kraut and flounder sandwich?"* He then

gave Sandy a deadly leer, hissing, "*I seem to be missing one.*"

"Why, I don't actually know," thought Delbert out loud. "We'll have to ask my dear sister that very same question."

They all looked over at Jake, begging him for his approval. "Can we? Can we?" they squealed hopefully.

Jake scratched his head, pondering their dilemma. "I don't know, you guys. We really have to get to Pirate's Point and find Captain Snappy. We do have a case to solve, you know."

"Oh, Inspector, I do believe you all have time," declared Delbert, fumbling with his favorite gold pocket watch. "After all, I should know. I am The Keeper of Time!"

Not wanting to insult Delbert's hospitality, Jake reluctantly agreed to a short visit to the kitchen for a spot of tea and a snack. They all followed behind Delbert as he led them down a dimly-lit hallway to the kitchen.

"Follow this way, everyone," echoed Delbert's voice in the halls of the museum. "Mrs. Panosh has been anxiously awaiting your arrival."

"I thought you said you didn't send for us," questioned Jake.

"I didn't, Inspector," he replied. "But just because I didn't send for you doesn't mean I didn't know you were coming! Things are always a little strange on this side of the magnifying glass. You, of all people, should know that by now, dear boy!"

"*Ya got that right!*" blurted out Rex, scurrying close behind, licking his whiskers in anticipation of what treats awaited them to eat.

"The animals hanging on the walls talk to each other, don't they, Delbert?" Alexa asked, knowing the answer to her own question.

A big smile of satisfaction grew across Delbert's face, and he started to giggle with the tickling that his moustache gave his nose. "Those animals do like to jibber-jabber all day long, Inspector Girl," he replied. "I'm glad to hear you figured that out! That shows the mark of a truly great detective. Those mounted animals help keep order to the worlds...I mean world."

The kitchen hadn't changed a bit since the children's last visit. It was still as magnificent as they'd remembered. It was a huge room filled with many antiques surrounded by multicolored stained glass windows reaching up to the sky. Copper pots and pans hung everywhere the children could see, while heavenly smells of cakes and pastries filled the air. There at the end of the long banquet table was the cobblestone fireplace with the roaring fire and their dear, old friend Jasper, the mounted moose head, hanging happily as ever above the mantel. His big, soulful, brown eyes shaded by his long, thick eyelashes brought a warm and comforting feeling to the children.

"Jasper!" they shouted out, ever-so-happy to see him.

Jasper became so excited he swirled his head knocking his enormous antlers on both sides of the fireplace, loosening some of the cobblestone, causing the stone to tumble to the ground. "Hello Inspector and Inspector Girl," he bellowed with a gust of stinky moose breath filling the air.

"I see your oral hygiene hasn't improved much since the last time we were here!" snapped Rex. *"Your breath **still** stinks!"*

Jasper glared down at Rex with utter distain. "Listen, you overgrown piece of lint. I'm a moose head. It's not like I can walk away to brush my teeth and gargle after I've had my snicky-snack, ya know!"

"Oooh, I do like him!" chutted Sandy. "He hates Rex just as much as I ddd—d—do!"

"Sandy, sweetie," scolded Alexa, "that is not very nice to say."

Jasper crinkled his brown, bristly snout, exploding at Rex in anger, "I just hang here all day long, seeing what I can see, when I see what I can see! You see!"

Sandy grabbed the last bit of Rex's grilled 'kraut and flounder sandwich from her tiny backpack and sat back nibbling away on it in complete delight as Rex and Jasper argued like two old enemies. "Oooh...I really, really do like that mmm—m—moose head. What's his name again? I forgot to write it down."

"Jasper, you scrumptious, little thing!" uttered Mrs. Panosh, passionately gliding from the back pantry into the room. Her long, flowing, golden-blonde hair glistened from the sunlight gleaming through the stained glass windows. "I like him, too!" she said to Sandy, giving her a linen napkin to wipe the sauerkraut from her tiny nose.

Gertrude, Mrs. Panosh's oversized pet goose, waddled across the red and black, checkerboard floor carrying a tray of freshly-baked pastries. "Jasper is one of the most lovable animals of all!" she declared, taking the tray from Gertrude and placing it on the kitchen counter.

A "*HONK*" and an "*AHCHOOOO!*" flew out of Gertrude's allergy-ridden beak.

"And I love you, too, Gerty," consoled Mrs. Panosh as

she wiped Gertrude's watery eyes with the edge of her clock apron. "I have enough love for you and Jasper!"

"My friend Grace, she has terrible allergies this time of year, too," Alexa said as she placed a pink, silk bow onto Sandy's head. "Whenever the wind blows against the sea grass, she sneezes up a storm."

"So I've heard, my dear," stated politely Mrs. Panosh. "So I've heard."

"We've all heard about Grace and her allergies, Lexy," snapped Jake. "Why, I bet the whole universe knows all about Grace by now!" he chuckled.

Mrs. Panosh flashed Jake a knowing look and giggled, "You can count on that, Inspector!"

"Huhhhh?" Jake grunted, confused by her remark.

Delbert gave his naughty sister the evil eye as he tried to distract Jake away from a conversation about the universe that he wasn't quite ready to hear yet. "Oh, don't pay any attention to Penny," he said. "She tends to babble so. Don't you—Penny?"

Mrs. Panosh quickly realized her mistake in discussing the universe with the children and tried to cover it up by agreeing with her brother that she, in fact, did tend to babble a bit. She then continued to gently pat Gerty's runny nose with her apron. "There, there, my dear. Allergy season is almost over with."

"*Is that hyper-allergic duck still here!*" barked Rex in a snit. "*Oh, brother, this is becoming a reunion of misfit animals: first pig breath, then that stinky moose head, and now this sniffling duck! Before you know it, there'll be a wise-cracking, yellow canary annoying the heck out of me!*"

"Well, if this is a reunion of misfit animals, you're the king of all of them, you knucklehead," Jake cried out in exasperation.

"*I resemble that remark!*" Rex declared. "*Besides, I'm not a king, I'm—**Divine!***"

Jake just covered his eyes in complete and utter despair. "Well, whatever you are, how many times do I have to tell you, it's resent, not resemble, and she's a goose, not a duck!"

"*Duck, goose, canary, what's the difference?*" Rex snickered, laughing himself silly. "*You've seen one stupid bird, you've seen them all!*"

"Big difference," argued Jake. "Is a turkey a duck...no! How about a parrot? Would you call a parrot a duck, too?"

Rex thought for a minute and replied, "*Well, that's just crazy. Everyone knows a parrot and duck aren't the same thing!*"

"Then why do you keep calling Gertrude a—duck?"

"*Because she—is!*"

"You are hopeless," sighed Jake as he jumped from one red-tiled square to the next, "completely hopeless!"

"It's so utterly delicious to see you young sleuths again," shouted out Mrs. Panosh. "Have you been keeping up with your knitting, my dear?" she asked Alexa.

"Oh, yes!" replied Alexa firmly. "My mom and I have been knitting away!"

"Scrumptious, my dear! Just scrumptious! Do you have time to play a game of House Detective?" Mrs. Panosh asked. "I just love screaming out 'General Ketchup, in the bedroom, with the rope!' "

"I don't think we have time," Alexa answered with a

frown. "We have a case to solve."

"How exciting!" Mrs. Panosh exclaimed as she poured some tea and plopped a heavenly dessert on the table. "Sit, sit, sit, and tell us all about it while you have some raspberry tea and some of my new north pole, south pole, coconut snowballs."

Everyone sat down at the table and started gobbling up the most delectable coconut snowballs the children had ever tasted, while they listened to the young detective's tale of Captain Snappy and the curse of Shipwreck Bottom.

"Where's Rupert?" Jake asked as he stuffed another coconut snowball into his already over-stuffed mouth.

"Oh, he's taking a nap in the library," Delbert sighed, wiping away some frosting and coconut shavings from his blue-grey moustache. "He spent all last night alphabetizing and categorizing a new shipment of books all filled with time."

"It can be just exhausting," added in Mrs. Panosh, pouring some more raspberry tea.

"Well, let him know that we used one of his gift certificates," declared Alexa. "You know...the ones that stop time!"

"*And, boy, did it save our sorry butts!*" Rex added. "*Right there at the edge of Comanche Canyon, Snodgrass was about to blow us into smithereens. Thunderbolts of lightning were flying everywhere.*"

"Alexa threw one of those certificates into the air, stopping time, and we were able to turn the tables on that evil Snodgrass," Jake explained, munching on yet another coconut snowball.

"So, Inspector," uttered Delbert with fatherly pride, "I gather you've done well trying to master the magnifying glass and dealing with the Baron Von Snodgrass."

"He was no match for Inspector Moustachio!" shouted out Alexa, licking the coconut off her snowball. "He never got the chance to steal Jake's magnifying glass. You should have seen him send his own lightning bolt at that evil villain."

"Well, let's not get overly confident now. The Baron has had years to master his own magnifying glass," Delbert reminded them.

"And you know what we found?" Rex was just about to tell them all about Grandpa Moustachio's secret journal, but Jake gave Rex a disapproving glare and a swift kick under the table.

"Ouch!" he cried, rubbing his hind leg.

"What was it that you found dear?" asked Mrs. Panosh, sipping ever so daintily from her tea cup adorned with tiny clocks.

Rex fumbled for the right words, trying not to give away their guarded secret. *"We...we...,"* he stuttered, *"we found... that... ah...strawberry milk comes from pink cows. Yeah, that sounds good...I mean, right, pink cows!"*

"You don't say," said Delbert in an unbelieving tone. "You don't say."

"I just love strawberry milk!" exclaimed Mrs. Panosh. "Why, come to think of it, I love all things pink: pink ribbons, pink clothes, pink yarn, and especially my hot-pink cupcakes filled with strawberry preserves. I'm entering them in this year's town baking contest. With that wicked Mrs. Smythe not poisoning my cakes and out of my way, I'm assured first prize this time around! Aren't I, Jasper?"

"Yepper!" he declared. "I just love Mrs. Panosh's

hot-pink cupcakes almost as much as I love her right-side, left-side, cherry, chocolate–glazed, marble pie," slurped Jasper, almost singeing his dangling tongue in the fireplace below him.

"Inspector," cried out Mrs. Panosh in a worried snit over winning the baking contest, "you don't think that horrible woman will show up here to poison my cupcakes, now do you?"

"Oh, Penny," Delbert assured his sister," I think Mrs. Smythe is far, far away from here by now. She'd be crazy to return. And if she does, I assure you that Gerard the giraffe at the jail house will make sure she stays put this time."

"How is Gerard's knotted-up neck, anyway?" Alexa asked, wiping some coconut shavings off of Sandy's nose.

"It took forever to untangle him after Mrs. Smythe tied his neck in a knot to prevent him from telling anyone she escaped with the Baron," explained Delbert.

"Do you have any leads on Mrs. Smythe's whereabouts, Inspector?" Mrs. Panosh inquired as she poured the last drop of tea.

"The only thing we know about her," Jake explained as he slurped some tea, "is that Snodgrass said she was floating around somewhere."

"Now, what do you suppose he meant by that?" questioned Mrs. Panosh.

"I'm not sure," Jake said as he scanned the time on the numerous clocks hanging on the walls. "I hate to eat and run, but I do believe we need to get onto our new case."

"By all means, Inspector," encouraged Delbert, "by all means. After all, mysteries don't solve themselves, now do they?"

Alexa stood up with a big grin and declared, "You got that right. Moustachio Investigations—Mysteries Are Our Specialty!"

"Oh, I just love your new slogan!" complimented Mrs. Panosh. "It's so—so delectable!"

They all said their goodbyes with hugs filled with love and gratitude.

Jake grabbed his magnifying glass and flung it high up into the vaulted ceiling of the kitchen. He commanded to it, "***Iratespay Ointpay.***"

The magnifying glass let out an enormous bolt of lightning. It hung suspended in mid-air, growing larger and larger as the funnel of wind exploded from its center, rattling the shimmering stained glass windows of the museum's walls.

"Time to go!" Jake shouted out through the howling wind.

"Evil lurks quietly beyond the glass," warned Delbert. "Snodgrass will stop at nothing to gain possession of another magnifying glass. The power is within you to stop him and any other evil force you come across. Just believe in yourself, use your magnifying glass wisely, and you will prevail, Inspector!"

"I will, Delbert," promised Jake.

"And he who possesses both magnifying glasses and is purest of heart and thought will be able to unravel the mysteries of the universe," reminded Mrs. Panosh, placing a big bag of coconut snowballs into Alexa's Inspector Girl backpack for the trip.

"One more thing, Inspector," continued Delbert. "Always remember that when fate collides with destiny, cataclysmic events can unfold."

"*How cataclysmic?*" shuttered Rex, thinking what could possibly go wrong.

"That, as you know, my good pussycat, will be revealed all in good time!"

With Sandy safely tucked away, Alexa grabbed her backpack and firmly held on to Jake's right hand as Rex held on to the other. The copper pots dangling from the ceiling clinked and clanked against the forceful wind, while the sounds of the cuckoo clocks echoed from beyond.

"On three," confirmed Jake.

"*I hope it's a little softer ride the second time around!*" spouted Rex.

They all shouted out goodbye, took a deep breath, and jumped into the magnifying glass.

Delbert and Mrs. Panosh just stood there in awe, watching the mysterious powers of the magnifying glass as it shrunk away, disappearing into the thin air from which it came.

"Delbert," she scolded, "shame on you for not telling them."

"How about you going on about everyone in the universe knowing all about Grace and her allergies!" he answered back.

"That was a simple mistake, dear brother," she babbled in a huff. "But you deliberately kept things from those children."

"I kept from them what they aren't ready to know yet, my dear sister."

"Do you think they have the book?" she asked inquisitively. "Or the letter?"

Delbert looked worried. Trembling in fear, two tiny clocks fell from his red suspenders. As he went to pick them up, he denied, "I haven't got the foggiest of clues!"

"Well, you better hope so," she warned. "The fate of our worlds and the universe depends upon it!" Mrs. Panosh then glided across the red and black, checkerboard floor to Jasper and announced, "Jasper, dear, I need a favor."

"Can I have another snowball?" he anxiously asked, filling the room with some more of his stinky moose breath.

"Why, yes, my bristly friend," she agreed. "But first I need you to tell the others that the Moustachios are on their way. They must keep them safe, and no harm must come to a hair on their heads. Do you understand?"

"Yepper!" he bellowed as his big, old antlers banged against the loose cobblestones of the fireplace. "No harm must come to the Moustachios! Got It!"

CHAPTER FOUR

Turkey! Turkey!

The children swirled once again down the gigantic, seemingly endless slide inside of Jake's mystical magnifying glass. Twisting and turning, they screamed for their young lives. Faster and faster with every bend, sparkles of colorful stars flew past their wide-awed eyes. Suddenly, a blast of light exploded from the glass as the mystery-solving group came shooting out one by one into a massive, pillowy cloud of powder-blue.

Rex frantically tried to claw his way out. *"We're dead!"* he cried. *"Dead, I tell ya! We've gone to the great beyond. There's nothing but clouds up here, and I can't see the light!"*

Jake popped his head out of the cloudy mess and yelled, "We're very much alive, you pesky pet."

"So we're not in the great beyond?" asked Alexa, pulling the fluffy, blue clouds out of her hair.

Jake proceeded to lick his sticky lips. "These aren't clouds, and we're definitely not goners."

Rex took a bite out of the pillowy clouds and exclaimed *"We're not!"*

Alexa and Sandy took a nibble themselves. "This tastes like..."

"Cotton candy, candy!" screeched a quirky, deep, drumming sound from above. "Get out of my cotton candy, candy! You've ruined it, it!"

Out of the blue clouds of the cotton candy popped the

head of the largest bird the children had ever seen. She had a blue-gray neck with enormous, twinkling, emerald-green eyes adorned with the longest fake eyelashes. She scooped each of them up with her beak, taking them one by one out of the vat of powder-blue cotton candy, plopping them each onto to the sandy boardwalk below.

"Hey, watch the fur, you overgrown turkey!" Rex shouted.

"Turkey, turkey?" she yelled back, stretching her long neck from the wall her head was mounted on. "I think not, not!" She then clunked each of them on the head for ruining her batch of blueberry cotton candy.

Jake wildly flung his arms in the air, swatting her head out of his way. "What'd you do that for?"

"Do you know how long it takes a mounted ostrich head to make blueberry cotton candy, candy?" she scolded, blinking her long, fake eyelashes endlessly.

"An—n—n hour?" replied Sandy ever so softly.

The very perturbed ostrich head leaned down really low. Her fanning eyelashes blew a cool wind up against Sandy's tiny face. "Why, no, you silly little thing, thing. It takes five hours, thirty six minutes and twenty two seconds, to be exact, exact. Now I have to start all over again, again. The amusement pier is about to open up, and I have nothing to sell, thanks to you all, all! How utterly rude, falling into a freshly-made batch of blueberry cotton candy, candy!"

"Sorry!" Alexa apologized as she grabbed Sandy and placed her safely into her Inspector Girl backpack. "We'll help you make more if you'd like."

"I'll make it myself, myself," she snapped, swirling her head around violently. "I have to do everything around here, anyway, anyway. But you might want to get that magnifying glass hanging up there in the air down, down. It's blocking my sign, sign. How is anyone supposed to find my booth, booth? Since you ruined it, I'll just have to sell my blueberry cotton candy cheaper since it is slightly used, you know, know!"

Jake reached out his hand, commanding his magnifying glass to come to him. After it was securely in his palm, he began combing the boardwalk looking for clues to their whereabouts.

"There, there!" clicked the ostrich as she dusted off her sign with her long, black eyelashes. "That's better, better. Now everyone will know where to find Penelope's worlds'-famous, blueberry cotton candy, candy. And you can only get it here on the boardwalk at Pirate's Point, Point!"

"Pirate's Point!" they all exclaimed.

"Well, where else would you find blueberry cotton candy, candy?" screeched Penelope. "Of course you're at Pirate's Point, Point!"

"We need to find Captain Snappy and the Krusty Katfish," explained Jake. "Do you know where he is?"

"Well, of course I do, do!" she snapped, pulling the old, slightly-used cotton candy out from her vat.

"*Well?*" yelled out Rex, expecting an answer.

"Well, what, what?" questioned the ostrich with a beak full of sticky, blue cotton candy.

"*Aren't you going to tell us?*" Rex hissed in a snit.

Penelope stretched her very long, slender, feathery, blue-grey neck and bellowed, "Tell you what, what?"

"Where Captain Snappy is," Alexa reminded as she rummaged through her backpack, looking for a wipey to wipe the sticky cotton candy off her and Sandy's hands.

"Well, you didn't ask me to tell you where he is, you know, know" confessed Penelope. "You just asked me if I knew where he was, was. Big difference, you know, know!"

Jake was exasperated from the crazy double talk, "*And?*" he shouted, desperately needing the information to the whereabouts of the ship.

Penelope spit out a huge wad of her blueberry cotton candy, pointed her beak down to the right, and proclaimed, "You'll find Cap'n Snappy and his ship at the end of the boardwalk, that-a-way, way!"

"Thanks—I think!" shouted out Jake as they all ran frantically down the boardwalk.

"I suppose you wouldn't want to buy a couple bags of slightly-used, blueberry cotton candy, now would ya, Inspector, Inspector?" yelled back Penelope.

"Sorry, don't have time," answered back Jake. "How do you know who I am?" he asked.

"*Let me guess,*" Rex uttered, springing down the boardwalk. "*Some other stupid mounted animal heads told you! Didn't they?*"

"Well, we all don't hang around on the walls for nothing, ya know, know!" she explained.

They all ran faster and faster down the boardwalk, gasping for breath. The salt water air rushed up at them from the storm that was brewing far out to sea.

"Hurry, you guys, hurry!" encouraged Jake. "The hurricane is getting closer!"

Alexa was trying to keep up with Jake, but the boardwalk was never-ending. "I don't think I can run any faster, Jake."

Seeing his sister struggling, Jake grabbed her backpack and flung it over his shoulder to help speed her up. Rex scurried close behind as they passed all the amazing stands and booths lining the boardwalk.

"Ooh, a candy wheel," squealed Alexa, her big, blue eyes now mesmerized by the spinning names on the wheel, *BOB, SANDY, MOM, DAD, GRANDMA, and GRANDPA.*

"And they have Clunky Chunky Bars!" drooled Rex. *"I just love Clunky Chunky Bars, almost as much as I love guinea pig sandwiches smothered in mustard and pickles."*

"I heard that!" grumbled Sandy.

"Lexy," warned Jake, "we don't have time to win any candy. We have a case to solve!"

"Just one spin of the wheel," she begged, running with determination towards the stand with Rex trailing closely behind. "I promise!"

"Alexa, this candy wheel addiction of yours is getting out of hand!" he scolded. "And Rex, you're not helping the situation!"

"I can't help it," she confessed. "Every time I see a candy wheel and smell a box of Clunky Chunky Chocolate Bars I go—crazy!"

"I could use a little bit of a Clunky Chunky Chocolate BBB—B—Bar myself," Sandy chutted from behind Jake's right ear.

Jake turned his head and glared at her with disapproving eyes.

Sandy trembled as she buried herself deep down into the Inspector Girl backpack. "Then again, I can always ggg—g—go without!" she mumbled in fear.

Frustrated and yet somewhat intrigued, Jake ran after

his sister over to the candy wheel. Hanging there on the wall were boxes and bags of the most delectable sugar treats they had ever seen before. The smell of chocolates, lollipops, and salt water taffy floated about the stand. The wheel was shiny white with black-lettered names to bet on. Surrounding the stand was a countertop painted with the matching names to place their bets on.

Alexa and Rex stood there mesmerized by the grand prize, a super-duper, mega-deluxe box of Clunky Chunky Bars.

"They're my favorite," she whispered, licking her ever-so-pink glossed lips.

"*Mine, too!*" he purred with dazed eyes as a tear of joy bounced off his whisker. "*Mine, too!*"

"Oh, brother!" moaned Jake in disgust. "We're never going to finish this case if we don't get started."

Suddenly, the spinning wheel violently turned around, revealing that crazy ostrich, Penelope, hanging from the other side.

"Well, hello there, there. Care to place a bet, bet?"

"*Hey—how did you get over here so fast?*" Rex pondered in awe.

"Like I said back there, I have to do everything around here, here," complained Penelope, bopping her head up and down, clunking Rex on his.

"*Knock it off, you over-stuffed turkey!*" yelled Rex. "*That hurts!*"

"Turkey, turkey?" Penelope protested. "I think not, not. Why, I'm an ostrich, ostrich! Why, I think you need glasses to see, you foolish feline, feline!"

"*You've seen one stupid bird, you've seen them all!*" he

snapped back.

Jake pulled out his magnifying glass from his back pocket and started examining every inch of Penelope. "Hey, not so close, close!" she uttered in protest. "You'll ruin my new eyelashes with that thing, thing."

"How did you get down here so fast?" he asked with a curious, yet suspicious, grin.

"Now, you of all people should know things are a little strange on this side of the magnifying glass, Inspector, Inspector," she said. "Now, everyone place your bets, bets. It's time to place your bets, bets!"

Alexa ran over to Jake and grabbed her Inspector Girl backpack. She quickly searched for her pink, satin change purse with the silver clip hook. "Sandy," she called down to the bottom, "do you see my change purse?"

Sandy ran all around till she finally bumped into it. "I think sss—s—so," she called out, dragging it up to the top.

Alexa dumped her change purse all over the counter, searching for a coin. Countless quarters, dimes, nickels, and pennies rolled everywhere.

"Lexy," asked Jake, "where did you get all these buffalo nickels from?"

"I've been collecting them ever since we met Chief Buffalo Hump on our last case," she explained. "It's not every day you get to change history and meet someone whose famous face is actually on a coin."

Jake started gathering up all the coins, looking for a quarter to place a bet with. "Here's one," he said as he dumped the rest of the coins back into her change purse.

Alexa then grabbed the quarter and placed her bet on the name "**GRANDPA**."

"That should bring us luck," declared Jake.

"Your Grandpa was always a very lucky guy!" announced Rex with a thoughtfully warm smile brewing under his whiskers.

"All bets are done, done!" Penelope exclaimed, spinning the wheel before flipping herself around. "No more bets, bets," she warned from behind the wheel.

They all watched the wheel spin around and around in anticipation of winning. It made a loud clicking noise passing each and every name till it barely landed on the name "**SALLY**" one notch just before "**GRANDPA**." They all took a short gasp of salty air and held their breaths as the wheel suddenly turned one notch further, landing directly on "**GRANDPA**."

"We have a winner, winner!" shouted Penelope as she spun around facing them. Pointing to the numerous boxes and bags of candy with her beak, she questioned, "What'll it be, be?"

Alexa had a huge smile across her face as she gave Rex a wink. "We'll have the box of Clunky Chunky Bars, please."

Rex became overwhelmed as his eyes grew wide with the anticipation of munching on the caramel-crusted, milk chocolate treat.

Penelope grabbed the very large box with her beak. She then stretched her very long neck and lowered it down to the children.

Within seconds of the box hitting the boardwalk, they all ripped it open, and each snatched up their very own Clunky Chunky Bar. "We have to get down to the end of the boardwalk," mumbled Jake, munching on his candy bar. "Captain Snappy is waiting for us!"

"Well, what are you waiting for, for?" yapped Penelope. "Mysterious cases don't solve themselves you know, know!"

Alexa quickly handed the rest of the chocolate bars to Sandy, who dragged them to the bottom of the backpack. Then they all took off once again, running down the boardwalk as fast as they could.

"*Do you always end every sentence with the last word twice?*" Rex annoyingly asked Penelope as he darted away.

"Whatever do you mean, mean?" shouted out Penelope, feverously blinking her long, fake, clumped-up eyelashes. "By the way, I suppose you wouldn't want to buy a couple of bags of slightly—used, blueberry cotton candy, now would ya, ya?"

"Sorry," yelled back Alexa, "we don't have time. We have to get to the Krusty Katfish and find Captain Snappy."

On their way down the boardwalk they passed by the most inviting arcades, snow cone stands, and a fun house, but there was no sign of the Krusty Katfish.

"Oh, my gosh!" shouted out Jake. "I don't believe it!"

"What is it? Do you see the ship?" asked Alexa in a panic.

"*I don't see a ship,*" added Rex. "*Where? Where?*"

"I ddd—d—don't see one, either!" chutted Sandy.

Jake became spellbound by one of the games directly ahead. It was his favorite game of all time, the squirt gun races.

"Jake," reminded Alexa, "we don't have time. You said it yourself; we have a case to solve."

"Just one turn, I promise," he proclaimed, running to the stand.

Alexa, Rex, and Sandy just stood there watching Jake

make a spectacle of himself. "But, Jake..." she yelled out.

"*Well, you can't play the squirt gun game alone, now can you?*" questioned Rex, scurrying off to join him.

"Do you believe those two, Sandy?"

"BBB—B—Boys and their ttt—t—toys!" exclaimed Sandy.

"They'll never learn," Alexa sighed. "We girls are so much more sophisticated!"

Sandy shook her short, golden-brown, furry little head in complete agreement.

"I guess a quick game couldn't hurt," Alexa determined, skipping to join them.

"Look at all the sss—s—stuffed animals!" gleamed Sandy as she counted them all one by one.

"Aren't they just precious?" squealed Alexa in delight. "Which one should we get?"

"There must be hundreds of them," Jake counted, examining each one carefully through his magnifying glass.

"*I like the brown wolf over there,*" ordered Rex.

"He looks scary and hungry," thought Alexa.

"*You know wolves love to eat little, tiny, annoying pigs,*" he said, glaring into Sandy's eyes.

"How many ttt—t—times do I have to tell you I'm not a pig-pig? I'm a guinea pig, you furry clod. And I'm not afraid of any bbb—b—bad old wolves, either. Why don't we get that big, hungry–looking, grey bulldog up there? I'll bet he would love to take a bite out of a scrawny, old pussycat like...*you!*"

"*Who you calling old?*" Rex snapped, licking his slightly-matted fur. "*Why, I'm not a day past one hundred and forty.*"

"You mean twenty," clarified Jake.

"No, no, I mean a hundred and forty."

"Rexy Cat, you can't be a hundred and forty," explained Alexa. "Cats don't live that long. It's impossible."

"Noooo, I'm pretty sure it's a hundred and forty," he protested.

"Listen, you crazy nut ball,. you measure cat and dog years by multiplying the actual years on the planet by seven. So you being about twenty years old, give-or-take, makes you about one hundred and forty in cat years, not real years."

"You're so old you must bbb—b—be getting confused!" stammered Sandy with a tiny grin.

"Now listen, you three. I may be a little long in the cat tooth, but I do know how old I am," Rex declared firmly. *"And it's a hundred and forty, give-or-take a life or two!"*

Jake put his hands over his face in complete exasperation. "Why do I even bother?"

Suddenly, out from the layers and layers of hanging stuffed animals, Penelope emerged, hanging from the back wall. Startled, they all screamed "Ahhhhh!"

Penelope became so frightened by their screams she let out one of her own "Ahhhhhs!" and sunk back into the layers of stuffed animals, too afraid to come out. "What did you do that for, for?" she mumbled behind a gigantic, pink elephant. "You nearly scared me to death, death. And I don't have nine lives, lives!"

"What's the big idea jumping out of nowhere and scaring us half to death, you wild, over-stuffed turkey?" grumbled Rex. *"I nearly lost one of my nine lives, and I'm not exactly sure how many I have left!"*

"Turkey, turkey?" Penelope protested, popping back out

to clunk Rex on the head with her beak. "I think not, not. Why, I'm an ostrich, ostrich! How many times do I have to tell ya, ya?"

Sandy scooted her head out of the backpack and snickered, "You know...I kinda like her! She talks a little funny, but she's quite ddd—d—delightful. Plus she hates the cat!"

Rex turned to Sandy, rubbing the bump on his head, and bellowed, "*I hope you and this stupid turkey are very happy together!*"

Jake grabbed his magnifying glass and started to examine every inch of Penelope. "How did you get over here so fast?" he asked curiously. "You have no body!"

"Inspector, Inspector, the greatest gift in life is your power to believe, believe," she proclaimed as she stuck her long neck out and clunked him on the head.

"Ouch!" he yelled out in frustration. "Would you stop doing that?"

"*My sentiments exactly!*" Rex hissed, still sore from his own clunk.

Penelope batted her long, black, clumpy, false eyelashes right over Jake's entire face. "So...ya gonna play the game, or what, what?"

"*How about we skip the game and just take the squirt guns and shoot her?*" suggested Rex. "*I'm sure it's Thanksgiving somewhere in the universe!*"

Jake became so mad his face turned redder than his hair. His yell could be heard to the depths of the ocean. "For the last time, she's an ostrich, not a turkey, turkey!"

"*Well, all right,*" Rex hissed. "*Ya don't have to get all huffy, huffy about it!*"

"Everybody grab your favorite squirt gun color, and let's get blasting away, away!" ordered Penelope. "And remember, squirting me is no way to win a prize, prize!"

Alexa ran to grab the hot pink squirt gun to the far left with Sandy close by her side. Rex jumped up between the children and snatched the blue gun while Jake nabbed a fire engine red-colored one.

"*Hey,*" shouted Rex, "*this isn't fair. My paws don't reach the trigger.*"

"Use your foot, you nut ball," suggested Jake.

Rex raised his right hind leg in order to grab the gun.

"Do you mind," scolded Jake, staring at Rex's behind.

"*What?*" Rex asked.

"I'm not going to be able to concentrate with your furry butt in my face."

"*Ooow, sorry!*" Rex then swapped his legs, raising his left one in Sandy's direction. "*What are you looking at?*" he demanded at her.

Sandy took one long look at Rex's furry butt facing her, sighed, "And you call me a ppp—p—pig!" She then stormed off down the counter to the other side of Alexa in an annoyed huff of her own.

"*No one told ya to look!*" Rex chuckled.

"Everyone ready, ready?" Penelope exclaimed.

"**Ready!**" they all shouted out.

"Now aim your guns right at your own seahorse's belly button, button," she explained. Penelope stretched her neck, looking right into Alexa's eyes. "Have you ever seen a seahorse's belly button, my dear, dear? They are the cutest things and very ticklish, too, too!"

"I didn't know seahorses had belly buttons," stated Alexa

with a perplexed look on her face.

"Well they do, they really do, do!" She then told them that the first one to get their seahorse to reach King Neptune's scepter, making it glow, would win a prize. The bell rang, and off they went, squirting away. Inch by inch, they jockeyed for the top spot. Up, down, up, down went the seahorses. Suddenly, Jake's gun spontaneously squirted out one gigantic blast of water that shot his seahorse right to the top, reaching the scepter first, followed by Alexa and then Rex.

"We have a winner, winner!" announced Penelope.

"Oh—Jake always wins at this game," complained Alexa.

"*Yeah, let's see if you could win using your foot!*" Rex smirked at Jake.

"Well, I know one thing. You're a poor loser," Jake yelled back to Rex.

"*What?*"

"I wouldn't be sticking my butt in your face if I had used my foot!"

Penelope clunked them both on the head for arguing. "Alright, Inspector, what's it gonna be, be? You can have any prize you want, want. Just name your prize, prize!"

Through his magnifying glass Jake studied each and every stuffed animal with the utmost precision. Not wanting to be too hasty in his decision, he carefully thought about each and every one.

"Well, well?" snapped Penelope. "Times a wastin', wastin'."

"I'll have the sea walrus!" he decided.

"I don't think so, so," replied Penelope, batting her eyes furiously. She then ducked under the booth and pulled out

an old, tattered, dirty, leather, brown book, very much like Grandpa's secret code book that Jake had hidden in his pocket. "How about one of these, these?" she mumbled with the book in her beak.

Jake looked at her like she was crazy.

"No, thank you. I'll take the blue-grey walrus."

"So you'll take the book then, then?"

"Nooooo," declared Jake. "I really want the walrus."

Penelope dropped the book on the counter and clunked Jake on the head with her beak.

"Ouch!" he screamed in pain. "What did you do that for?"

"What's the matter, matter?" she asked. "Do you already have a little, dirty, brown, leather book, book?"

"*Well, actually...*" Rex started to confess before Jake swooped in and covered his mouth. "*I can't breathe,*" he mumbled.

"You're not going to be able to do a lot more, you foolish fur ball, if you don't keep quiet about Grandpa's book!" Jake whispered as he slowly removed his hands from Rex's mouth.

"*You're the boss!*"

Jake stretched his neck out over the squirt guns and looked Penelope right in her clumped, eyelashed eyes, ready to protect his secret. "I don't have any such book, and I don't need yours."

"Oh, yes, you do, do!" she squawked.

"He does?" asked Alexa surprised.

"He sure does, does," squawked Penelope again.

Jake grabbed the book and his magnifying glass and started to examine the pages. **This looks just like**

Grandpa's secret book, he thought.

"Why?" he muttered. "Why do I need this book?"

Penelope started to explain since Jake supposedly didn't have such a book in his possession, having this one might come in handy. "It's filled with Ostrich Greek, Greek, and," she explained, "it's very similar to Pig Latin, Latin. One might say, Inspector, if someone was to be given this book, he would not be able to tell the difference between Ostrich Greek and Pig Latin, don't you know, know?"

"We don't need your stinkin' book!" shouted out Rex. *"We want the stuffed walrus."*

"Yeah, the www—w—walrus!" added in Sandy as she made room for it in the Inspector Girl backpack.

Penelope got right down into Jake's face. He could smell the left—over, blueberry cotton candy on her breath. Her fake eyelashes ran up and down his face with each blink she made. "You know, when fate collides with destiny, cataclysmic events can happen, happen. You never know when a book like this might come in handy, handy. What's it going to be, Inspector...the useless walrus or the potentially lifesaving book, book?"

Jake thought to himself, having a second book similar to the one he had just might come in handy if he ever were up against the evil Baron Von Snodgrass again. "I'll take the book," he keenly agreed.

Penelope tried to blink her right eye at him, but the glue from her false eyelashes made her eyelids stick together. "Wise choice, Inspector, Inspector!" she winced as she pulled her eyelids apart. "A very wise choice, indeed, indeed! Now hurry, hurry. You don't want to keep Cap'n Snappy waiting, waiting. The storm is brewing more fiercely out at sea, and Jezebel is moving fast up the coast, coast. You need to set sail before she finds ya, ya!"

As they took off down the boardwalk, Penelope tried once again to get rid of that bad batch of blueberry cotton candy they fell into. "I suppose you wouldn't want to buy a couple bags of slightly-used, blueberry cotton candy, now would ya, Inspector, Inspector?" yelled back Penelope.

"Sorry, you know we don't have the time," called back Jake. "You do know there's a gigantic hurricane coming, don't you?"

Penelope gathered up her bags of slightly-used, blueberry cotton candy and squawked, "That's what I've been trying to say, say!"

The crazy ostrich just hung there shaking her feathered head. "I hope they know what they're getting themselves into, into!" she muttered to herself.

CHAPTER FIVE
Come Sail Away!

They all frantically hurried to find the Krusty Katfish. At the end of the boardwalk there was an empty marina, except for one ship they could see docked at the end of the pier. It was a magnificent, hundred-foot long pirate schooner with sails reaching high up into the sky. Its fore and aft white, linen sails fluttered in the wind, which blew violently in from sea. The mahogany hull was shiny and newly-stained with scary, black cannons sticking out from all sides, just waiting to blast an enemy into smithereens.

"Wow, that is some ship!" exclaimed Jake as he ran closer and closer.

"I can't wait to get aboard!" shouted Alexa, grabbing her pink and white, seashell scarf from her backpack and tying it through her windblown hair.

"MMM—M—Me, too!" chutted away Sandy.

Rex ran behind, drooling in anticipation of a restaurant on board. *"I'm hungry. Can we stop at the restaurant and get some food?"*

"Rex, it's not a cruise ship," explained Alexa. "It's a pirate ship."

"They don't have a restaurant, you fur brain," yelled Jake. "They have galleys to grab your grub!"

"Well, whatever you call it, kitchen, galley, or restaurant, I can't wait to sink my teeth into a juicy, delicious, crusty, catfish sandwich. And pig breath is getting nowhere near this one! And why are you talking pirate?"

"Krusty Katfish is the name of the ship, you knucklehead, not a sandwich," declared Jake. "And I be not talking pirate... well, maybe I am!"

"*You mean I'm not going to get a crusty, catfish sandwich to replace the grilled 'kraut and flounder sandwich that that stupid pig ate?*" argued Rex. "*Then why am I here?*"

Jake, with an annoyed look on his face, uttered, "I was wondering that same thing, myself."

"*Very funny,*" snarled Rex, "*very funny! Hey, is it my imagination or does that ship look vaguely familiar?*"

Suddenly, a large, horizontal pole swung over their heads from behind the majestic ship. And there was Penelope hanging from the end of a boom from another ship, squawking away. "Whatever are you doing over here, here?" she questioned, clunking them each on the head.

"Would you knock that off!" yelled Jake. "What do you mean, what are we doing here, here? Great, now I'm talking like an ostrich. We're getting ready to come aboard the Krusty Katfish. That's what we're doing over here!"

As she pointed her beak towards the grand ship, she exclaimed, "That's not the Krusty Katfish, Katfish! That's the Lady Lilac, the queen of the sea, sea!"

"Where's the crew?" asked Alexa, applying a new coat of strawberry lip gloss to her chapped lips.

"*And the captain?*" Rex questioned next.

Penelope explained that no one had ever seen the crew or the captain. "It's almost like it's a ghost ship, just sailing the high seas all by itself, itself."

"Where's the Krusty Katfish?" Jake asked, scratching his head perplexed and somewhat confused.

"It's right over there, behind the Lady Lilac, silly boy, boy," pointed out Penelope. "Can't you see where I'm hanging from, from? And you call yourself a detective, detective. Why, I'm hanging from the boom at the bottom of its main sail, sail! Jump on, and I'll swing you over, over."

They all jumped onto the long, rickety pole and held on for their lives as Penelope swung it around, right over the Lady Lilac's massive deck. They gasped in horror as the Krusty Katfish came into full sight. It was a crumbling, old, brigantine ship with tattered sails hanging haphazardly off its mast. Seaweed and tape filled the array of holes, barely keeping it afloat.

"Is this thing safe?" worried Alexa as they all got whipped around one hundred feet off the ground passing over the aft of the Lady Lilac.

"Well, I've never had a problem in the past, past!" proclaimed the repetitive ostrich. "Then again, I've never done this before, before!"

"Don't look down! Don't look down! Don't look down!" Rex cried out in fear as he, of course, was looking down.

The boom, with them barely hanging on, whisked right over the ocean, almost dumping them into the treacherous, shark-infested waters below. With the wind blowing ferociously in from sea against the sail, they all let out a terrifying scream. "Ahhhhhh!" Penelope lost control of the sail as she tried to guide the boom over the deck of the Krusty Katfish so they could jump off. But the wind kept spinning the sail around and around with them all dangling from the bottom boom's wooden pole for their young lives.

"Oh dear, dear!" Penelope uttered in distress.

"We're doomed! Doomed, I tell ya!" wailed Rex. *"I'm too*

young and handsome to die! Plus, I still haven't used my coupon for a free bag of Perrrfect Petz, diamond-crystal, multicat, super-absorbent, clumping cat litter yet. It expires soon!"

"What do you mean, you're too young? You were just telling us you were a hundred and forty," blurted out Jake, grasping on to the pole. "Where do you get young from? We're the ones that are too young to die!"

"Ahhhhhhhh!" they all screamed.

"O.K.—maybe I'm just too darn handsome to die!"

The boom with the sail attached kept spinning around and around as it flew over the Krusty Katfish, then over the ocean, and then over the Lady Lilac, only to begin again over the Krusty Katfish. The faster they spun, the dizzier and more out of control Penelope got. The weight of their bodies started to crack the rotted wood of the boom they were hanging from.

"We have to jump!" screamed out Jake. "It's our only hope!"

"Are you crazy?" screeched Rex. *"One false move and we're goners, I tell ya—GONERS!"*

"We have no choice. The boom is about to snap!" confirmed Alexa. "And that crow's nest lookout tower at the top of the mast will fall over, killing us all!"

"Unless the sharks eat us fff—f—first," Sandy squealed.

"I'm so dizzy I think I'm going to throw up my lunch. Ohhh, yeah, I forgot—I didn't get to have my lunch, thanks to the stupid pig eating my grilled 'kraut and flounder sandwich!" complained Rex. *"Hey, speaking of throwing up, throw the pig off. That'll lighten the load."*

Alexa screamed out in protest that they were not kicking

Sandy off the boom to save their own lives.

"She doesn't even weigh a pound, you crazy cat!" Jake uttered against the wind as they still kept spinning around and around. "Kicking her off doesn't change a thing."

"Maybe it wouldn't for you, but getting rid of her would just make my day!" Rex smirked.

Staring at his watch, Jake explained that every twenty-two point nine seconds they were flying in a circle over the Krusty Katfish. Their only chance of surviving this predicament was to jump into a bunch of old sails piled up towards the front of the ship. He instructed them to jump at his command.

"And if we miss?" frantically cried out Rex.

"Then I hope you can swim because those sharks look hungry!" he replied, ordering them to jump.

And jump they did as the boom flew over the deck of the Krusty Katfish. Every sea creature to the depths of the ocean could hear Rex screaming as he jumped, ***"We're doomed!"***

One by one, they plopped face down into the pile of linen sails.

"You know," mumbled Jake, "we really do have to work on getting to places more easily than this!"

"Ya think?" grumbled back Rex from beneath the sails.

Alexa just lay there draped in a white, linen sail with Sandy more dazed and confused than usual. "I don't even want to think about what my hair must look like!" she said. "Are you alright, sweetie?"

"I think so!" chutted Sandy. "I forgot to write it down. Where are we—again?"

Looking up at what was coming their way, Rex sighed,

"We're in deep cat litter. That's where we are."

A circle of piercing eyes surrounded the children. The smell of stinky breath loomed over the children's heads. "Ye be on the Krusty Katfish," said a squeaky voice.

"Arrrrr, on the Krusty Katfish, that's what he said," repeated another very scary voice.

The mystery-solving foursome slowly looked up and saw to their surprise that they were surrounded by a group of the tiniest band of pirates the world had ever seen. The teeny-weeny, treacherous lot held long, pointy swords to their backs, just waiting for them to make one false move.

"Ye be friend or foe?" asked a stocky, little one with a wooden leg.

Staring down at the end of one of the surrounding swords, Rex's fur puffed up as a dribble of nervous sweat ran down his nose, bouncing off his right whisker. Shaking, he cried out, *"Ohhhhh, definitely friend!* **Friend, Friend, Friend...Friend!** *Did I mention friend? No foes here!"*

"Are ye sure?" questioned a tiny, bald one with a hook for a hand. "The little pig looks shifty ta me—yo-ho-ho!"

Sandy got really mad and exploded, "I'm nnn—n—not a pig, you..."

Rex immediately cut her off from finishing her sentence as he covered her mouth with his paw. *"Are you crazy?"* he whispered into her ear. *"We're about to be diced and sliced into smithereens, fed to those sharks, and you're arguing with the littlest one with the hook!* **Do you want to become shark bait?"**

Sandy started trembling as the hooked pirate smirked at her, just waiting for a fight. "I see your ppp—p—point!" she whispered back to Rex.

Sandy smiled for her life. "That's a lovely hhh—h—hook you have, Mr. Pirate," she said, wincing in horror.

"My name be Spike Longsliver, but me buckos be calling me Spikey!"

"Of course they do!" Rex trembled. *"What else would it be?"*

All the tiny pirates let out a roar of laughter as the children and their pets joined them with nervous, hesitant laughs.

"I be likin' the pig!" announced Spikey. "She be havin' spunk." He looked Sandy squarely in the eye and smiled. "I be likin' spunk!"

Alexa turned to Jake and whispered, "These pirates, they look like children!"

Jake grabbed his magnifying glass from his back pocket, trying to inconspicuously examine their faces. "You're right. They're toddlers—younger than us!"

"But they sound and act like adults!" she confirmed.

Confused, Jake exclaimed, "I don't get it!"

Suddenly, they heard a familiar, gravelly voice echo from behind the motley crew of teeny-weeny pirates. "That be the bloody curse, Inspector!" The voice then commanded the crew to make a gangway. Quickly, they complied, stepping aside for their leader as he came trudging barefoot through the unruly crowd. He was the tiniest of captains, with a burgundy scarf tied around his head. His oversized, dirty–white, second-hand, linen shirt was carelessly tucked into his tattered, burlap pants that were just barely held up by an old piece of nautical rope. "The curse of Shipwreck Bottom," Captain Snappy explained. "Now, me hearties, raise ye swords and give a proper Krusty Katfish welcome ta the one and only Inspector Moustachio and his crew," he ordered.

"Hip-Hip-Hurray!" the pirates shouted out to the sea. "Hip-Hip-Hurray!"

"What's the curse of Shipwreck Bottom?" asked Alexa, admiring one of the pirate's shiny, gold, hooped earrings.

"What ya see, lassie!" snarled Captain Snappy, stomping about his deck.

"*I'm confused,*" Rex declared.

"Me, ttt—t—too!" added Sandy as she grabbed her notepad and her purple crayon from her tiny backpack to take notes.

"I'm not," Jake said as he walked all around the tiny pirates and their broken-down, dilapidated ship, examining everything like the world-class detective he was growing into. They all spoke and acted like cranky, old pirates, but they looked more like a bunch of cranky toddlers overdue for their afternoon nap. "Jezebel, the sea witch, cursed you all backwards in time, didn't she?"

"That's how she be getting' rid of all the ships and crews that sail the Seven Seas, me boy," bellowed the wooden pegged-leg pirate, Stumpy.

"Like all the ships cursed before us, we be gettin' younger and younger by the day, Inspector," explained Captain Snappy. "When we be reachin' the youngest of our days— '**Poof,**' we be vanishin' into thin air. Half me crew is gone already. Once a ship is empty, Jezebel sucks it into the depths of the ocean to be buried at Shipwreck Bottom."

"And when the last ship sailing sinks to the bottom..." announced Jake.

"*Jezebel rules the sea...*" added Rex.

"And that's when she takes over the—**WORLD!**"

71

whispered Alexa.

"Are you the last ship sailing?" Jake asked in fear.

"Besides the Lady Lilac over thar, we be not seein' another ship for days!" explained Snappy. "We best be weighin' anchor and gettin' underway. The storm, she's a-brewing nasty out at sea, and Jezebel be headin' this way. Everyone to ye posts!"

All the teeny-weeny pirates ran, crawled, and toddled around the deck, preparing the ship to leave Pirate's Point upon their captain's commands.

"Are you sure this thing can float?" Rex asked Jake as he gazed at a gigantic piece of tape covering a hole in the side of the ship.

"That doesn't look ggg—g—good!" Sandy trembled, searching for some extra tape at the bottom of Alexa's backpack just in case.

"Oh, how bad could it be?" reasoned Alexa as she, too, rummaged for some spare tape.

"Yeah, if we get into trouble, we can always stop time or jump back into the magnifying glass!" proclaimed Jake. "Don't worry. Nothing bad will happen to us, I promise!"

"Are you sure?" worried Rex. *"Because every time we get into one of these predicaments, I'm the one that has to suffer!"*

"Usually it's because you deserve it!" Jake smirked.

"I resemble that remark!" Rex hissed back at him, swatting some annoying flies.

"It's not resemble...it's...never mind," sighed Jake. "Why do I even bother?"

Rex grabbed Jake's cheeks with his paws, giving them a loving squeeze. *"You bother because I'm your best pal in the whole wide universe! You love me—then again, what's not to love?"*

Suddenly, they a heard a loud bang of clanking pots and pans as the nastiest looking little girl appeared from below the ship's deck. Her dark, dingy hair was braided into two pigtails sticking straight out each side of her head, right over her big, floppy ears.

"**LUNCH!**" she screamed, banging her pots against the hull of the ship. "It's time for lunch!"

The pirates were so busy setting sail that they paid absolutely no attention to her. Her eyes nearly popped out of her head as she became enraged from the lack of attention she was getting. Having a big, old toddler hissy fit, she grabbed a long, sharp sword and scurried up one of the gaffs, a lengthy pole sprouting out from the deck of the ship. In one impressive swing, the annoyed, little girl chopped right through the gaff's rope, letting a humongous sack of sand, dangling from the rope, drop down to the crowd. It made a gigantic hole in the decaying deck, barely missing the children.

"*I thought you said nothing bad would happen to us?*" Rex whined over to Jake, diving out of the way.

Ducking for cover, he shouted, "I didn't plan on her!"

"Did she mean to do that?" Alexa questioned in a huff.

"I'm not sure," he answered as they all bent over really low so they could look down into the gaping hole she had made in the deck.

"*She nearly killed us!*" Rex uttered in frustration.

"This ship has mmm—m—more holes than a piece of Swiss cheese," squeaked Sandy.

"When I say lunch—it's **LUNCH!**" she bellowed down to

the unruly lot.

Captain Snappy started to climb up in a tizzy after her. "Are ye crazy, old woman?" barked Snappy. "Izzie, come down from thar! Tis my ship, and I be givin' the orders! One more outburst from ye and you be walkin' the plank."

As the cranky girl climbed her way down, she never let up screaming at the captain. "How dare you...I've been cooking all day, and someone's going to eat my food whether they like it or not."

The entire ship's tiny, toddler crew stepped back in the horror at the thought of having to eat one more bite of Izzie's, the ship's cook's, food.

"I made crab cakes for lunch. Why, everyone loves my crab cakes," she hollered, waving the sword in the air. "Do any of you know how hard it is to cook when you're trapped in the body of a five–year-old girl? I had to get up on a stool and six cookbooks just to reach the stove!"

"*Crab cakes sound delicious!*" purred Rex. "*I mean, it's no grilled 'kraut and flounder sandwich, but it'll do—let's eat!*"

"She be not makin' the crab cakes ye be thinkin' of, Mr. Pussycat," Captain Snappy ranted about his ship. "She be makin' cakes shaped like little crabs, red frostin' and all. Thar be not a piece of real crab meat in 'em. The only thing she be ever makin' morning, noon, and night is cakes, pastries, and pies! How much sugar can we eat, woman? Just look at our teeth."

The crew reluctantly smiled at the children, who gasped in horror at the sight of what was left of their rotten, decayed, black teeth.

"*I gather there's not a dentist on board?*" Rex smirked

under his breath. *"A little floss maybe?"*

"You are the rudest man I've ever worked for!" she complained, as she swung the sword over the captain's head. "If it wasn't for you and being on this stupid, decrepit ship, I never would have been cursed with the rest of you fools. After all, look at me, just look at me. I'm a five-year-old, little girl!"

"And not a pretty one, at that, I might add!" Rex whispered under his breath.

"Now I'm stuck here till you fix it!" Izzie screamed at the captain.

Captain Snappy got right under Izzie's nose and yelled back, "I don't know what I'll be happier about, gettin' rid of Jezebel and this curse or the likes of—**you!**"

"With any luck, Jezebel will sink this floating junk pile and take you all down with it!" Izzie screeched back.

"Well, if she does, she be takin' ye with us!" he shouted back at her.

"Don't be too sure about that!" she warned as she stormed back down below to the ship's galley.

With his teeny-weeny face all sweaty and red, Captain Snappy gave a deadly stare at his crew, who were just standing around stunned. He then exploded at the top of his lungs to the bunch, "Well, what are ye lookin' at? Swab the poop deck, fill the guns, raise the sails, and get back ta work!"

"Penelope, where are ya?" he called out.

Penelope, still hanging from the boom, swung around. "Right here, Cap'n Snappy, Snappy!" The captain, ready to set sail, ordered her to pull up the anchor. "Aye-aye, skipper, skipper!" she sang out.

Rex looked up at Jake with a fearful look spreading across his furry face. *"Are you **still** sure nothing **bad** is going to happen to us?"*

"Well...not sure-sure," Jake hesitated, "but sort of sure!"

"That's what I was afraid of!"

CHAPTER SIX

Pete Want A Quacker

As soon as Penelope pulled up the anchor, the wind took hold of the ship's sails, and off went the Krusty Katfish, heading far out to sea—destination unknown, or so the children thought. The teeny-tiny crew feverishly ran about the broken-down ship, doing what they do, when they do what they do.

Captain Snappy came scuttling up to the children and whispered as he placed his stubby, little finger over his dry lips, "Shhh, follow me down the hatch over thar by the quarterdeck to me captain's cabin below. Don't let me crew see ya!"

"You know, he really does need some lip balm over his dry lips," noticed Alexa as she rummaged through her Inspector Girl backpack looking for a spray bottle of sunblock.

"SSS—S—So true," agreed Sandy. "You always have to protect your skin!"

As they conspicuously followed Captain Snappy down the hatch to his cabin, Alexa started spraying everyone with her super-duper, twelve-hour, waterproof sunblock.

"*What are you doing to me?*" Rex coughed up in a cloud of sunblock.

"Oh, stop complaining, Rexy Cat," she answered. "I'm protecting your fur. We redheads can't be too careful with the sun's rays. We don't want to age before our time!"

"*Speak for yourself—sister,*" he snarled. "*I'm already*

over a hundred and forty!"

"For the last time," argued Jake, "cats don't live that long!"

"You wanna bet?"

"You are hopeless!" Jake exclaimed.

"Do guinea ppp—p—pigs live that long?" asked Sandy, bopping around the backpack, ready to write the answer down in her tiny notebook.

"Not a hundred and forty years, sweetie," Alexa replied.

"Well, there's something to be grateful for!" snickered Rex.

"Rexy, be nice!" she scolded.

They all hesitantly followed Captain Snappy down the hatch to a deep, musty, dark hallway that led to his cabin. "Close the hatch," he ordered.

As Jake pulled down on the cold, rusty, steel doors of the hatch, he could see off in the distance Spike Longsliver and the wooden peg-legged pirate, Stumpy, smiling ever-so-treacherously at him.

"Hurry, we be not havin' much time! Jezebel be breathin' down the back of our necks," Captain Snappy bellowed, shoving them all into his cabin. "Who left me door open and unlocked? And what in the worlds happened to me cabin? Pete!" he screamed.

"How rude!" Rex uttered as they all went stumbling in.

The teeny captain locked the door from the inside. They all stood there with eyes wide open and glistening in the candlelight, too afraid to move. There were nautical maps and a compass thrown haphazardly about the splintery table located in the center of the torn-apart, messy room. They heard a rustling coming from inside an old, brown, weathered treasure chest in the corner of the cabin.

"Quackers! Quackers!" went the unknown voice. "Pete want a quacker!"

"Arrrrr, Pete," the captain yelled out. "Did ya go and lock yourself in that bloody chest again?"

"Quackers!" answered Pete "yes."

"That parrot be always gettin' himself into a heap of trouble," declared Captain Snappy. He then ransacked the cabin looking for the key to the chest. "I keep forgettin' where I be puttin' me keys. I had two sets of keys to me cabin and to me chest. Now I be only havin' one if I be lucky enough to be findin' 'em."

They all helped the captain search for his keys in the dimly-lit room. Jake grabbed his magnifying glass and combed every inch of the cabin. As he felt along the wall, he noticed a freshly-made notch in the wood panel. With his hand he followed the notch all the way to the floor where he found two long, slender, rusty, brass skeleton keys dangling from a round, metal ring.

"Is this the set?" he asked the surly captain.

"Aye, ye be a good detective, Inspector!" answered Snappy. "I could have sworn I put them thar keys under me pillow. I be thinkin' the other set be lyin' around here somewhere."

Captain Snappy snatched the keys out of Jake's hand and quickly opened the padlock to the chest. Out flew Pete, a frazzled, teeny-weeny, grey duck. He had a green-feathered head with a black patch over his right eye. Pete landed directly on Captain Snappy's right shoulder. "Quakers!" he quacked.

"That's no parrot!" Rex exclaimed. *"That's a—DUCK!"*

79

"Shhh!" warned Captain Snappy, covering Pete's ears from Rex's harsh words. "He be not knowin' that!"

"The duck doesn't know he's not a parrot?" asked Jake in utter confusion as he scanned every grey and green feather of the peculiar bird.

"What do you mean he doesn't know he's a duck?" wondered Rex.

"When Pete was still inside his egg, a huge storm be comin' in off the coast. The storm become so ferocious it blew his egg right out of his mother's nest, and rolled it off a cliff into the nest of a mother parrot sittin' right on top of her own lot of eggs. She be havin' no idea she be sittin' on an extra egg. And when her young'n hatched, there was Pete. Well, not knowin' what to do with him, she raised him as one of her own."

"Are you telling us that duck was raised as a parrot?" uttered Rex in a baffled snicker.

"Aye!" confirmed the captain.

"What happened to his poor eye?" questioned Alexa as she stroked Pete's slightly-bent beak.

Captain Snappy explained that Pete was in an unfortunate cracker accident. "But we be not speakin' of it! It upsets Pete so!"

"Oh, how sss—s—sad!" chutted Sandy. She then grabbed her gigantic, purple crayon and proceeded to feverously write every bit of this information down in her tiny notebook.

"Now, let me get this straight," Rex smirked, stomping all around the cabin in a tirade of disbelief. *"Gertrude from The Museum of Time is a duck?"*

"No, she's a goose," declared Jake.

"Then...Penelope is a turkey?"

"Noooo, she's an ostrich," explained Alexa.

"Then pig breath over there is a pig—right?"

"How many times do I have to ttt—t—tell you?" Sandy exploded. "I'm not a pig. I'm a guinea pig from Peru. Big difference!!!!"

Rex's fur puffed up as the skin on his back tightened from his outrage and exasperation. *"Are you all going to stand there and tell me that one-eyed duck is a—**Parrot?**"*

Captain Snappy gave them all a deadly evil eye while caressing a large sword hanging on the wall. They all trembled in fear for their lives if they dared to say otherwise.

The hairs on the back of Jake's neck stood straight up as he felt the captain breath from behind. "Well, if it walks like a parrot...," " he said in a high pitched nervous tone.

"And—d—d, talks like a parrot..." stuttered Alexa, too frightened to disagree with Snappy.

Captain Snappy once again covered Pete's ears so he wouldn't hear and bellowed out firmly in his gravelly voice, "**He be a parrot!** And if anyone be sayin' otherwise, they'll be walkin' the plank!"

Rex just stood there shaking, trying not to cough up a nervous fur ball. *"Wo—wo—works for me!"* Rex succumbed as he went to pet Pete, who immediately snapped at him with his beak. *"And a lovely parrot...he is! Truly...charming, I might add!"*

"And he be a smart one, too!" the captain bragged while searching through the chest. "Pete's been helpin' me figure out these riddles so we could gather up the seven sandstones of the Seven Sea Gods: Tethias, Herus, Eos, Sethena, Rhus, Endoseidon, and Aryas. Once ye be helpin' me figure out the last three riddles, we'll be able to find the last three stones. Then we'll be able to put the pieces of the puzzle together and figure out the course to **Earth's End!**"

Suddenly, a crack of lightning crashed over their heads as a rumbling clap of thunder shook the ship violently to the right and then to the left. Captain Snappy let out a seemingly-endless, wicked laugh as they were all tossed about the cabin. Pete quacked away as the children and their pets screamed out in horror.

"*We're doomed!*" cried out Rex. "*Doomed, I tell ya!*"

The wave that almost tipped the Krusty Katfish over left as quickly as it came, and they all regained their balance. Captain Snappy was still laughing himself wickedly silly.

"You four gotta' grow some better sea legs if we're goin' to be solvin' this puzzle. Once we get to **Ear...**"

"Don't say it!" they all screamed out, petrified at the outcome of his words.

Rex, looking a tad seasick, blurted out, "*I think by now we all know where we're going!*"

"Well, once we be gettin' thar, we'll find the right conch shell and trap Jezebel back in it. That be breakin' the curse of Shipwreck Bottom—aye!" announced Snappy.

"And the crew will return back to their rightful age?" guessed Jake.

"You be right thar, Inspector," answered Snappy. "And all the ships buried at Shipwreck Bottom will be risin' from the depths of the sea and be saved from thar death!" He then carefully gathered up all the sandstones he found from the chest and spread them far and wide across the table. He showed the children the stones of Herus, Rhus, and Eos. He told them that all seven stones, when put together, make a giant puzzle that forms one large map that leads to their final destination.

Jake grabbed his magnifying glass and carefully examined each and every one of the sandstones. They were very old and worn, each having a trail leading off its stone to an unknown other piece of the puzzle, which, when complete, would lead to Earth's End. "There's one missing, isn't there?" he asked, looking around the room. "You said you found four sandstones."

Captain Snappy got an alarmed look on his cursed, young face as he ransacked the cabin searching for the other sandstone, which was the third piece to the puzzle. "Pete," he hollered about, "where is the third stone of Sethena? We be only havin' the first, second, and fourth puzzle pieces. "

"Quackers!" shouted back Pete, meaning it was missing.

"What do ya mean, it's missin'?" Snappy grunted. "I thought I told ya to be keepin' your good eye on all four of them sandstones!"

"Quackers!" Pete announced. "Quackers!"

"What do ya mean ya left to get a snack?" Snappy snarled back.

Pete explained in his own unusual way that he left the cabin and waddled down to the galley to get some salt water taffy. He just loved salt water taffy. Upon his return, he heard a rustling coming from the cabin. The cabin was pitch black when he entered. Someone grabbed him from behind, threw him into the treasure chest, and locked him inside.

"They must have taken the third sandstone!" exclaimed Jake.

"What are we going to do?" pondered Alexa, "Without Sethena's stone to complete the puzzle, we only have numbers one, two, and four. Now we'll never find our way to **Earth's End!**"

"*Oh, no—not again!*" Rex whimpered.

The ship rocked back and forth as the thunder and lightning exploded over their heads. For a second time they were tossed about the cabin like beach balls bouncing in a sand storm. Once again the waters calmed, and the ship steered steady on its voyage.

Rex gasped, almost coughing up a fur ball from being seasick. "*Alright...*" he scolded, "*I can't take anymore of this tossing around. No one mentions the name of that place again until we get off this floating popsicle stick...agreed?*"

Feeling seasick themselves, they all agreed not to mention Earth's End again until they hit dry land.

Captain Snappy just moaned and groaned as he stomped about the cabin in a tirade. "Me thinks me got a treacherous traitor among me crew who must have snatched that third stone. That be mutiny!" he uttered. "Why, they'll be shark bait for this!"

"Maybe we should ggg—g—go?" chutted Sandy as she scurried out of the way of the ranting, mad captain.

"*For once I'm with the pig!*" whispered Rex. "*Let's blow this joint!*"

They all started to inch their way closer and closer to the door to escape when, suddenly, Pete noticed their slow progress towards the door. "Quackers! Quackers!" he quacked.

"*Stool pigeon!*" Rex hissed.

"He's not a pigeon. He's a parrot!" whispered Jake.

"*Oh—please. He's a one-eyed, annoying, baby duck who thinks he's a parrot!*" snapped Rex. "*Am I the only one who can see that?"*

Captain Snappy turned abruptly to the exiting group and yelled out in a commanding, treacherous tone, "Where do ya think you be goin'?"

Frozen in fear, they all just stood there.

"Ahhh—nowhere," explained Jake, "absolutely nowhere!"

"Yeah, nn—n—nowhere, stuttered Alexa. "We were just admiring this ***beautiful*** door! Weren't we guys?"

"*Stunning!*" shouted out Rex. "*Mahogany, isn't it?*"

"Truly!" proclaimed Sandy nervously.

In the glimmer of the oil lanterns, Jake quickly scanned the door with his magnifying glass, getting ready for a quick exit. "They just don't make doors like this anymore!" he skittishly chuckled.

"Enough about that blasted door," blasted Snappy. "If ya help me find that thar third missing stone of Sethena and Jezebel's shell, I'll let ya have the bloody door if it be meanin' that much to ya all! Though I don't know what ye all be wantin' with me door— anyways."

"*Now, let me just get this straight...*" announced a confused Rex. "*You want us to find a stolen sandstone that is the third piece in a puzzle for which you already have the first, second, and fourth pieces. And when that missing piece is combined with the pieces you **do** have, plus three other pieces, numbers five, six, and seven, which you apparently **don't** have, we'll then be able to solve this mystery.*"

"Aye, Mr. Pussycat!" confirmed the captain.

Jake carefully examined the writing on the fourth sandstone. "So even though we are missing the third piece to the puzzle, which is Sethena's stone, we can find the fifth stone by solving the riddle written on this fourth stone—right?"

"Aye, Inspector!" agreed Snappy. "That's what I be needin' ye for!"

"So solving the riddle on one stone leads you to the next one?" wondered Alexa.

"Aye, lassie, you be gettin' it now!"

"Well, we'll just solve the riddle on the fourth stone, leading us to the fifth stone. Then, we'll figure out the riddle on that fifth sandstone to find number six. Once we solve that riddle on number six, it should be simple enough to find that last, seventh, sandstone," determined Jake, "and solve the puzzle."

"*Excuse me!*" snickered Rex, raising his hand as if he were in school. "*Aren't you all forgetting something?*"

"What?"

"*We don't have the third, stolen, stone!*" exclaimed Rex in a huff. "*How do you expect to solve the puzzle and build a map without it?*"

"We'll just have to find it!" announced Jake, glaring angrily at him for his lack of faith in their detective skills.

Rex paced back and forth in the cabin, shaking his head in disbelief with a mask of concern on his fuzzy face. "*You expect us to find the stolen sandstone that is the third piece in the puzzle for which we already have the first, second, and fourth pieces. Then, find the three other sandstones by solving the riddle from the fourth stone, which will lead us to the next stone with the next riddle—and so on—until we find the seventh stone. Then, if we are lucky enough to find all seven stones, which, by the way, could be hidden anywhere on the planet, solve a mysterious puzzle created*" *by the Seven Sea Gods, which will lead us to—don't worry, I'm not going to say it. Once we get there, we have to find a mystical conch shell that King Neptune used to capture Jezebel, the evil sea witch. Then we have to recapture her in that shell and throw her back into the ocean before she sucks up every floating ship on the high seas and covers the planet completely in water. Once we do that, all the sunken ships will rise up from the bottom of the sea and the curse of Shipwreck Bottom will be broken, which will allow all these teeny-weeny, little, toddler pirates to return to their normal size and age. We have no idea who took the third sandstone or where the other three are, let alone who let Jezebel out of her shell in the first place!* **Are you all crazy?"**

They all gasped in fright as Captain Snappy grabbed a sword and pointed it right under Rex's dangling, helpless, furry chin and grunted, "That be exactly what ya be needin' to do. And if you be callin' me crazy one more time, ye be shark bait—Mr. Pussycat!"

Instantly Rex's fur puffed up fearing for his life. "N—N—N—No p—p—problem!" he stammered. **"*Moustachio Investigations: Mysterious Crimes*,** *after all,* **Are Our Specialty!** *Right, you guys?"*

"Right!" they all confirmed. "Mysterious Crimes Are Our Specialty!"

"Well, I be hopin' so..." Snappy declared. "That be what ye card be sayin'!"

"What card?" inquired Jake with a curious look.

"The card that be fallen out of the sky," he answered. "That tis be what card!"

"Do you still have it?" wondered Alexa.

Captain Snappy told them he thought that the card was in the cabin somewhere, and he started his search. While he looked about, he began to explain that while he was docking his ship next to the Lady Lilac, a gust of flowery wind blew across the bow of the ship. Suddenly, out of the sky, the Moustachio's card drifted down from the heavens. He called the number on the card and spoke to a woman who claimed to be their secretary, and she told him how to contact the children.

"Ye secretary be sayin' you can solve any crime!" Snappy growled, glaring down at the young detectives. "Tis be why I be contactin' ya!"

In a huff, Jake took his magnifying glass and started searching for the card himself, hoping this time to get a good look at it. "If we can find the card, call the number on it, and speak to this mysterious woman, we can get some answers as to why we have a detective agency, a secretary, and don't know anything about it!"

Captain Snappy dug deep into the chest as Sandy scurried around him and pulled out the card. "Here she be!" he proclaimed. The children were ecstatic finally having the opportunity to get closer to solving the mystery of the unknown woman and why she was sending them all these mysterious cases. As the captain went to hand Jake the card, Pete let out an enormous "**Quack!**" and gobbled up the card. "Quackers!" he sputtered as he swallowed it up.

"**Noooooo!**" the children cried out.

"Pete, that be not a quacker...I mean cracker," scolded Snappy.

"Now we're never going to get that phone number," Alexa sighed.

Jake had a long face. "This is one mystery even I can't seem to solve."

Sandy was feverishly writing something down in her notebook with her big purple crayon. "SSS—S—Six, SSS—S—Six..." she mumbled.

"What are you writing down, you annoying pig?" Rex grunted to Sandy.

"Eight..." she whispered under her breath.

Rex grabbed the notebook out of Sandy's paws causing her favorite, purple crayon to go flying across the room. *"Give me that!"* Rex then read the numbers 668 out loud. *"What the heck is this gibberish?"*

Sandy snatched her notebook back as she retrieved her lost crayon. "It's the number on the ccc—c—card, you furry clod," she snapped.

"Sandy!" exclaimed Jake with wide open eyes. "You saw the phone number before Pete ate the card?"

"Oh, my gosh!" squealed Alexa.

"Well!!!!!!!" chutted Sandy. "I did sss—s—see it."

"And?" demanded Rex.

Sandy just sat there nervously trying ever-so-hard to remember the other seven digits. "Now let me think. Six six eight...ummm...two, no that wasn't it. Maybe it was four. No...not four...seven, yeah...no, not seven."

"I don't believe this!" shouted out Rex in exasperation. *"You can't remember all the numbers! Of all the stupid..."*

"Now, now, Rexy Cat, you know Sandy has short-term memory loss!" scolded Alexa as she snuggled Sandy for comfort. "It's O.K., sweetie. At least you got the first three numbers. We'll eventually get the other seven and figure out this mystery. Won't we, Jake?"

Looking down at the table, Jake had a blank look on his face as he stared at the fourth stone and its riddle.

"Won't we—Jake?" Alexa encouraged, trying to make Sandy feel better. "Jake!"

Jake wasn't paying any attention to her as he read the fifth riddle on the bottom of that fourth stone. "Huhhh?" he questioned.

"Jake, you're not paying any attention to me," she complained with a blank expression on her face. "Tell Sandy it will be O.K."

As he carefully reread the riddle over and over, he mumbled under his breath, "It'll be all right." He then asked Captain Snappy which of the sea gods wrote the fifth riddle on the fourth sandstone.

"Arrrrr—tis be Endoseidon, the supreme ruler of all the sea gods. That be the riddle me and Pete be stumped on!" he grunted in confusion.

Jake grabbed his magnifying glass and read the fifth riddle of Endoseidon out loud.

"Who swings above the World of Old and New, climbing the vines far and wide, from fruit to fruity tree? Erupting mountains above fiery seas the sandstone you seek will be."

"What the heck does that gibberish mean?" Rex snickered. *"We'll never figure that out."*

"Quackers!" quacked Pete as he waddled around the room, bumping into walls in utter confusion.

"Don't be gettin' your tiny feathers in a snit, me boy," bellowed Snappy to Pete. "The Inspector will be figurin' out the riddle any minute now! Then we be on our way to be findin' the fifth sandstone."

The captain, tiny as he was, scooted right underneath Jake's chin and looked curiously up at him as Jake read through the riddle a few more times. "You can solve the riddle, can't ya—matey?"

"Uhhhh—no problem," Jake stuttered, looking at his sister for any help, having absolutely no idea what the fifth riddle meant. Alexa shrugged her shoulders back at him, having not a clue herself.

"Help me out!" he silently mouthed over to her.

"I have no idea!" she soundlessly mouthed back to him over the Captain's and Pete's heads.

Rex just stood there with desperation written on his fuzzy face as he mouthed to them, *"Then we're... doomed!"*

Jake and Alexa just glared at him for his continued lack of faith in their detective skills.

"All right..." Jake reasoned, "let's break the riddle down into smaller parts."

"Yeah..." Alexa agreed, "how hard could this be?" She then directed Sandy to take some notes as they worked through the riddle.

"Now, let me see..." Jake thought out loud.

Sandy feverishly wrote down his every word.

"What in the world are you doing, you foolish rodent?" Rex hissed at her.

"I'm ttt—t—taking notes!" she chutted as she scribbled away with her purple crayon.

"He hasn't said anything worth writing yet. Write the important stuff—not every word everyone says!" he

snipped. *"Just—the important stuff!"*

"How am I supposed to know what that is?" she squealed.

Rex got right down into Sandy's face and grunted in annoyance, *"We'll tell ya...that's how you'll know!"*

Jake, frustrated by the distraction of his pesky pets, asked them if they were both finished arguing and proceeded to continue trying to make heads or tails of the fifth riddle. "Fruit trees, fruit trees," he called out. "Everyone start naming some fruit trees."

"Apple?" announced Alexa with confidence.

"How about pear?" added Rex as he stared down fiercely at Sandy, who was just staring off into space. *"Now would be a good time as any to start writing something down, pig breath!"*

"Now?" asked Sandy of the group. Jake and Alexa nodded "yes" as she started listing all the fruit trees. "Oranges?" she chutted.

"Maybe," thought Jake, "but they don't fit with the beginning of that sentence... **'Who swings above the World of Old and New, climbing the vines far and wide.' "**

"Maybe the fruit is a grape, Jake," thought Alexa.

"The lassie may be on ta somethin'," Captain Snappy snarled.

"Quackers!" quacked Pete in agreement.

"Yeah—the duck, I mean parrot, is right. Grapes do climb on vines!" Rex exclaimed.

"But not from fruit to fruity tree, they don't," Jake explained.

"My friend Grace..." Alexa started to say.

"Not another story about Grace!" Jake moaned, shaking his head into the palm of his hand in utter exasperation.

Alexa just rolled her eyes at her brother who so rudely interrupted one of her famous stories about her friend... Grace. "Anyway...Grace just loves grapes. She's not allergic to any fruit, whatsoever, just peanuts. We were at lunch, and Grace was very happily munching on some grapes, not the red ones with the seeds, but the seedless, green ones. The seeds stick to her teeth...not pretty!"

Rex collapsed on the floor and yawned in boredom. *"Does this story have an end; we do have a case to solve, ya know."*

Alexa smirked at her pesky pet, trying to ignore his contempt for her stories. "As I was saying...Grace was eating her grapes when Oliver grabbed them and started tossing them across the lunch room to the boy's table. And, boy, did that get the boys in trouble. Mrs. Barshey yelled at them good. Oliver had to give Grace his banana to make up for the loss of her grapes. Grace doesn't like bananas, so she traded Lainee for her watermelon. Grace just loves watermelon. I mean the seeds can be a little annoying...but..."

"That's it!" Jake cried out.

"Watermelon?" questioned Alexa.

"That makes no sense," smirked Rex. *"Watermelon doesn't grow from trees. Does it?"*

"Not the watermelon, you nut ball...the **banana!**" he shouted with confidence.

"Banana!" they all gasped.

"Banana!" Jake confirmed. "Bananas grow on trees!"

*"Then what's up with '**climbs the vines far and wide?**' "* asked Rex.

"And what ddd—d—does '**swings above the World of Old and New**' mean?" asked Sandy.

They all pondered the question. Silence filled the air as they thought and thought for an answer. "**Monkeys!**" Alexa declared. "Monkeys swing above '**the World of Old and New!**' We just learned that in science class."

"And '**climbs the vines far and wide**' " announced Jake.

"Monkeys!" they all gasped.

A smile sprang across Jake's face from his sister's brilliant detective skills. "Right you are, Inspector Girl—monkeys! Monkeys are members of two main groups of classification, the New World monkeys or the Old World monkeys. Two of the three groupings being simian primates and the third group being the apes."

"See, Pete? I be tellin' ya the Inspector would be able to solve the riddle," proclaimed Snappy.

Alexa, in a snit, cleared her throat. "Hmmmmm!" she glared at him, deserving some praise, too.

"Arrrrr, and the lass, too!" he added.

"That's better!" she smirked.

Sandy read back her notes affirming that they had two clues to solving the riddle—banana and monkeys. "Now what?" asked Sandy. "We still have the last half of the rrr—r—riddle to solve."

"Yeah," added Rex. "*I always hate to admit it, but the pig is right! So what the heck does, '**erupting mountains above fiery seas the sandstone you seek will be?**' *"

Jake had a perplexed look on his face as he kept mumbling the phrase back and forth trying to make sense of the second half of the riddle. "Fiery seas...fiery seas?" he questioned.

"What do you think, Jake?" Alexa asked.

Jake's eyes grew wide with excitement as he shouted out, "**Lava!** It has to be lava!"

"And lava erupts from mountains called..." Alexa concluded, as they all shouted out the answer together "...**Volcanoes!**"

Alexa turned to Sandy and asked her to read back the clues to the riddle. Sandy chutted away as she read from her teeny-tiny notebook: monkeys, banana, lava, and, finally, volcano.

"Captain," Jake questioned, "does that mean anything to you?"

"Arrrrr," he thought, "I be thinkin', I be thinkin'." The captain toddled around his cabin with Pete perched on his little shoulder as they whispered to each other under their stinky breaths.

"Quackers, quackers, quackers," Pete argued with the captain.

"It truly can't be, Pete!" Snappy protested.

"Quackers!!!!!!!!!!" the parrot-duck exclaimed.

"What is it?" shouted out Jake. "What does it mean?"

"It be meanin' Moneke Island," the captain slowly whispered to the group.

"*I'm confused!*" blurted Rex. "*What's Moneke Island?*"

"Tis be where the clues from the riddle be pointin' to, Mr. Pussycat," he explained. "The island, she be havin' a volcano and trees from one end to the other covered with bananas."

"Is it a live volcano?" questioned Alexa, worried for their safety.

"You'll be safe, lassie. The volcano, she be not spittin' out for centuries," Snappy grunted.

"*Are you sure?*" trembled Rex. "*Because I'm not going anywhere near an erupting volcano! My fur is way too delicate to get singed!*"

"I be as sure as the parrot on my back!" Captain Snappy declared as his duck quacked away.

Rex just looked bewildered at the one-eyed, baby duck pretending to be a parrot and whimpered, "*We're so, so doomed!*"

Suddenly, they heard a loud bang from outside the cabin's door.

"Quickly, Lexy, the stones," Jake cautioned as he and his sister gathered them up, dumping them and Sandy into her Inspector Girl backpack.

Wanting to discover what all the commotion was about, Captain Snappy stormed in anger towards the door and nearly ripped it off its hinges as he opened it.

"*Wow, he's really strong for a little kid!*" Rex chuckled.

To their surprise, they found Izzie hanging from a large meat cleaver stuck in the door.

"What in the worlds are you doin', woman?" he snapped.

"Well, what does it look like I'm doing, you fish—smelling, old fool?" she scolded. "I'm trying to get my meat cleaver out of the door."

The children and their pets just stood there in awe at the spectacle of the little girl trying relentlessly to pull her meat cleaver out of the captain's door.

"How did it get thar in the first place?" he grumbled. "And what ye be doin' snoopin' around me cabin?"

Izzie gripped tightly onto the cleaver's handle, leveraging

her baby-sized feet against the wooden door, and pushed and pulled with all her toddler might. Without warning, the meat cleaver popped right out of the door. The children, Rex, and Sandy let out a horrified scream as it went flying across the room, nearly missing their heads.

"Like I said," Rex groaned, checking his head for any missing parts, *"I have delicate fur!"*

"DDD—D—Did she mean to do that?" stammered a frazzled Sandy, diving deep down into the backpack for cover.

"I think that nasty, little girl meant to do that!" Rex cried out.

"I'm beginning to think you're right," sighed Jake.

"Oh, don't be ridiculous," Izzie mumbled. "I wouldn't hurt a hair on your precious heads—well, maybe the cat's," she said with a half-hearted laugh. "None of this would have happened if I hadn't had butter all over my hands when I was chopping up some gummy worms for my crab cakes. My meat cleaver just slipped right out of my hand and went flying this way. Imagine that! I didn't even know you all were in here. By the way, what are you doing in here—anyway?"

"Never ye mind, woman!" Snappy grunted, running past her in a hurry. "Come on," he ordered the children. "We be needin' to turn the ship about if we be headin' towards Moneke Island."

They all ran after the captain as he bolted up to the top deck of the ship. "What about the last clue?" Jake reminded from behind.

"What clue ye be belly-achin' about?" the captain shouted back.

"The monkeys!" exclaimed Jake. "What about the monkeys?"

"Well—where thar be bananas, there's sure to be some monkeys," Snappy snapped.

Alexa got a huge smile across her face and squealed, "I just love monkeys. They're so, so cute. You know they show love by picking bugs off of each other's fur."

Rex just shook his furry head back and forth, whining, *"Oh, joy—something to look forward to!"*

CHAPTER SEVEN

My Purple Crayon!

Upon reaching the top deck, the captain ordered Penelope to turn the ship about and head into the sun. "Aye-aye, skipper, skipper!" she repeated.

"Where we be headed, Cap'n?" snarled Spikey as he hoisted up the sails into the wind.

"Yes..." shouted out Izzie, wanting to know their destination, "where are...we going?"

"Moneke Island," he declared.

"MONEKE ISLAND!" the crew grumbled in protest.

"Is it me, or do they look a little worried?" Rex wondered as he started to panic, himself.

Snappy stomped about the rotted, wood planks of the deck, barking, "Tis be me ship, and we be goin' where I be sayin'!"

Scratching his little peg leg, Stumpy questioned, "But what about the monkeys?"

"Arrrrr—stop your whining. Ye be acting like a bunch of babies."

"Well, technically half of them are actually babies," Jake whispered to his sister.

"Yeah, and I think some of them are actually crying as we speak," giggled Alexa back to him.

"We all got jobs to be doin'," Captain Snappy ordered his disgruntled crew. "The Inspector be tryin' to break the curse, ye all be gettin' us to that island, and I be takin' care of the monkeys! Anybody who can't follow me orders can walk me plank right here and right now. I be bettin' the sharks are ready for a snack about now, anyway." The captain then let out a dastardly laugh.

There was dead silence among the teeny-weeny pirates. "Now, get back to work!" Snappy ordered. "Swab the poop deck, fill the guns, raise the sails, and get back ta work!" He then noticed Izzie slithering around the children, wide-eyed as she became fixated on Jake's magnifying glass sticking out of his back pocket.

"What an unusual looking magnifying glass," she inquired interestedly. "Wherever did you get it?"

Jake jumped nervously out of her way as she tried to take it out of his back pocket. Rex slid between them, protecting Jake and the magnifying glass from the crazy, messy, little girl.

Looking her straight in the eyes, the annoyed cat hissed, *"What do you think you're doing?"*

Izzie started having a fit, ranting and raving like the toddler she was, having not gotten her way. "I just wanted to see it! Why can't I look at it?"

Jake then politely, but firmly, explained that the magnifying glass was a family heirloom, never to be touched by anyone but a Moustachio. He then pulled out his grandpa's secret book from his front pocket, sandwiched it with his magnifying glass, and stuck them both back into his pocket for safe-keeping. Glaring at the annoying girl with the greasy, braided pig tails sticking out of both sides of her head like antennas, Jake thought to himself, **There's something awfully disturbing about her!**

Izzie just stood there watching Jake's every move, paying extra attention to where the brown, leather book was located.

"Woman—what you be lookin' at?" Snappy echoed into the wind. "Get down below and fix us somethin' we actually can eat!"

She scowled at him with the nastiest of looks. "You are the crudest man I've ever cooked for!" she uttered in disgust. "I'll go start dinner—I'm making a banana cream pie!"

"For dinner—?" he hollered back. "Can't ya fix anythin' besides desserts? I barely have one tooth left that not be rotten from all the sugar!"

Her bug-eyes nearly flew out of her head as she screeched, "The moment the curse is reversed, I am so off this floating piece of junk!" Before storming off the deck, she grabbed a hatchet and chopped another piece of nautical rope in half, causing another sandbag to fall from above. As it fell from the sky, it nearly missed the children once again.

"*She is so trying to get rid of us!*" announced Rex.

"I'm with Rexy Cat on that one!" confirmed Alexa.

Sandy popped her tiny, frazzled head out from the backpack and very nervously stuttered, "I sss—s—second that! Or is it third? I can't remember!"

"*Whatever!*" Rex moaned at her.

"But why?" thought Jake. "She needs us to reverse the curse. Without us, she'll just get younger and younger until she goes—'**Poof**' and disappears."

"Maybe she's the one who swiped the third piece to the puzzle?" pondered Alexa.

Looking over at Stumpy and Spike Longsliver smiling

toothlessly at him, Rex added, smiling back, *"My bet's on those two."*

"But it doesn't make sense for any of them to have the third sandstone. If we can't put them all together and solve the puzzle, we'll never get to..."

"Don't say it..." they all screamed, covering his mouth.

"I wasn't going to!" he mumbled under their hands. Jake then annoyingly shushed them away from his face as he continued. "Like I was saying before you rudely interrupted me...if we can't get to you-know-where and find that conch shell and trap Jezebel in it, they'll all be goners."

"And the ship will be sucked down to the depths of the sea to be buried at Shipwreck Bottom for all of eternity," confirmed Alexa.

"DDD—D—Don't forget the world being completely engulfed in water!" chutted Sandy as she was reviewing her notes.

"Well, that's just crazy," Rex snickered. *"Preventing us from solving the case wipes them off the face of the planet."*

"Or does it?" pondered Jake, caressing his cleft chin ever-so-cleverly.

"What do you mean?" Alexa asked.

"Maybe whoever swiped the third puzzle piece thinks they're protecting themselves," surmised Jake.

"How?" questioned Rex, now caressing the tuft of fur under his chin with his left paw.

Jake had a curious grin sprouting across his face. "By stopping us, they would be helping Jezebel take over the world, now wouldn't they?"

"Oh, I get it!" Alexa exclaimed. "Jezebel would reward

them and protect them from her destruction."

"Very ccc—c—clever!" whispered Sandy, writing every word down so she wouldn't forget. "The culprit who stole the third sandstone might be working for the sea witch!"

"*Or culprits!*" Rex announced, thinking there were two.

"Don't you guys remember when Captain Snappy was arguing with Izzie, she wished Jezebel would sink the ship," Jake mentioned curiously.

"Oh, yeah," whispered Alexa. "He yelled at her that if that was to happen, she would go down with the ship, too!"

"*But she said, don't be too sure about that,*" added Rex.

Alexa smiled confidently, "She's not worried about going down with the ship at all. Is she?"

"It's almost like she's planning something," thought Jake.

"*Or hiding something!*" Rex pondered as he looked nervously once again over at his two new pirate friends still smiling toothlessly at him. "*But what about those two pint-sized morons?*"

"I'm not sure what game those two are playing," wondered Jake, staring at Stumpy and Spikey. "But they are definitely up to no good."

"Why's that, Jake?" Alexa asked.

"Because when we were searching the captain's cabin for the keys to unlock the chest, I was feeling around the walls and found a freshly cut notch in the wall leading right down to where the keys were on the floor. That notch definitely could have been made from Spike Longsliver's hook! "

"Do you think Spikey and Stumpy locked Pete in the chest and took off with the third stone of Sethena?" his sister asked.

"I'm not sure, but my detective skills are telling me those two over there, Izzie, and this entire mystery are somehow connected."

"FFF—F—Fascinating!" announced Sandy, feverishly writing every word down with her purple crayon so she wouldn't forget anything.

"Well, whoever actually stole the third stone wasn't all that clever," Jake explained. "Since each sandstone has a riddle to finding the next stone on it, snatching the third puzzle piece only gives us a missing piece to the overall puzzled map because Captain Snappy, thank heavens, already found the fourth stone with the fifth riddle on it. So we can still move forward with the case and find the next, fifth, piece to the puzzle."

"You're right, Inspector," added Alexa. "If the culprit had taken the fourth sandstone with the riddle to the whereabouts of the fifth stone, the chain of riddles would have been broken, and we would never be able to find the fifth missing piece to the puzzle without knowing the fifth riddle written on that fourth stone."

"Right you are, Inspector Girl!" exclaimed Jake. "The Seven Sea Gods were very smart putting the riddles to finding the next stone on the proceeding numbered piece to the puzzle."

"It's a chain that can be easily broken," Alexa stated.

"And a puzzle almost impossible to solve," explained Jake. "They must really want to keep the location of those conch shells an unsolved mystery."

"*But the Moustachios are smart enough to figure it out!*" announced Rex with pride.

Jake gave Rex a scruffy rub on the head and declared,

"That we are, my furry friend—that we are!"

"So..." reviewed Rex, "*let me get this straight...all we have to do is discover the culprit or culprits who stole the third sandstone and get it back. Then, find the fifth stone on a volcanic island inhabited by monkeys and figure out the sixth riddle on that sandstone to find the sixth missing piece to the puzzle, which, if we're lucky enough, will lead us to the seventh one. We then need to put all those stones together to make one large puzzle map, which will lead us to you-know-where. Once we get to you-know-where, we have to find the right conch shell, trap the wicked sea witch in it, throw her back into the sea, which will then, hopefully, reverse the curse, and save the world.*"

"That's about right," Jake declared with complete faith.

"**Are you crazy?**" blasted Rex. "*Doesn't anybody think that might be just a teeny-weeny bit impossible, even for—* **us?**"

Alexa picked up her frazzled cat, gave him a big snuggle to calm him down, and said, "There, there, Rexy Cat. Remember what Grandpa used to say, '**the greatest gift in life is your power to believe.**' "

"And I, for one, believe we can do this!" exclaimed Jake, raising his magnifying glass in the air like a sword.

"Me, too!" declared Alexa.

"MMM—M—Me, three!" Sandy added. "Or is it four? I forgot!"

Rex just stood there shaking his furry, golden, red head in disgust at their hopefulness and sighed, "*We're doomed! Doomed as doomed can be!*"

Suddenly, they heard Stumpy screaming from the crow's nest atop the ship's tall mast. He peered out into the horizon through a one-eyed, brass-plated telescope and shouted, "Land ahoy...Cap'n! Land ahoy!"

Captain Snappy grabbed his own telescope and took a look for himself. He then handed it to Pete, who was perched upon his shoulder. The duck, who thought he was a parrot, carefully squinted through the scope with his one good eye and verified their location.

"Quackers!" announced Pete, confirming that the island they were seeking lay straight ahead.

"Are ye sure?" asked Snappy of his one-eyed, baby duck. Pete affirmed they had, indeed, found Moneke Island. The captain then ordered Penelope to drop anchor.

"Aye-aye, skipper, skipper" Penelope squawked. She slid the long boom that she was still hanging from over the upper deck of the ship to reach the anchor. She then stretched her long neck out, grabbed hold of the steel crank with her beak, and lowered the rusty, barnacle-infested anchor into the sea. The massive anchor took hold at the bottom of the ocean as the wind continued to pull the ship forward. The tiny crew quickly pulled all the sails down just as the ship snapped back like a yo-yo from the pull of the anchor's chain. The ship shook violently, rattling backwards and forwards as if an explosion erupted from inside. Everyone went flying backwards, rolling on top of each other as the Krusty Katfish came to an abrupt stop.

"Oh nnn—n—no!" cried out Sandy, as her purple crayon went flying into the air, falling down a hatch to the hull below.

"What's wrong, sweetie?" asked Alexa.

"My purple crayon slid down those steps," she chutted. "I'll be right back!"

Before Alexa could stop her, Sandy ran after her purple crayon down the hatch. She scooted along a very wet beam, jumped over a large bag of flour, darted down a gigantic wooden spoon, and ended up on top of a pile of dirty pots and pans. There she saw her favorite purple crayon teetering on the edge of the handle of a frying pan, seesawing up and down. It was about to fall into the depths of the kitchen sink's drain. Just as she was about to grab it from being lost forever, she looked up and to her surprise saw a gigantic magnifying glass looming over her. Knowing Jake was up on deck with **his** magnifying glass, she feared for her life and jumped into a pot to hide. Hearing a commotion erupting in the room, she slowly raised her tiny head up from the bottom of the pot to get a peak at who was arguing below. She gasped in terror as she saw Izzie arguing with the evil Baron Von Snodgrass.

"Look what's happened to me," she screamed at him, waving a frying pan under his scarred face. "And it's all your fault for dumping me on this ship to hide."

"But you've never looked younger, my dear!" he exclaimed with a maniacal grin.

"Younger? I'm five years old and getting younger by the day, you fool!" she bellowed. "You have to help me. If the curse is broken, and I'm on this rotten ship, those annoying children will find out I'm me and send me back to prison. And I am not spending the rest of my days cooking with that stupid giraffe, Gerard, ordering me around."

Snodgrass slithered about the room plotting his next move. "My dear Mrs. Smythe, how was I supposed to know the ship would be cursed?"

"You mean to stand there and tell me you had no idea

about the curse and the Moustachios ending up here," she ranted and raved, "before you dumped me on this floating pile of junk? Do you take me for a fool?" She then grabbed her meat cleaver and swung it in the air.

"Merely an unfortunate coincidence...my dear," he sighed as he took a distasteful bite out of one of her overly-frosted crab cakes. "Merely a coincidence. I had no idea that meddling boy and his annoying sister would end up here, I promise. Besides, you should be more grateful. After all, it was I who helped—**you** by plucking you out of that zoo-infested jailhouse Delbert put you in." He then quietly glided across the room as his yellow, linen duster jacket dragged on the sugar and baking powder-covered wood floor. "You know..." he coughed, trying to swallow the dry cake, "I think these need just a little less sugar and a little more butter... don't you?" he asked as he tried to hand her one.

Mrs. Smythe knocked the crab cake right out of his hand, and it went flying across the room, heading directly for Sandy, who ducked deeply into the bottom of the pot she was hiding in. "How dare you! I've been baking for royalty for years! Everyone just loves my crab cakes!" she exclaimed in a fit of anger as she threatened to whack him in the head with her skillet.

"Ah, ah, ah—my dear Izziedura," he protested. "I wouldn't do that!"

"Give me one good reason why I shouldn't!" she demanded.

"Because I can help you!" he snarled.

Her greedy eyes lit up. "How?"

"The moment the curse is broken, I will swoop in and get you off this ship."

"You will?"

"Of course—why, it's the least I can do," he said, dusting the dry crab cake crumbs from his thin moustache. "But one favor deserves another, my dear! Don't you think?"

"What do you want?" Mrs. Smyth asked. "Anything—anything!"

"Young Moustachio and his companions have no idea who you are?" he questioned, curling the tip of his overly-waxed, black moustache.

"Yes—yes, that's true!" she confirmed.

"Excellent, then!" Snodgrass announced. "The boy has something that belongs to me."

"What is it?"

"A small, brown, leather book," he explained. "During our last encounter he stole it from me, and it must be returned. Does he have it?"

Mrs. Smythe smiled, knowing Jake, indeed, had the book that Snodgrass wanted. "Why, yes—yes, he does!"

"Excellent, Izziedura—excellent," Snodgrass grimaced as he pranced arrogantly around the room. "Get me that book, and I'll get you off this ship the moment the curse is broken and you are returned to your former, older self!—Agreed?"

"Agreed," she replied. "But I thought you wanted the other magnifying glass?"

Snodgrass bent slowly down, looking Mrs. Smythe directly in her cold, dark eyes. "I still do, my dear, but young Moustachio's powers grow stronger. You'll never stand the chance of getting that magnifying glass away from him. I, on the other hand, have the powers to fight him. You let me worry about the magnifying glass. You just get me that—**book!**"

He then activated his magnifying glass and escaped into a vortex of wind, disappearing from her sight. But before he completely vanished, she yelled out, "What's in the book?"

"Never you mind, my dear—just never you mind," he echoed. "Get the book, and I'll be back to destroy the Moustachios." And with that said, the Baron's magnifying glass let out a burst of light and a rumble that shook the ship from stem to stern as it disappeared into the thin air from which it came. The violent vibration caused Sandy's purple crayon to fall into the galley's tarnished, metal sink, making a loud clanking noise.

Upon hearing that sound, Mrs. Smyth curiously started to make her way over to the sink and the unwashed pots and pans. Sandy trembled in terror as she clung to the bottom of the greasy pot she was hiding in. She was fearful that she would be discovered by Mrs. Smythe, who was crazedly searching the room for the possible cause of that odd sound. She finally looked down into the sink and saw the big, purple crayon just sitting there, now seesawing next to the edge of the drain. She then sniffed around the galley and her pots and pans, wondering where and how this crayon came to be in her sink. The wickedly evil cook took a deep breath and flicked the crayon into the drain to be lost forever to the depths of the sea. She then stumbled into the pantry, violently swinging all the cupboard doors open and shut, searching for some bananas to make her banana cream pie. **"Where are all my bananas?"** she screeched. **"How does anyone expect me to make a banana cream pie without any bananas?"**

Sandy, shaking like a leaf, raised her tiny head out from under the pot and scoped out the room for any signs of that crazy, little girl. "Oh, boy, I need to get back to the gang and let them know that Izzie is Mrs. Smyth and she's going to steal Jake's book!" She jumped out of the pot, repeating constantly, "Izzie's Mrs. Smythe. Mrs. Smythe's Izzie. Izzie's Mrs. Smythe." Sandy feverously ran along the top shelf, going over everything she just found out, trying not to forget any of the details. Over and over she sang in her head, "Snodgrass is here, Snodgrass is here. Snodgrass is Izzie. Izzie wants the magnifying glass. No, Snodgrass wants the book. Maybe he wants my crayon. That's it—Snodgrass wants my crayon." She then slid down a hatch repeating a thousand times, "Snodgrass wants my crayon, Snodgrass wants my crayon. I just loved that crayon." Sandy ended up following a beam of sunlight, calling out to herself, "I lost my crayon. I lost my crayon." Sandy finally leaped breathlessly out of a hole to the top deck above. Frazzled and confused, she lost any memory of the meeting between Mrs. Smythe and Snodgrass and their dastardly plans as she ran in a daze toward the children.

Alexa, alarmed at Sandy's despair, snatched her right off the deck. "What's wrong, sweetie?"

Trying to remember, she chutted, gasping for air, "I have horrible news!"

"**What?**" they all shouted in utter hysteria.

Sandy just stood there with a blank look on her face, thinking and thinking and thinking.

"*Well,*" scolded Rex, "*we don't have all day, ya know!*"

"Tell us, Sandy," Jake encouraged as they all held their breaths in anticipation.

Sandy's heart was racing like a speed boat as she blurted out the news, "My ppp—p—purple crayon is missing!"

"That's the horrible news?" Rex chuckled, falling down onto the deck, laughing himself silly. *"Well, let's stop everything we're doing. We don't have to save the world from complete destruction. Let's solve your case...the case of the missing purple crayon! After all, mysteries are our specialty!"*

"Rexal Moustachio!" scorned Alexa.

"Now you're in big trouble," announced Jake. "She called you Rexal!"

"Rexal Moustachio," she continued, "can't you see Sandy's upset?"

"Oh, brother—you must be kidding me. The pig only lost a stupid crayon," he snickered, grabbing Alexa's Inspector Girl backpack, ransacking it for another crayon. *"Look,"* he shouted as he pulled out an orange one, *"Mystery solved!"*

Sandy looked like she was about to cry, sighing, "BBB—B—But that's not my purple crayon!"

"Well, we'll just have to look again, now won't we?" Rex continued as he rummaged through the backpack again.

"Give me that, you crazy fur ball," demanded Jake as he snatched the backpack from Rex's paws. Jake searched and searched for another purple crayon without any luck. "Sandy, we have a red one, the orange one, or a blue one. We'll get you a new purple crayon when we get home."

"Oh, brother!" sighed Rex. *"I lost a toy mouse last week; I don't see anyone replacing that!"*

"You know, if you cleaned up your own toys, you wouldn't lose anything!" scolded Jake.

Alexa held out the assortment of crayons and asked Sandy to choose one.

Sandy reluctantly agreed to use the blue one until she

got a new purple one. While Sandy was trying out her new crayon, Jake took the unnoticed opportunity to switch his grandpa's book in his pocket for the one Penelope gave him in Alexa's backpack for safe keeping.

Suddenly, the hatch flew open and Izzie came storming through, ranting about her missing bunch of bananas. "Who took my bananas?" she yelled while flinging a meat mallet wildly into the air. Everyone ducked for their lives as she accused each and every crew member of snatching her crate of bananas. "Just how am I supposed to make dinner now?"

Captain Snappy ran over to the side of the ship, gesturing to the open sea. "There's an ocean filled with fish...woman," he bellowed. "Why don't ya use some of them for ye dinner?"

"Fish," she scowled, "now who ever heard of baking with fish?"

As Izzie and Snappy were arguing over the dinner menu, Jake noticed Stumpy and Spikey laughing themselves silly. "Would you look at those two?" he motioned to Alexa and their pets.

"Do you think they took the crate of bananas?" she asked.

"*Wouldn't you?*" Rex pondered. "*How many cakes, pastries, and pies can you eat in one day? Why, if I don't get some fish soon, I'm going to go crazy myself. Ah, my grilled 'kraut and flounder sandwich, how I miss you so. Just remember, I never did get to have my lunch, thanks to that pint-sized, flounder-stealing pig, ya know!*"

"We'll eat later," stated Jake. "We need to figure out how we're going to sneak onto that island and look for the fifth piece to the puzzle."

Overhearing the conversation, Penelope swung over their heads and bopped Jake right on the head. "Use your magnifying glass, silly boy, boy!"

Jake waved his hands violently over his head, trying to swoosh her away. "Would you stop hitting me on the head!" he shouted.

"Well, well?" she said.

"Well, well what?" he smirked.

"What are you waiting for, for?" she cackled. "Skipper, Skipper, the Inspector said he's going to use his magnifying glass to make it on to the island, island."

"I didn't say that," barked Jake, "you crazy bird!"

She stretched her neck all the way out and batted her big, long, false eyelashes over his face and clunked him right on the head again. "Are you sure...because I could have sworn I heard you say so, so! It really would be the best way to go, you know, know! The monkeys will never know you were there, there! Just pop over, find the fifth sandstone with the riddle to the next stone, and pop back to the ship, ship!"

Jake just stood there, grimacing at her. He hated being shown up by an ostrich. **But she was probably right**, he thought to himself. "Do you really think it is going to be that easy?" he asked her.

"You'll never know if you don't get going, going!" she clacked away.

"*Are you trying to get rid of us?*" questioned Rex. "*Because it sure looks that way.*"

Penelope bopped Rex on the head and spewed, "Why, of course not, but Jezebel's hurricane is coming after us, you know, know! Time's a-wasting, wasting!"

"Well, then," announced Jake to the crew, "we'll jump over to the island using my magnifying glass and bring back the fifth puzzle piece!"

"It would be the safest way to go!" agreed Alexa.

"Yeah—" chuckled Rex. "*I'm so glad you thought of it!*"

"Very funny," smirked Jake, "very funny!"

Captain Snappy ran around the deck, recruiting his disgruntled crew to make the journey onto Moneke Island. But in fear for their young, toddler lives, no one would budge. "What's the matter with ya? Why—you've all turned into a sniveling bunch of yella-bellied cowards!"

"But skipper—the monkeys!" exclaimed the group. "We're just little kids!"

Captain Snappy was infuriated by the lack of bravery from his crew. He told them even though they had been cursed into the teeniest of toddlers, they were still a treacherous lot of pirates who should let nothing stand in their way. "All those willin' to take the journey," he yelled, "take two steps forward." The entire crew took two steps backwards, including Rex.

"Get back here, you crazy cat!" exclaimed Jake as he snatched him from the cowardly group. "You don't get to decide whether you get to go or not!"

"*Hey, it was worth a try!*" Rex declared.

Captain Snappy was crazed in anger. "That be mutiny!" he proclaimed. "You'll all walk the plank for this! And I'll be gettin' me a new crew braver than brave can be!"

"Ah, skipper, skipper?" announced Penelope.

"What is it?" he snapped.

"They're the last of the pirates on the high seas, seas!" she explained. "Remember the curse, curse. All the other ships are at the bottom of Shipwreck Bottom and their crews— *'Poof* disappeared into thin air, air! There's no one to replace the crew with, Cap'n, Cap'n!"

Upon hearing that, Izzie strutted around the deck gathering up support from the crew. "Well...well...well, what are you going to do now?" she spouted at the captain. "Looks like your crew has the upper hand now, doesn't it— Snappy? Without them you can't sail this broken down ship. Now, can you?"

"Ye be right thar, woman," he mumbled. "But without me stones to break the curse, ya all go— *'Poof* into thin air like the rest, never to be seen or heard from again!" He then walked among his crew, warning them they had best stay loyal to him and the ship, not Izzie, if they ever want to be turned back into full-blown, manly, swashbuckling pirates again. He then gestured to Jake that they would go without the crew. He then pointed over to Izzie. "But we be takin' her!"

"Her?" the children exclaimed, not wanting the nasty girl tagging along.

"Me?" Izzie shrieked in a panic, not wanting to go.

"Aye—you!" Snappy bellowed. "I'm not goin' to let you stay on me ship and turn me crew against me! I'm goin' to make sure Pete keeps his one good eye on ya at all times!"

"*Wow*," chuckled Rex, "*I've heard of a watch dog but never a watch parrot-duck. This is going to be good!*"

"Quackers!" Pete quacked, knowing he, too, could help find the fifth stone on the island.

Jake grabbed his magnifying glass from his pocket and threw it towards the sky, commanding, "**Onekemay Islandway!**" A flash of light exploded from the center of the glass, burning a hole in the ship's deck.

"What ye be tryin' to do, burn me ship down, matey?" winced the captain.

"Ahhh, sorry about that," echoed Jake through the wind. "We'll tape that up later!"

The crew quickly doused the fire with some water and stomped the smoke out with their little feet. An enormous gust of wind shot out of the magnifying glass as it hung suspended in mid-air, growing larger and larger. The sails of the ship intensely swung back and forth as Penelope was spun around and around from the force of the magnifying glass's ominous whirlpool.

Having jumped through Snodgrass's magnifying glass before, Mrs. Smythe pushed everyone out of her way, "Well, I guess I can always look for some bananas," she mumbled as she jumped into Jake's magnifying glass.

"How rrr—r—rude!" snapped Sandy, hanging out of Alexa's backpack.

"My sentiments exactly, sweetie. Someone has to teach that snotty girl some manners, and I'm just the girl to do it! " affirmed Alexa as she jumped through after her.

Holding Pete in his arms, Captain Snappy ordered Penelope to take care of his ship and to keep an eye on his back-stabbing crew before he made his leap into the center of the glass.

"*Shouldn't we rethink this?*" Rex complained to Jake. "*We don't know what we're getting ourselves into. This could be very dangerous. I don't like monkeys; they're very, very nasty creatures, you know. Not to mention very uncivilized!*"

"Get—going, you nut ball!" Jake ordered as he gave Rex

a good, swift kick in the butt.

Rex reluctantly went soaring into the magnifying glass, screaming, *"We're dooooooooomed!"*

"I certainly hope not!" Jake shouted out, jumping through right behind him. "I certainly hope not!"

CHAPTER EIGHT

Monkey Business!

They all rolled and tumbled over each other within the gigantic whirlpool of the magnifying glass. Twisting and turning, they made the leap from the Krusty Katfish over to whatever terror awaited them on Moneke Island. Suddenly, a blast of light lit up the sky as the magnifying glass spit them out one by one.

"Arrrr, what parts of tis island do ye suppose we be at?" asked Captain Snappy.

"I think we are at the base of the volcano," Jake confirmed as he stood up and commanded his magnifying glass into his hand. "Rex, where are you?"

"*I'm up here!*" he called down.

"Where's here?" echoed Jake's voice up to the sky. "Oh, brother, come down from there, you crazy cat!" he demanded.

Rex was stuck in a palm tree, just dangling from a lovely bunch of coconuts. "*Uh—oh!*" he exclaimed, falling from the tree. All the coconuts showered down with him, violently clunking everyone on the head, and then bounced haphazardly to the ground.

"Quackers!" exploded Pete as Rex plopped right on top of him.

"Rex, get off the duck, I mean parrot—you're squashing him!" Alexa pleaded as she darted out of the way of another falling coconut. "Would you just look at my hair? What a mess! Every time I jump through that thing, I have to redo my hair."

"Oh, stop complaining about your hair!" snickered Izzie. "How can anyone be that obsessed with their hair?" She then mischievously grabbed a baby coconut and threw it at Alexa, just missing her newly-coiffed head.

"Watch it!" yelled out Alexa. She was mad as mad could be. She grabbed Sandy and her backpack and stormed right over to that nasty toddler. "Listen, missy, I have had just about enough of you. You're mean, rude, and you need to get some manners—not to mention a brush for your **own** hair."

Izzie was paying little attention to Alexa as her eyes nearly popped out of her head, glaring down at the ground. She unexpectedly, but with conniving delight, noticed Jake's brown, leather book just lying there helplessly, waiting for her to snatch it up.

"Are you listening to me?" Alexa shouted out in frustration.

"I heard you—I'm mean, rude, and need to get some manners—not to mention a brush for my **own** hair," Izzie grumbled as she started inching her way towards the book, trying to grab it before Alexa noticed it.

"Well, that's better," Alexa declared as she, too, noticed the book, quickly picking it up before Izzie could grab it.

"**Drat**," Izzie mumbled under her breath, having failed to snatch the brown, leather book that time.

"Ummmm," Alexa whispered to herself, "Jake must have dropped this when he fell through the glass." Alexa then carried the book off through the tropical jungle, ready to scold her brother for not being more careful with it. Worried about the monkeys and her brother's clumsiness, she decided it would be safer to keep the book tightly hidden in her backpack where Sandy could keep an eye on it. She never knew that Jake had thought the exact same thing just before leaving the ship when he, himself, switched the books. She quietly, without knowing, switched the books back. She put Penelope's book back into her Inspector Girl backpack and handed Jake Grandpa Moustachio's secret book instead.

"Jake, you need to be more careful with this," she scolded.

Jake wasn't that worried about the book, thinking that he had switched them earlier, hiding the real one in the backpack. "Sorry," he said. "I'll keep better tabs on it!" But what Jake didn't know was that Alexa had just unknowingly switched them back.

"*So what do we do now?*" asked Rex, sniffing around the jungle.

"We best be startin' to search for the fifth sandstone!" exclaimed the captain.

"*Are you kidding me?*" chuckled Rex. "*Hello—have ya seen the size of this place?*" Rex picked up the first rock he could lay his paws on and smirked, "*Look, here it is! We're done—let's go home!*"

"That's not a sandstone, you knucklehead!" scolded Jake.

"Quackers! Quackers! Quackers!" quacked Pete, pointing north.

"Pete says we be needin' to go that-a-way!" Snappy declared.

"*You mean to tell me we're supposed to just follow that one-eyed...**BIRD**,*" Rex smirked, "*and hope he leads us to the stone? What is he, psychic?*"

"Well, how do ya think he'd be findin' all the other pieces to the puzzle?" argued the captain.

"That's crazy!"

"I agree!" shouted Izzie. "I, for one, am not crawling all over this island following that quacking duck who thinks he's a parrot!"

Captain Snappy glared down at Izzie and blurted out, "That's what you be doin' woman, if ye don't want to be dumped on this island alone and left for the monkeys to get at ya." He then started shoving her on her way.

"Well—you don't have to be so rude!" she shrieked, pondering the predicament she was in. Facing the probability of being left behind, she reluctantly agreed to follow the parrot. "You are the rudest man I have ever had the displeasure of working for. I hate you!"

"Tell me somethin' I be not knowin', woman," grumbled Snappy. "Pete led me to the other four stones, and he'd be leadin' us all to the fifth one. I'd bet me ship on it!"

"I certainly hope so," Jake whispered to Alexa, following the captain and Pete's unstoppable quacking.

"Me, too!" she sighed. "Me, too!"

Pete sniffed the salty air and directed them around the north face of the volcano. The explosive eruptions of molten lava over time had created a hard, mountainous shell over the accumulated debris, forming rugged, steep cliffs into the volcano. Its peak reached high into the heavens, looking ominous and deadly. A hot breeze blew in from the ocean as the palm trees waved in the wind. "Quackers!" Pete commanded. "Quackers!"

"Are ya sure?" Snappy asked.

Pete nodded his head, flapped his wings, flew off the

captain's shoulder, and made an X with his webbed foot right there in the sand.

"Start diggin', me buckos," ordered the captain.

"Start digging with what, my paws?" whined Rex.

"Aye, matey!" muttered Snappy.

"Do you know how delicate my cat paws are?" complained Rex. *"What do I look like, a stupid dog? I am a domesticated animal on the top of the pet chain— I don't dig!"*

"Whatever it be takin', Mr. Pussycat," snapped Captain Snappy.

Alexa started rummaging through her Inspector Girl backpack, searching for something to use to dig up the fifth sandstone with. "Sandy, sweetie, do you see any of the garden tools Mom and I were using to plant daisies?"

"I think sss—s—so!" she exclaimed as she pulled out a miniaturized hoe, rake, and two shovels.

"You wouldn't happen to have a spare grilled 'kraut and flounder sandwich in there, would ya?" inquired Rex.

"I don't think so..."chutted Sandy. "But I do have some left-over pizza fishy crackers!" she tempted.

"**NOOOOOOOOOOOO!**" screeched the children.

"**Quackers!!!!!!!**" cried Pete, afraid of losing another eye.

"Now what's wrong with a bunch of smelly, pizza fishy crackers?" asked Izzie.

"Well, for one," Snappy barked, "it was an unfortunate cracker accident that led poor Pete to be wearin' that one-eyed patch in the first place."

"And pizza fishy crackers give Rex gas—bad gas!" declared Alexa, sticking the bag back into her backpack.

Jake rolled his big, green eyes as he started digging and added, "Really bad gas!"

Everyone dug away in the spot, trying to find the fifth piece to add to the puzzle that would lead them to Earth's End and Jezebel's shell. They dug and dug and dug without any luck.

"This is hopeless," complained Izzie. "That ridiculous excuse for a parrot is wrong—dead wrong."

"Pete's never wrong, woman," yelled Snappy. "It be here. I can feel it in me bones!"

"Well—I don't know if I'm feeling the stone in my bones, but I am feeling something. Do ya ever get the feeling you're being watched?" asked Rex as his fur started to puff up.

Jake cautiously scanned the area and whispered nervously, "I know exactly what you're feeling. I think Pete's right about the sandstone being here, but I don't think we should be digging down," he sighed.

"What do you think we should be doing?" whispered back Alexa.

"I think we should be looking up!" her brother said reluctantly.

They all slowly turned their heads up into the palm trees, fearful at what they would find. Jake's fear was well founded, for as they looked up they were surrounded by monkeys, not just ordinary monkeys, but sea monkeys. They were the most notorious, wise-guy sea monkeys that ever sailed the Seven Seas.

"Hey—how youse doin'?" chuckled one of them as he dangled upside-down from a vine. He then pulled out what looked like a sandstone and tossed it up and down in the air.

"Youse lookin' for this?" he smirked.

"Ahhhhhhhhhhhh!" they all screamed in terror, sprinting into the depths of the tropical jungle.

"Get 'em, boys!" ordered the monkeys' ring-leader.

All the monkeys swung from vine to vine, chasing them as they ran for their lives.

Huffing and puffing as he ran, Rex yelled out breathlessly, *"Now would be a good time as any to use the magnifying glass to jump out of here! Don't ya think?"*

Jake was running as fast as he could with his sister right behind him. "Not without that stone! The Moustachios aren't quitters."

"Speak for yourself!" Rex cried out through the jungle. *"And by the way—have I mentioned we're—doomed?"*

The nimble sea monkeys were gaining on them as the group of twelve swung feverishly through the trees, determined to capture the young detectives.

Sandy shook uncontrollably as she poked her teeny-tiny head out of Alexa's backpack, mesmerized by the hairy, green and brown monkeys. They had webbed hands and feet and the longest of dragon-like tails poking through the back of their surfer board shorts, which made their flight through the air easy. The scaly, flapping gills on the side of their necks enabled them not only to survive on land but to also thrive in the sea. "They're ggg—g—gaining on us," she squealed.

Alexa looked back and screamed out in terror as one of them swooped down, nearly snatching her up.

"This way!" Jake exclaimed as he turned down a lavender orchid-infested path. Pete flew right behind them as they all ran fast and furiously, following Jake to what they thought would be safety. "Oh—no!" he cried, abruptly turning around. "Wrong way—dead end—dead end! Turn around— turn around!" They all made an about face, but it was too late. The sea monkeys had them cornered.

The unruly group of monkeys hung off the trees, suspended by their long tails, bouncing up and down like a bunch of yo-yos, laughing themselves silly. Their leader plopped to the ground, followed by two other dopey-looking ones. He had a thick, gold chain wrapped around his neck. Dangling from it was the largest of engraved letters with the name "*Ma.*"

"Well, well—well, if it ain't the cursed, teeny-weeny Captain Snappy and his one-eyed duck," he smirked. "How da ya like being a little kid? By the looks of your size, it'll be just a matter of time before youse go— '*Poof*, and vanish into thin air."

"Yeah—'*Poof*," repeated the other two wise-guy monkeys.

"And who might these two redheads be?" the boss monkey asked.

Jake glared into his simian eyes and declared, "I'm Inspector Jake Moustachio, and this is my sister..."

"Inspector Girl," Alexa affirmed. "And who might you be?"

"Well—I'm very insulted my reputation is not known by youse two. Why, I am Tony Bannana, and these two bubble heads are my baby twin brothers, Little Johnny and Little Johnny."

"*Both your twin brothers have the same name?*" inquired Rex, sniffing around.

"Ma was only expecting the stork to bring one bubble

head, but he apparently made a mistake and dropped off two dumbos instead!" Tony explained. "What was she ta do? It wasn't like she could return one or nothin'!"

"Yeah—he dropped off two," repeated both the Little Johnnys.

Alexa had a perplexed look spreading across her face. "How do you tell them apart?"

"It don't matter!" Tony shrugged. "These two bubble heads don't have one brain to share between them."

"Yeah—we don't have one brain between us," the Johnnys repeated.

"Apparently so!" Izzie exclaimed.

"Would youse two stop repeating everything I say?" ordered Tony to his brothers. "After all—I am the boss of the family!"

"Yeah—Tony's the boss now!" the brothers agreed.

"Where's your crooked mother? I thought she be the boss of the family," Captain Snappy growled out in disgust.

"Haven't youse heard?" declared Tony. "Ma's on a... well, how shall I put this, a...a long and much-deserved vacation!"

"Yeah!" echoed the twins. "A long and much-deserved vacation!"

"When is she coming back?" asked Jake, staring at Tony clutching what looked like a piece to the puzzle in his slimy, webbed hand.

"She ain't as long as I keep this sandstone!" announced Tony with a big silly dribbling smile.

"Yeah—Ma's trapped in the conch shell," the brothers blurted out.

Tony got really mad at his brothers' constant interruptions

and shoved a banana into both their mouths. "Put a cork in it, youse two!" he scolded.

"My bananas," bellowed Izzie. "Where did you get my bananas from—you slimy, green ape?"

"I resemble that remark!" Tony sputtered. "And these ain't your stinkin' bananas," he denied. "These bananas belong to the family."

Izzie went ranting and raving about in hysteria over her lost bananas. "What do I look like, a fool?" she exploded.

"Well..." laughed Tony.

"Those are rare Brazilian-Dwarf-Apple bananas," she uttered. "I had a crate of them sitting right on the deck of that dilapidated ship, the Krusty Katfish, when we were docked at Pirate's Point. They were right next to my prize-winning watermelons. And when I went to bake my banana cream pie, they were gone."

"The Bannana Brothers ain't no thieves," protested Tony.

"Yeah—we ain't no thieves," mimicked the brothers.

"We are legitimate businessmen of the sea," declared Tony as he munched on one of the stolen, rare bananas.

"Who you be kiddin'?" barked Snappy. "Your family be filled with nothin' but double-crossin' scoundrels, stealin' anything and everything you be gettin' your slimy, webbed hands on."

"Quackers!" agreed Pete, flapping his wings in an uproar.

Alexa turned to Jake and Rex, whispering, "Do you think they stole the bananas?"

"Maybe," Jake thought. "Come to think of it, these guys might have been the ones that jumped Pete in Captain

Snappy's cabin, locked him in the chest, and took off with the third piece to the puzzle."

"And then took the bbb—b—bananas!" Sandy concluded.

"But what would they want with the third stone to the puzzle anyway?" asked Rex. *"They don't have the first, second, or fourth pieces."*

"And the bbb—b—bananas, too!" announced again Sandy.

"Enough about those stupid bananas," Rex mumbled under his whiskers. *"We have to get that sandstone he's holding and get out of here still in one piece ourselves."*

"But is that the third one he's holding, that he stole from the Krusty Katfish?" questioned Jake. "Or did these wise-guys stumble upon the fifth piece to the puzzle that we are searching for and that's what he's clutching in his hand."

"I think it's the fifth one," Alexa whispered. "That snotty girl's got my vote as the culprit who locked poor Pete in the chest and stole the third stone."

"I still think those toothless pirates back at the ship are the ones who stole the third piece to the puzzle," Rex disagreed. *"That drooling monkey probably has the fifth sandstone in his slimy, webbed hand."*

"BBB—B—But what about the bananas?" chutted Sandy.

That's exactly what I was thinking!" Izzie ranted as she marched angrily over to the two Johnnys, plucking the Brazilian-Dwarf-Apple bananas right out of their overstuffed mouths. "Give me those!" she demanded. "Now, just look at my precious bananas. They're covered in monkey drool. ***Ouch!!!!***" she cried out in pain. "Did you just pinch me?"

"You'll have to excuse my brothers," apologized Tony.

"They ain't got no manners. Stop pickin' flies off the little girl, youse two!" he yelled. "Since Ma's been gone, these two bubble heads have been quite a handful!"

"We miss Ma. She's trapped in the conch shell," the brothers repeated out of their banana-free mouths.

"What conch shell?" Jake suspiciously asked.

Tony became exasperated by not being able to keep his bubble-headed brothers from blurting out what happened to their mother.

"Youse know...the shell that kept that evil sea witch trapped!" the twin monkeys blurted. "Now it's got Ma!"

"Jezebel!" they all gasped.

"Yeah, yeah, yeah," Tony finally confessed, "that crazy sea witch Jezebel. Personally, I found her to be very annoying."

"I'm confused," Alexa thought.

"*Me, too!*" added Rex.

"I'm not!" stated Jake. "You were the ones who let her out—weren't you?"

"It was most certainly not yours truly," Tony denied. "I ain't that dumb! Now, those two nincompoops are another story. The Johnnys found that stinkin' shell and started tossing it around like a beach ball, and they dropped it, releasing that crazy witch. And there she was, an ugly lookin' thing, if you ask me. She was huge, with long, slimy, green, suction-cupped octopus tentacles trying to snatch us up."

"Where did ya get the shell from?" grumbled Snappy, glaring at the ruthless monkeys.

"I don't seem to recall that information!" recalled Tony as he was picking some banana out of his teeth with a toothpick.

133

"You ruthless monkey," declared the captain. "You stole that shell!"

"Quackers!" agreed Pete.

"Hey—youse pint-sized pirate," Tony proclaimed, "like I said before, the Bannana Family ain't no thieves. We are legitimate businessmen of the sea. That crate of shells fell off that boat. How were we supposed to know there was a crazy sea witch living inside one of them shells?"

"Which boat did ya steal it from?" Snappy demanded.

"Ya know, I don't appreciate your tone!" Tony remarked. "If youse ain't careful, youse are goin' to be findin' your short, little self at the bottom of the ocean—*capisce?*" he warned.

"It was the Lady Lilac," confessed the twins.

"What is it with youse two? Can't you keep your bubble-headed traps closed?" scolded Tony to his brothers. "Geeze!"

They all gasped in disbelief. "You mean you stole a whole crate of mystical conch shells off the Lady Lilac?" interrogated Jake.

"Arrrrr—are ye crazy? You be messin' with the Lady Lilac and the Seven Sea Gods! Not ta mention the natural order of the universe," warned the captain. "You be cursin' us all ta Shipwreck Bottom."

"You know, hidden inside each and every seashell lies an undiscovered, mysterious world of the sea just waiting to be discovered," announced Alexa.

"Don't forget the trapped sea monsters!" Rex winced.

"Quackers!" agreed Pete.

"Hey, I'm Tony Bannana. I ain't afraid of nobody!"

"Except for Ma," announced one of the twins.

"Yeah—except for Ma!" repeated the other.

Tony grabbed two more Brazilian-Dwarf-Apple bananas and plugged up both his brothers' mouths. "Shut up—already!"

Jake thought to himself that this was all starting to make sense. The Bannana Brothers, after stealing the shells, must have accidentally released Jezebel into the sea, and somehow their mother wound up getting trapped inside Jezebel's shell. Tony's now the head of the family with his mother gone. But there are definitely some missing pieces to this mystery. Jake just had to find out which sandstone Tony had in his hairy, webbed hand. Was it the third stone stolen off the ship? Or did the monkeys find the fifth one here on the island? Tony obviously wanted to keep anyone from finding that shell and releasing his mother. But why? Was this all about being the boss of the family, or was there more?

"Tell me, Tony...may I call you Tony?" Jake asked. "How did your mother end up in Jezebel's shell?"

"Well...Ma and that crazy sea witch got into a scuffle over the shells."

"A scuffle?" inquired Alexa.

"Yeah—ya know—a fight. Jezebel wanted the rest of the shells," he explained. "Apparently, she had friends trapped in some of the shells she wanted to let loose."

"*Friends?*" asked Rex.

"Ya know—buddies, henchmen, cohorts, flunkies, gumbas that work for her!" Tony explained, spitting out some left-over banana. "Like my boys here!"

"I'm ccc—c—confused!" Sandy confessed, quietly munching on a pizza fishy cracker.

"Arrrr, it must be true," grunted Snappy. "Pirates for generations, they be tellin' stories about the storms that brew in the sea. They be sayin' that they be comin' from all the sea witches and warlocks working for Jezebel. For centuries the Seven Sea Gods have been gatherin' them up and banishin' them into those mystical conch shells to prevent them from destroyin' the worlds. But once in a while, a shell drifts with the tides, and one of the witches or warlocks be let loose by some fool who stumbles upon thar shell."

"Yeah, like us!" exclaimed the little Johnnys with foolish pride.

"Like I be sayin', once a fool lets one of them out, they swirl around the sea, growin' stronger and stronger, destroyin' everythin' in thar path until the sea gods trap them back into thar shell."

Jake and Alexa gasped in disbelief. "***Hurricanes!***" they exclaimed.

"You be right thar—Inspector!" confirmed the captain.

Alexa cleared her throat, "Hmmmmm?"

"You too, lassie!" he added.

"That's better," she sighed. "You know occasionally I would like a little credit for something—thank you very much!"

"*So that's why hurricanes have names,*" Rex boasted. "*They are the names of all the sea witches and warlocks running amuck around the globe!*"

"And that's why hurricanes pop out of nowhere and then suddenly dissipate, disappearing from where they came,"

Jake explained. "Someone finds a mystical conch shell and unknowingly lets out a sea witch or warlock. Their anger storms the seas in the form of a hurricane until the Seven Sea Gods trap them back into their mystical shell and banish them back into the depths of the ocean."

"That's probably what the Lady Lilac was doing," thought Alexa.

"*Yeah,*" exclaimed Rex, "*helping the Seven Sea Gods by gathering up any renegade conch shells floating out to sea!*"

"Arrrrr, and some of those witches and warlocks be mighty strong," Captain Snappy imagined. "Those be the ones that must cause most of the destruction as they must fight the sea gods fiercely."

"What happened next?" Jake asked Tony Bannana.

"As I was sayin' before I was so rudely interrupted...Ma wouldn't let that witch have them shells. Ma was plannin' on making a lot of clams selling them, ya know. That witch grabbed the shell she was in, yelled out a couple of mumbo-jumbo words and— '**Poof**, Ma was gone, sucked right into that shell."

"*Where are the shells now?*" wondered Rex.

"What do I look like—a stupid gorilla?" laughed Tony. "I ain't tellin' ya that!"

Knowing he was about to be covered in monkey dribble, Jake quickly jumped over to the twins and pulled the bananas out of their mouths. "Spill it," he ordered them as Alexa handed him a wipey to clean off the drool.

"*Eeeeeew, that's nasty!*" hissed Rex.

They confessed that after Ma was captured into the conch shell, Jezebel went to gather the rest of the shells up. There was a horrific roar of thunder in the sky and then— '**Poof**, the shells, including Ma's, vanished into thin air. Jezebel kicked up a storm in anger, not getting her tentacles on the shells, and blew out to sea, searching for them.

"The shells, they must had been sent back to **Earth's End!**" Snappy declared. Suddenly, a massive ray of lightning blew across the heavens, followed by the tumultuous clap of thunder that shook the island.

"Precisely!" Tony declared. "And that's exactly where they're goin' to stay!"

"But if Jezebel finds those shells and sets all the sea witches and warlocks free..." said Alexa in a panic.

"*There will be hurricanes popping up all over the place...*" feared Rex.

"And that's how she intends to take over the world!" declared Jake.

"With each ship cursed to lie dead at Shipwreck Bottom, and no pirates left to be stoppin' her, she be growin' stronger and stronger," explained Snappy.

"We have to stop her!" shrieked Alexa.

Jake pointed to Tony and demanded his stone. Tony told them there was no way he was giving it up. "If youse find that shell and capture that sea witch, youse be lettin' out Ma. She'll be madder than a wild orangutan when she finds out! There's no tellin' what she'll do to me!"

"Finds out what?" bellowed Izzie as she tried to gather up the rest of her precious bananas.

"Tony married Savannah," blurted out one of the twins.

"Yeah—Tony married Savannah," repeated the other bubble-headed twin.

"What's wrong with that?" questioned Alexa. "I just

love weddings. There are pretty flowers, you get to dance, and there's wedding cake. My friend Grace's aunt just got married. It was beautiful. They had ice sculptures and little hot dogs in a blanket."

"Ma hates Savannah," the brothers squealed. "She forbade Tony from marrying her!"

"Ohhhhhhhhh!" they all sighed while Pete flapped around Tony's head.

"Precisely, and get that duck outta' my face." Tony shouted. "That's why you ain't gettin' this sandstone. If Ma finds out I got married to Savannah, my goose is cooked!"

"*Wait a second!*" spouted out Rex. "*I thought Gertrude was a goose, and he's an ape?*"

"She **is** a goose, you fur brain," Jake declared. "*My goose is cooked* is an expression for being in serious doo-doo!"

"And I ain't no ape," murmured Tony. "I am a monkey! Like I was sayin' before I was once again so rudely interrupted—Youse people really need to get some manners! Ma can never find out I married Savannah. Plus, I'm the boss of the family now, and I ain't givin' that up!

"BBB—B—But Jezebel is going to destroy the world!" chutted Sandy, now nibbling away at a Clunky Chunky Bar.

"That ain't my problem!" Tony shouted. "Sea monkeys can survive on land and on sea. And it's a good thing'cause when that crazy witch gets done, they'll be nothin' left of the worlds but water and a few wise-guy sea monkeys!"

"Are you telling us that you're going to let her destroy us all because you're afraid of your mommy?" bellowed out Jake.

Tony just stood there tossing that sandstone up and down

in the palm of his hairy, green and brown, greedy, webbed hand thinking of an answer. "Come ta think of it—**YEAH!**"

"Yeah—that's what he's gonna do!" repeated little Johnny and the other little Johnny. "That's what he's gonna do!"

CHAPTER NINE

Kaboom!

Suddenly, out from the depths of the tropical jungle, they heard an awfully scary, high-pitched, nasally screech. *"TONY!!!!!!!"*

"WHAAAAAT?" he yelled back.

"I thought youse was goin' to take me to get somethin' ta eat!" screeched the voice.

Tony had an exasperated look across his simian face. "I'm workin' here!" he shouted back.

The voice got closer and closer and scarier and scarier. "Let me guess, somethin' fell off a boat, and you're trying to sell it! What else is new?" All of a sudden, out from behind an aloe bush popped Tony's wife. She was a pink and brown-haired ape with the reddest of lips and greenest of eyes. She was wearing enormous pearl earrings dangling from her big, floppy ears and a piece of sandstone hanging from a thick vine around her equally thick neck.

Jake immediately noticed it and realized not only did Tony have one of the missing pieces to the puzzle but so did Savannah.

Savannah was paying absolutely no attention to anyone but her husband. She was infuriated he didn't even notice her new coconut swimsuit.

"Tony—" she yelled. "Does this suit make me look like a gorilla?"

"Doll face, please, not now...I'm doin' business here," he informed her. "Ya look great! Youse could never look like a gorilla. Youse the most beautiful and delicate ape in the universe!"

She then gave him a sweet kiss and picked a fly off his fur, which she ate right up.

"I think I'm going to be sick!" Rex moaned, swatting at the array of annoying flies circling the monkeys.

Upon hearing Rex, Savannah immediately turned around and finally noticed the group. "Oh, pardon my rudeness. I didn't know we was entertainin'!" she exclaimed. "I'm Savannah Bannana, and who might you all be?"

Jake and Alexa introduced themselves to the less-than-beautiful ape.

"Charmed, I'm sure," she said with a dribbley-drool smile. She then strutted over to Alexa and asked "What do you think of my new bathing suit? Do ya think the coconuts are too much?"

"I like the coconuts," Alexa replied politely.

"You're cute," she said, picking a fly off Alexa's shoulder and then eating it. "Tony, I'm starving. If you're not goin' to take me out ta eat, I'm goin' to order a pizza pie!"

"Make mine with anchovies!" Rex shouted out, licking his whiskery lips.

"Rex!" scolded Jake. "We're not here to eat pizza, you crazy nut ball. We're here to solve a case. Besides, pizza gives you gas!"

"Doll face, me and the Inspector have some unfinished business to attend to," Tony announced. "Why don't ya get on the shell and call over to Dolphino's and order us up a couple of pies and some root beers!"

"O.K., Tony," she said as she started to walk off into the jungle.

"**Wait!**" Jake yelled out at her. "You can't go!"

"Hey," scolded Tony. "That's no way to talk to a lady!"

Rex started laughing himself silly, smirking under his breath, *"That ain't no lady!"*

"That's a pretty necklace you have there. Where ever did you get that unusual piece of sandstone?" Jake inquired as he grabbed his magnifying glass trying to get a better look at it.

Alexa, Rex, Pete, and the Captain gasped as they, too, realized that Savannah had another missing piece to the puzzle just dangling from her hairy, pink and brown, thick neck.

"Arrrrr—you scoundrels," grunted Snappy, "so ya did go robbin' me ship. That other sandstone be provin' it."

"Yeah!" quacked Pete.

"Hey," Tony yelled back, "we didn't go stealing nothin' off your stinkin' ship."

"But Tony, what about the bananas and the other stuff?" confessed the twins.

Tony was infuriated at his bubble-headed twin brothers. He stuffed two more Brazilian-Dwarf-Apple bananas into their dribbley, chatty mouths and yelled, "Would youse two shut up—already!"

"O.K., so maybe we did steal the bananas and...a few other things," admitted Tony. "But we didn't take any of your sandstones. And for the last time, youse ain't gettin' any of mine," Tony said as he ordered his boys to get them.

"Ahhhhhhh!" screamed Alexa in terror.

"**Wait!**" yelled out Jake in protest. "Maybe we can make a deal?"

Tony held up his big, old, hairy, webbed hand and ordered

his boys to hold up their attack. "I'm listening," he curiously said.

Jake explained to Tony that he understood him not wanting anyone to find their way to Earth's End because if they did and found Jezebel's shell, they would, ultimately, release his mother from her own captivity. And that would spell trouble for Tony. But he only had two of the pieces to the puzzle, and they had three. If they or any of the Krusty Katfish's crew were able to find the last two missing pieces to the puzzle, numbers six and seven, having only five sandstones to build the puzzled map to Earth's End might be just enough to make the map readable.

"You seem like a gambling monkey, Tony," Jake asked. "How about we play a little game of cards? If I win, you give us your two pieces of sandstone, and we walk right out of here—unharmed."

"Well, that would be awfully stupid of me to let ya release Ma," Tony smirked. "Now, wouldn't it?"

"What's the matter?" Jake laughed "You afraid of losing? Are you sure you're a monkey because I'm smelling a chicken!"

"Hey, wait a second—I thought he was a monkey, not a chicken," Rex mumbled in confusion. *"So the parrot **is** a duck?"*

"Quackers!" Pete exploded, denying he was a duck.

Jake glared at his pesky pet in annoyance and yelled out, "He **is** a monkey—*smelling a chicken* is an expression. When are you going to get all these animals straight in your furry brain—you fur brain?"

"Sorry—got it!" Rex mumbled in shame. *"The duck's a parrot, and Tony's a chicken—I mean monkey!"*

"Hey—" screeched Savannah, "no one calls my Tony a chicken. He's ain't afraid of nothin'. Are ya, Tony?"

Tony told Jake that he accepted his challenge. But if he won, not only would Jake have to give up all of his stones, Tony would get to toss them all into the volcano.

"Are you crazy?" bellowed Rex hysterically. *"You can't throw us into that volcano. We'll be goners!"*

"Hey—Mr. Pussycat," he announced, "if I win, it don't matter because Jezebel and her sea witches and warlocks will destroy the worlds. Youse all will be goners anyway. But at least I will get the pleasure of seein' youse all...go first!"

"Well, that makes sense!" Rex reasoned. But as he thought more and more about the predicament, his trembling fur puffed up as he collapsed on the ground crying out, *"What am I saying! We're doomed, I tell ya—DOOMED!"*

Izzie huffed and puffed as she toddled over to Jake. "Are you sure you know what you're doing because I have no intention of being cooked alive in that silly volcano."

"Don't worry," whispered Alexa, "Jake is a card shark."

"Besides, that volcano doesn't even look active!" Jake declared.

"Ah...words of comfort!" Rex sighed. *"The end is near!"*

"Oh, stop being so dramatic, you knucklehead," Jake scolded. "Come over here. I have a plan!"

While the Bannana Brothers set up for the card game, Jake, Alexa, Rex, and Sandy were in a huddle as Jake explained his plan for getting out of this deadly mess. "Plan-A: it's very simple...we'll play a quick game of cards. I'll win...we'll get the stones and get the heck out of here!"

"Do you really think he's going to let us just walk out of here with them?" Rex asked, completely frazzled from the

chain of events.

"I ddd—d—don't" shuddered Sandy.

Alexa just shrugged her shoulders in disbelief. "Come to think of it, Jake, I don't think we're getting out of here that easily either."

"*What's Plan-B?*" inquired Rex.

Jake just stood there contemplating his next move. "I don't think I really have a Plan-B."

"*What do ya mean, you don't have a Plan-B. You just said you had a Plan-A. Everyone has a Plan-B when they have a Plan-A. What's the matter with ya?*" hissed Rex in a fright.

"Oh, all right!" retorted Jake. "Must I think of everything?"

Huddled, they all exclaimed in a silent whisper, "Yeah!"

"O.K., Plan-B, if I lose...Alexa throws one of the gift certificates into the air that Rupert gave us, and we stop time for one minute. I'll grab the stone from Tony, and Rex, you grab the one off of Savannah's thick, hairy neck. And then we'll run out of here like the terrified kids we are."

"*Wait just a blueberry-cotton-candy-pickin' minute,*" Rex argued. "*Why can't pig breath go get the stone off of Mrs. Bannana?*"

"Because," Jake needlessly needed to explain, "except for us, Sandy, along with everyone, else will be frozen in time— remember?"

"*Oh—Yeah!*"

"Are youse comin', or what?" Tony called over to Jake.

The brothers pulled over the crate of what was left of Izzie's bananas for a table to play on and two medium-sized rocks for them to sit on. Izzie became mad as could be looking at all the banana peels lying at the bottom of the crate.

"So what's it gonna be..." Tony asked, "Seven Card Stud? A little Texas Hold'em? Or maybe some Bridge?"

Alexa became so excited at the talk of playing Bridge. "You know our Grandma was the state Bridge champion seven years in a row."

"Ya don't say!" Tony snickered.

Jake looked him square in the eyes and declared in a very serious tone, "Let's play a *man's* game—*GO FISH!*"

"Well, well, well, Inspector, it looks like you're a guy who knows his way around a deck of cards," Tony announced as his boys laughed up a storm, hanging from their tails in the palm trees. "Go Fish it is," he agreed.

Alexa quickly rummaged through her Inspector Girl backpack looking for another deck of Go Fish cards. Remembering she only had the one deck they were playing with back at Grandma's cottage, she signaled to Jake she was fresh out of cards. Tony signaled his boys to drop him down a deck of cards from the trees. He then shuffled the deck and started dealing them each out seven cards from the deck filled with lobsters, crabs, dolphins, whales, and numerous other creatures of the sea.

Tony started the game as he winked at his wife like a world-class card shark himself. "So, Inspector," he asked, "do ya have any lobsters?"

Jake was very nervous playing cards for such an important prize. He ever-so-carefully scanned his cards, hoping not to make a match for the ruthless monkey. Jake popped a grin off the side of his mouth. He had a dolphin, a sea turtle, a walrus, two goldfish, and two octopuses, but no lobster. "**GO FISH!**" he smirked with delight, having not given Tony a single match.

Tony had no intentions of losing this game and releasing his mother from that conch shell. He made sure when he shuffled the cards that he would end up with the most lobsters. Without anyone noticing, he thought, he pulled an extra lobster card out from the side pocket of his surfer-board shorts. He palmed it, hiding it from everyone's sight under his big, gooey, webbed, monkey hand. With that card in hand, he very carefully pulled a new card from the top of the deck, which was stacked on Izzie's crate of half-eaten, rare Brazilian-Dwarf-Apple bananas. He slowly slid the card under his sticky, webbed hand towards himself face down across the wooden crate so no one would see that he had two cards. Tony then raised the cards, slipping the lobster into the cards he was playing and hiding the one he pulled from the deck into the side pocket of his shorts. An evil, satisfied, monkey-dribble smile grew across his green and brown, hairy simian face. **"BADA-BING, BADA-BOOM!"** he exclaimed, smiling up at his boys dangling from the trees.

"Do you think he has a match?" Alexa whispered in fear to her group as she rummaged through her Inspector Girl backpack, searching for the gift certificates to stop time.

"*We're so doomed!*" Rex cried quietly, covering his eyes with his paws. "*I can't look—I'm too young to die!*"

Jake looked over nervously at them, only having one pair of seahorses.

"What's the matter, Inspector?" Tony chuckled. "Ya look a little nervous!"

"You must have a good hand," Jake questioned.

"Maybe I do, and maybe I don't!" he smirked back.

Jake then glared at him with the determination of a

world-class card player and promising detective. He asked the crime monkey boss if he had any seahorses. Tony's dark, chocolate-brown eyes pierced down at the cards he was holding for any signs of a seahorse in his hand.

"Why, yes I do!" he exclaimed as he started to hand Jake the card. Jake's group had a sigh of relief, hoping the end would not be so near.

"Oops!" Tony shouted. "I made a mistake. This ain't no seahorse. It's one of those annoying jumbo shrimp. Sorry pal—**GO FISH!**"

Sandy, Snappy, Izzie, Pete, and Rex gasped in fear for their lives as Alexa firmly held onto that gift certificate, waiting for Jake to give her the signal. Jake then pulled a card from the top of the deck, praying it was a seahorse. His hand shook as he read the card. "**Darn it!**" he said to himself. "**A lobster!**"

Tony knew the deck was full of lobsters. He was holding three in his hand already and only needed one more lobster to make a full house for a win. But Jake, being the detective he was and knowing the scoundrel he was playing against, hadn't put it past him to cheat.

"Ya know, Inspector," Tony chuckled, "you play a mean game of Go Fish! If my boys weren't about ta drop youse down that volcano, we could become buddies!"

"*I really am too young to die!*" Rex wept uncontrollably.

"The game's not over yet—Bannana!" Jake smirked back.

"Oh—I do believe it is!" Tony spit, knowing the answer to his next question. "Do you have any lobsters—Inspector?"

Before handing Tony the lobster card, Jake signaled over to Rex and Alexa to get ready to jump into action. He then reluctantly handed Tony the card. Tony laughed himself silly as he threw his four lobsters on the crate, winning the game. He clumsily fell backwards, knocking over the crate of bananas. The deck of cards went flying all over the ground, exposing all the extra lobster cards with which he had unscrupulously filled the deck.

They all gasped in disbelief. **"You cheated!"** Jake exclaimed.

"Hey—" Tony uttered, "I ain't no cheater—a thief, a liar, and a no-good criminal, but I ain't no cheater. Youse didn't think you were getting out of here alive—did yas?"

"Like I said, Bannana," Jake exclaimed, "the game's not over yet!"

"Get 'em—boys!" Tony ordered.

"Quackers!" echoed Pete, flapping his wings in fear.

"Now Alexa—now!" Jake shouted.

"Hurry!" screamed Rex as he ran towards Savannah.

With the monkeys almost upon them, Alexa tore one of the certificates from the booklet and threw it into the air. A blinding flash of light burst forth, spreading across the tropical sky, freezing all in its path except Jake, Alexa, and Rex. Time had stopped, but only for a minute.

The Bannana Brothers just hung by their scaly tails in mid-air, right before Jake's eyes. "Run, Lexy!" he yelled out. "Run! We only have a few seconds! Rex, grab Savannah's stone from her neck."

Rex made a brave, flying leap into the air and snatched the sandstone dangling from her neck. Jake then nabbed the other one that Tony had in his pocket. The three of them ran as fast as they could out of the jungle with Sandy frozen in time, stiffly bouncing around in Alexa's Inspector

Girl backpack. As they ran faster and faster, Rex tossed his sandstone to Jake, who read both of them.

"Oh, my gosh, these are the fifth and six missing pieces to the puzzle," he screamed out in delight as he tossed them into Alexa's backpack. "They never had the third sandstone of Sethena, after all!"

"But we're still going to have to find the third, stolen, sandstone in order to complete the map!" exclaimed Alexa.

"Yeah—" shouted out Rex. "*And we also have to find the last and seventh stone!*"

Jake explained, as they frantically fled for their lives, that having the last riddle on the sixth stone would make finding the seventh and final piece to the puzzled map a snap.

"But we won't be able to read it without the third sandstone?" questioned Alexa, huffing and puffing.

"The third stone has to be somewhere back on the ship!" her brother declared. "My detective skills are telling me it just has to be there! We'll find it!"

After escaping death by volcano, time fell back into place. They kept running and running in order to get far enough away from the Bannana Brothers and be able to jump back into the magnifying glass, which would return them to the safety of the Krusty Katfish.

"Hi ggg—g—guys!" Sandy chutted as she fell back into time. She quickly grabbed her notebook and her new blue crayon while asking them what she had missed.

"*Well*—" Rex spouted, huffing and puffing, himself, as he ran. "*After Alexa threw one of those time-stopping certificates into the sky, I leaped up and grabbed that sandstone around Tony's wife's neck. Then Jake snatched the one Tony had. We have all the sandstones but number three, the stolen one, and number seven, and we are about to jump the heck out of here."*

Sandy started flipping the pages of her notebook in a nervous snit as she read back her notes. "Ahhh, ggg—g—guys?" she squealed while they ran feverishly through the jungle. No one paid very much attention to her. Sandy became quite annoyed at the lack of attention, so she nose-dived into the backpack, looking for something that would get their attention. At the bottom she found a pink metal whistle, dragged it up to the top, and blew it with all her might. Shocked and alarmed by the noise, they all stopped dead in their tracks.

"What did ya do that for?" snarled Rex *"You scared us half to death."*

"Not to mention bringing attention to where we are!" exclaimed Jake, just about to toss his magnifying glass into the air to activate it.

"What's wrong, sweetie?" asked Alexa. "You're trembling."

Sandy just kept flipping through her notes, going over and over and over them. "I know I sometimes fff—f—forget stuff, but weren't there seven of us when we arrived on this island?"

"**Uh—oh!**" Jake cried out. "We forgot Izzie, Pete, and Captain Snappy."

"Oh, no!" sighed Alexa. "We have to go back."

"Are you crazy?" screamed Rex. *"We can't go back; those stupid, hairy sea monkeys will feed us to that volcano."*

"But if we don't, Izzie, Pete, and the captain will be goners!" declared Jake.

"Better them than us!" Rex uttered.

"Jake, we just can't leave," Alexa urged. "It wouldn't be right. We have to go back and get them; well, at least the captain and Pete. I, for one, think that Izzie is a horrible little girl. It would just serve her right if we left her to the Bannana Brothers. Do you know she threw a coconut at me?"

"What do you expect to do, just walk right in there and say 'Excuse me, sorry for stealing your stones, but can we have the captain, the duck, and the snotty girl back?'" Rex blurted out.

"Well, not exactly!" Jake shouted. "We'll have to go to Plan-C."

Rex was panicking at the thought of having to go back and deal with the Bannana Brothers again. *"Plan-C! What makes you think a Plan-C will work? We haven't done so well with A or B, ya know! When did we get a Plan-C, anyway?"*

Jake told them not to worry. Since they already had the sandstones, he would use the powers of his magnifying glass to get Captain Snappy, Pete, and Izzie back. "We'll just walk around the other side of the volcano and come up behind them. I'll throw a few lightning bolts at them. That should scare them enough to give us back the captain, the duck, and that annoying little girl."

"I certainly hope so," Rex snapped at Jake, *"because I, for one, have no intention of being dumped into that volcano!"*

"It's not even active!" Jake stated.

"With our luck, do you really want to take that chance?" Rex moaned.

153

Jake thought for a minute about the possibility of the volcano actually being alive and uttered, "No!"

"Neither do I!" confessed Alexa as Sandy nodded her head in agreement, too.

So the mystery-solving foursome made an about face and headed back in the direction from which they had come. They climbed up onto the cliffs of the mountainous volcano in order to surprise the monkeys from behind. From the top of the volcano they could see poor Captain Snappy, Pete, and Izzie all tied up in vines. The brothers were just about to drag Snappy, Pete, and Izzie up to the top of the volcano and dump them to their doom.

"This is all your fault!" Izzie shrieked at the captain. "If you didn't force me to come to this monkey-infested island, I wouldn't be in this predicament."

"The only good thing about bein' dumped into that volcano, woman," Snappy yelled back, "is I be not havin' to listen to the likes of you—**no more!**"

"Quackers!" agreed Pete, who was all tied up with his captain.

Just that moment the children jumped out from behind some bushes, surprising the lot of green and brown, hairy monkeys.

Stunned at what he thought was Jake's complete stupidity for returning, Tony smirked, "Are youse crazy messing with me? Give me back my stones!"

"Not on your life!" Jake defied him.

"And people call me a thief!" Tony shrugged his shoulders and over-confidently announced, "Have it your way, Moustachio! Get 'em, boys."

Alexa and Rex hid behind Jake as he raised his

magnifying glass into the air and shouted, "Don't anybody move!"

"Help!" quacked Pete.

All the monkeys started chuckling uncontrollably at Jake, holding what they thought was a silly, little magnifying glass up as a weapon to stop them. "What are you gonna do, bop us on the head with that thing?" Tony laughed.

"Yeah—he thinks he's gonna bop us on the head with that thing!" the twins repeated annoyingly.

"Face it, Moustachio, you ain't no match for Tony Bannana," he boasted. "Though I must say, ya do got a lot of coconuts coming back here to save your friends."

Tony nibbled on a fly off of his wife's shoulder and sneered, "It looks like I got the last laugh!" He then ordered his boys to grab the stones and toss them all into the volcano.

"There's where you're wrong, Bannana," announced Jake, "because I'm going to have the last laugh." Jake then swung his magnifying glass around his head and commanded, *"Ightninglay oltsbay endsay!"*

An array of fiery lightning bolts blasted out from the center of the magnifying glass as everyone took cover. Tony grabbed Savannah and scooted up a palm tree as the other wise-guy monkeys darted about trying to save themselves. The lightning rays flew wildly through the air, slamming into anything and everything in their paths, including the base of the volcano.

"Quackers!" screamed Pete in fear.

"*Wow!*" Rex giggled, "*I don't think those slimy, fly-eating dudes will be messing with us anymore!*"

"Quickly, you guys, untie Snappy, Pete, and Izzie," Jake yelled out, "while I cover you so the monkeys can't get at you!"

Rex and Alexa, with Sandy flopping away in the backpack, went dashing up to Captain Snappy and Pete to untie them. It was a scene of utter chaos with the lightning bolts blasting all about. The monkeys were screeching as they ran for cover. Izzie was yelling for help, while Pete, having been freed, went flying madly around so as not to get hit. Tony was ordering his boys to get them while hiding in the trees. Suddenly, the island started to rumble from deep within, tossing everyone about.

"What is that?" Jake called out as he grabbed on to a vine to keep from falling to the ground.

"Is that an earthquake?" Alexa yelled back, shaking, as she untied the last knot on the vine around Captain Snappy's legs.

"**Tony!**" Savannah screamed, pointing up to the top of the volcano in a panic.

"**Oh—geeze!**" Tony grimaced in terror as he and his wife got clunked on their heads from falling coconuts. **"Boys, it's time to make like a banana and split outta' here!"**

"But what about the stones?" the little Johnnys asked, shaking about.

"Forget about 'em for now!" ordered Tony. "The volcano's about ta blooooow!" Tony ordered his boys back to their ship before they were goners. The entire bunch of monkeys hightailed it off the island.

"We be needin' to get out of here, too!" barked Snappy. "The volcano, she's about to explode!"

157

They all started running with all their might away from the volcano for their lives.

"Ahhhhh!" screamed Alexa and Sandy through the wind.

"Run guys, run," Jake yelled out as he raised his magnifying glass, about to throw it into the smoldering sky for their escape.

"*I thought you said that volcano was dead!*" Rex scolded Snappy as they ran and ran and ran to save themselves.

"Apparently I be wrong. Then again, I didn't be expectin' ya to go blastin' fire balls at it—ya know!" snapped Snappy, holding onto Pete for dear life. "Ya made it angry enough ta spit!"

"Hey—we saved your life!" Jake exclaimed.

"Remind me to be thankin' ya if we be gettin' out of here alive!" Captain Snappy uttered, ducking from the falling rocks, "cause this island's about to be blasted into smithereens!"

"**Help! Help!**" they heard a cry through the rumbling.

"Do you hear something?" Jake asked.

"*The only thing I hear is music playing at our funerals if we don't get the heck out of here!*" bellowed Rex, scurrying as fast as four paws could go.

Sandy, feeling something was wrong, started checking her notes again in a frenzy. Page by page, she read every last crayoned word she had written. "Ahhh, guys—?" she squealed.

Skedaddling as far away from the soon-to-be erupting volcano as possible, like usual, no one was paying any attention to her. Sandy became once again ever-so-annoyed. She grabbed that pink, metal whistle again, taking the deepest of breaths, and blew into it with all the power her tiny body could muster.

"*What's the matter this time?*" Rex hissed, panting away as he ran.

"What's wrong, sweetie?" huffed and puffed Alexa as she ran and ran frantically through the jungle.

Sandy just kept flipping through her notes, going over and over and over them. "Like I said before, I know I sometimes fff—f—forget stuff, but weren't there seven of us when we arrived on this island?"

"**Uh—oh! Not again!**" Jake cried. "We forgot Izzie. I thought I told ya to untie her?" he asked Alexa.

"I thought Rex was untying her!" she exclaimed "I took care of the captain and Pete—that was my job!"

"**Rex!**" Jake called out in a disapproving tone.

"***What?** I thought Lexy was taking care of Izzie!*" he denied under his whiskers.

"**Help! Help!**" Izzie shrieked, jumping after them through the jungle, still all tied up in vines. "**You can't leave me!**"

"We have to go back!" Jake declared.

"*Are you crazy?*" Rex screamed hysterically. "*We can't go back! We'll be blasted into cat litter by that volcano!*"

"But if we don't, Izzie will be a goner!" Jake declared, feeling a little responsible for her.

"Let her be!" Snappy yelled out into the jungle. "She be of no use to us anyway!"

"Quackers!" fluttered Pete in agreement to leave her.

"*Yeah!*" Rex agreed. "*I'm with the bird. Leave her!*"

Jake looked over to his sister, looking for some support. She shrugged her shoulders and stated, "Well—she really is nasty!"

"**Lexy!**" he grumbled.

"Oh—all right!" she agreed reluctantly. "Let's go get her."

They all ran like the wind with Pete quacking away and Rex screaming through the jungle, "***We're doomed! Doomed, I tell ya!***"

Upon bumping into Izzie, instead of her being a grateful, little girl for them coming back for her, she did nothing but bounce all around, yelling at them for leaving her not once, but twice.

"Untie me this instant—you fools!" she ordered.

"*See—I told you we should have left her!*" Rex reminded them.

Izzie just kept yelling and yelling and yelling at them. Jake got a very annoyed look on his face and declared to Rex, "You know—you had a point!" he then turned to the group and said, "**Let's go!**"

As they started running back off into the jungle, Izzie screeched, "**Wait—you can't leave me!**"

Jake turned his head in a huff and asked, "Give me one good reason why I shouldn't?"

Izzie just bounced up and down, thinking and thinking and thinking. "**Because! Because!**"

"Because, because why?" he questioned.

"Because I know where the third stolen piece to the puzzle is!" she proclaimed. "**That's why!**"

"Where it be—woman?" demanded Snappy.

"Take me with you off this exploding island, and I'll tell you where when I am safe and sound back on that pathetic excuse for a ship of yours," she bargained.

By the smoke and fire brewing at the top of the volcano,

Jake knew they only had seconds before they would be goners. "**Deal!**" he agreed. With all the strength in his body, he threw the magnifying glass into the sky and commanded—"***Ackbay otay ethay Ustykray Atfishkay!***"

An enormous bolt of lightning shot out of the magnifying glass as it soared through the air. A pool of blinding light radiated from it as it grew larger and larger. The wind spun from the glass, blowing everything and everyone in its path as it hung in the air.

"Jump!" he ordered. "Jump!"

Alexa, Sandy, and Rex jumped into the magnifying glass. Captain Snappy followed, diving right in behind as he clutched tightly onto his beloved parrot.

"Well, aren't you going to untie me?" uttered Izzie.

Not sure if she was telling the truth about knowing where the stolen third sandstone of Sethena was, Jake smirked, "**No!**" He then grabbed her by her tightly wrapped vines and pulled her with all his might into the blustery center of his magnifying glass.

Within seconds of their escape the volcano erupted——

KABOOM!

CHAPTER TEN

Drat!

The magnifying glass appeared high above the ship as Moneke Island was being engulfed by the erupting volcano's hot, molten lava. One by one they all tumbled out, hitting the rotted, wood deck of the Krusty Katfish. As Jake fell out of the magnifying glass with a thud, his grandfather's tattered, secret book popped out from his pocket, sliding across the deck of the ship. It slid right under the wicked nose of Izziedura Smythe. Still wrapped in the vines the Bannana Brothers had tied her up with, Izzie rolled her way towards the book, trying to grab it with her teeth. The eruptions from the volcano caused a humongous wave to crash up against the ship, which sent her and the book off in two different directions.

"**Drat!**" she mumbled, rolling and rolling like a rolling pin about the deck.

"*Pull up the anchor! Pull up the anchor!*" Rex cried out as he ran for cover from the falling debris.

Penelope swung around from the ship's boom and squawked, "What's the matter, matter?"

"*Bad sea monkeys, exploding island, stolen sandstones,*" Rex warned. "*We need to get out of here!*"

Penelope looked out to sea at the exploding island, sighing, "Oh dear, dear!"

They all looked back and screamed in horror as a massive, black ship came speeding towards them. It was decked with the fanciest of silver, chrome trim and sails with black and white fuzzy dice embroidered on them

"Arrrr, it be those bloody, pillagin' monkeys," grunted Snappy. "Penelope, weigh anchor and do it with plenty of bite. They be gainin' on us!"

"Aye-Aye, skipper, skipper!" she exclaimed as she cranked up the anchor with her beak.

Izzie managed to stand herself up when she saw Jake's brown, leather book lying there helpless and unnoticed by an old barrel of apple juice. She hopped her greedy, tied-up self over to it, but just as she was about to snatch it up, one of the little sailors kicked it clear across the deck. "**Drat!**" Izzie grumbled, not able to grab it that time. The crew was scuttling around the ship in a mad frenzy, letting out the sails as they tried to get away from the charging monkeys' ship. It reminded the children of the playground the moment the school bell rang in the afternoon.

Izzie hopped about the ship, still tied up in vines, madder than ever, trying to find that book. "Isn't anyone going to untie me?" she shrieked.

"**NO!**" they all yelled back at her, to her discontent.

Alexa's eyes nearly popped out of her head as she became mesmerized by the fast approaching ship. "What type of ship is that?" she yelled out above all the chaos.

"That be the Caddo Escargot," Snappy explained, "the meanest, fastest ship ever to be sailin' the Seven Seas. Why, it be almost a match for the Lady Lilac. It has a 578-seahorse-powered engine."

"*And how many seahorses does your engine hh—h—have?*" Rex stuttered, looking warily at the Escargot ripping through the waves towards them.

"I got me a one-seahorse-powered engine, mighty fine

stallion...a little old, though," the captain declared. "His name's Fred. Ya want ta meet him? He's down below."

They all gasped in terror, knowing there was no way they were going to outrun the Bannana Brothers' ship. Rex collapsed on the deck and bellowed, "*We're Doomed!*"

Jake held out his hand and commanded his magnifying glass to return to him. As it flew into his hand, he asked, "Where in the world did they get a ship like that?"

"Arrrrr—" moaned Snappy. "Those fly-eating, slimy monkey scoundrels be stealin' that thar ship!"

Suddenly, out of the Escargot, a white cannonball shot directly towards them. Sandy panted breathlessly, being the only one to see it, facing backwards in Alexa's backpack. "GGG—G—Guys!" she nervously chutted. But as usual, they weren't paying any attention to her. She tried a second time to get their attention, but her tiny voice was no match for all the commotion going on about the ship. So she once again grabbed her pink, metal whistle, took the deepest of breaths, and blew it like never before, knowing their lives depended on it.

"**What?**" they all yelled.

Sandy, with her whistle still in her tiny paws, pointed up to the sky and screamed, "**BBB—B—Big! BBB—B—Ball!**"

Shocked, their eyes grew wide as they, too, let out a scream, watching the white cannonball fly right past them, plunging a hole deep into the already hole-riddled deck of the ship. "Ahhhhhhhh!"

"*We're never going to get out of this alive—I tell ya!*" cried out Rex, staring at the gaping hole. "*We need some masking tape! Where's the tape?*"

Jake got a determined look across his face. "I've had just

about enough of those Bannana Brothers." He angrily raised his magnifying glass and was just about to send a shockwave soaring at the Escargot.

"Are ye crazy—boy!" scolded Snappy. One more blast outta' that thing towards that island and you'd be sending a tidal wave through these waters that will kill us all."

"Oh, come on—it wasn't my fault one of the lightning bolts hit the volcano!" snarled Jake. "I'm just getting the hang of this thing."

"We be better off taken' our chances with the monkeys," Captain Snappy grunted. He then ordered the crew to man the cannons as the Escargot shot another white cannonball their way, nearly missing the Krusty Katfish.

Izzie was jumping all around, trying to find the book and get loose from the knots of her vines. "Ooow, ooow," she uttered, "If you let me loose, I can help!"

"**No!**" they all shouted.

Izzie bounced around in a toddler fit. Once again she saw the book across the deck. She knew when the curse was reversed she would never get off that ship without the help of the evil Baron Von Snodgrass as the children would quickly find out she was Mrs. Smythe. She hobbled her way over to it as fast as she could. Finally, she would have that book, give it to Snodgrass, assuring her safe passage off the ship once she grew back to her older and slightly uglier self. She bent way over and was just about to grab it with her teeth when suddenly the ship turned abruptly about as a renegade, white cannonball came shooting towards her. She gasped looking up at it. "Oh-no!" she uttered. "Why me—why do these things keep happening to me? I try to be a good person. I know I'm a little evil, but I'm not all that bad." The cannonball was a direct hit, striking her like a lonely bowling pin. Still all tied up in vines, she went flying into the air, landing right on top of a crate of overflowing watermelons. "**Drat!**" she cried out.

"**Fire!**" ordered Captain Snappy. Nothing happened. Not a cannonball came shooting from his ship. "What's wrong?" he bellowed.

"We be all out of cannonballs!" exclaimed Spikey.

"What does ya mean, we be havin' no cannonballs?" asked the captain. I loaded them meself back at Pirate's Point. I be puttin' them right next to that case of watermelons over thar."

Just then another white cannonball came shooting at them from the monkeys' ship, Stumpy pointed out into the sky and declared, "Thar's your balls, skipper!"

Captain Snappy became enraged when he realized the Bannana Brothers were firing at him with his own cannonballs. "Is there anything left on me ship that those ruthless monkeys be not stealin'?"

"Quackers!" quacked Pete, "no," in anger.

"We have watermelons skipper, skipper!" announced Penelope as she stretched her long neck out, scanning about the deck for something to load the cannons with.

Izzie was just lying there helplessly on top of the watermelons. "These are prize-winning, Saskatchewan watermelons. I was going to make my award-winning, top-to-bottom, bottom-to-top, watermelon cake. Everyone just loves my top-to-bottom, bottom-to-top, watermelon cake," she protested. "Don't even think about it—you stupid ostrich!"

Rex turned to Jake and declared, "*Is it me, or does this*

all sound vaguely familiar?"

"I'm beginning to wonder that myself!" Jake thought.

Snappy darted over to Izzie, jumped up on top of the pile of watermelons, and gave her an annoying kick in the butt as he rolled her down the pile like an unraveled piece of carpet. "Tis me ship, woman!" he bellowed, "and I be given the orders—not the likes of you!"

"How dare you," she whimpered, rolling and rolling away. "You are the rudest man I've ever worked for! Isn't anyone ever going to untie me?"

"**No!**" they all exclaimed again.

"I'm sick of her cakes, pies, and pastries," Snappy sniped. "We be not needin' the watermelon anyway. Load 'em up, boys."

Izzie let out a horrified scream as the teeny-weeny crew loaded all of her precious, prize–winning, Saskatchewan watermelons into the cannons. "Not my watermelons!" All of a sudden, as she lay there on the deck, she saw once again Jake's brown, leather book just a couple of inches beyond her sniveling nose. Her eyes lit up in delight at the prospect of finally snatching it. "I have you this time!" she giggled in a girlish screech.

"Now—I know things are a little strange on this side of the magnifying glass, but does anyone really think a bunch of watermelons are going to stop those criminal-minded monkeys?" Rex asked as he plopped his furry butt down on top of the book, scratching himself with his back leg.

The children agreed, no. "We need a plan," thought Jake, running towards the end of the ship to get a better look out to sea. Alexa ran after him, curious as to what he was going to come up with.

"*Yeah, preferably a plan that keeps us alive,*" Rex yelled out sarcastically as he wiggled his red and golden, furry butt, finally noticing the brown, leather book he was sitting on, "***Now, how did this get here?***" he thought to himself. Realizing Jake must have dropped the book out of his pocket when they fell through the magnifying glass, Rex snatched it up and ran after the children to give it back to him.

Seeing him do that, Izzie just lay there crying in utter despair, whimpering, "Why me—why do these things keep happening to me?—**Drat!**"

Rex was just about to yell out that he had the book and then thought to himself the book might be safer if he hid it in Alexa's Inspector Girl backpack. So he quietly, without anyone noticing, switched the real book for the fake one Jake won at the boardwalk.

He then gave Jake the fake book back instead. "*You do know you dropped this?*"

Alexa scolded Jake for being careless with the book again. She remembered switching the books, thinking she was putting the real one safe and sound in the backpack while Jake carried around the fake one that Penelope gave him. Not knowing Jake did just the same thing earlier, she mistakenly switched the real one Jake put in the backpack for the fake one he won at the boardwalk. The book that Rex just found lying helpless on the deck was indeed the real book.

Without any of them realizing it, Rex had just wound up swapping them back, placing Grandpa Moustachio's real secret book safely into Alexa's backpack, while giving back Jake the fake book to keep in his pocket.

"We need to hurry. The Bannana Brothers are gaining on

us," Alexa exclaimed. "What's your plan, Jake?"

"I'm thinking!" he said as he caressed his magnifying glass. **Jake wondered, if people could jump through the magnifying glass...could a ship?**

Rex ducked as a cannonball went flying in one direction while a watermelon went flying in another. *"Well—think faster!"* Rex hollered in despair. *"What are we up to—Plan-D?"*

Alexa had an idea of her own as she started searching through her backpack for the sixth sandstone. "Got it!" she cheered, handing it to Jake.

"That's my smart sister!" he praised. They had a plan. Quickly solve the last riddle on the sixth sandstone and use the magnifying glass to jump to that location to find the seventh and last sandstone of the Seven Sea Gods before the Bannana Brothers destroyed the ship.

*"**Are you two—CRAZY?**"* Rex bellowed in an outburst of unwilling emotion. *"You want to send this ship through the glass? It's nothing more than a bunch of popsicle sticks taped together!"*

"YYY—Y—Yeah!" chutted Sandy, nervously watching Stumpy duct taping up another hole in the ship that had been made by the last cannonball.

"And, what about those stupid monkeys?" Rex shouted. *"Don't ya think they already read the riddle and know where we would be going?"*

Jake thought that if, in fact, the monkeys had figured out the last riddle and knew the whereabouts of the final piece to the puzzle, they would never beat them to it if he used the magnifying glass. He then read the last riddle out loud so they could begin to figure out what it meant. " 'What paddles so green in the sea and eats its grass by night—that basks in the sand by the glow of the sun's light?' "

Pete flew right over to them and landed on top of Jake's left shoulder to help with the riddle. He quickly snapped up a piece of watermelon that had fallen into Jake's hair, quacking away as he read the final riddle on the sixth sandstone, too.

"Do you mind not eating off of my head?" Jake snapped as Pete clapped his duck wings in Jake's face reading away. They all read over and over the riddle, trying to come up with an answer as watermelons and the white cannonballs flew back and forth across the sea. "So...'What paddles so green in the sea?' " Jake asked.

"Oh, I got it!" exclaimed Alexa. "A green oar."

"Quackers!" quacked Pete, "no."

"An oar from a boat doesn't eat sea grass—does it?" scolded Jake to his sister.

Alexa got an annoyed look on her face and smirked back at him, "Do you have a better idea—hmmmmm?"

"Sorry!" he shouted, holding his hands up in the air, having not a clue to figuring out the riddle.

Suddenly, the ship jolted as it stopped dead in the water.

"What happened?" screamed Rex, looking at the Escargot gaining on them. *"Why did the ship stop?"*

"Oh—bloody no!" stammered Captain Snappy as he ran to the hatch that covered the ship's one-seahorse-powered engine.

In a panic they all rushed behind him to see what the problem was. Snappy opened up the heavy, steel hatch and found Fred, his one seahorse, moaning and groaning in a pool of water with orangey-red frosting drooling from his snout.

"**FRED!!!**" he yelled down as they all stuck their surprised faces in the hatch. "Ya didn't go eatin' any of those darn awful crab cakes—did ya?"

"***Burp!***" went Fred, nodding his head, "yes." He just lay there, moaning and groaning, sick as could be, having just gobbled up a dozen or so of Izzie's orangey-red, frosted, super-sugared crab cakes. Snappy became enraged as he scuttled about the ship looking for Izzie. She heard the commotion and was trying quickly to jump far, far away, still all tied up, to hide as he approached.

"Are you crazy—woman," he shouted, "ta be givin' a seahorse **FROSTED CAKES?** Every man, woman, and child who sails the Seven Seas knows ya don't go feedin' no seahorse—**FROSTED CAKES!**"

"Help!" she cried out in fear, hopping about the deck. "Someone untie me this instant!"

"**No!**" they all shouted out.

"I did no such thing, you fool," she argued, still trying to untie herself. "What possible reason would I have to get this sorry excuse for a ship stuck in the middle of nowhere? Furthermore, my crab cakes are not awful. They are delicious. Maybe a little dry, but still delicious!"

Snappy swung around, flashing a deadly glare at his crew. "Well, if Izzie not be sabotaging me ship, then we be havin' a good-for-nothin' traitor on board. When I be findin' the scallywag who fed me seahorse those frosty cakes, ye be walkin' the plank! This is mutiny, I tell ya—mutiny!"

"Don't you have a spare engine?" Alexa asked, ducking from a cannonball that just whizzed by.

"Like I be tellin' ya—" Snappy snapped, "tis be a one-seahorse-powered ship. We ain't got any more seahorses."

Upon hearing that, Rex and Sandy leaped over to the sails and started blowing on them, hoping to move the ship.

"Are you nuts?" Jake asked at the uselessness of the two of them blowing air into the sails. "That's not going to do anything."

"*We have no engine, no wind, and we're being chased by a bunch of ruthless monkeys who want to whack us for stealing from them,*" Rex hysterically bantered as he continued to blow and blow even faster into the sails. "*You have a better idea?*"

"Well...not really!" Jake uttered in a panic as he, too, joined them. "But just for the record, we stole those stones to save the world!"

"*Try telling that to them!*" Rex hissed back at him. "***Now blow!***"

The entire ship's crew started blowing and blowing and blowing into the sails, trying to get the ship to move.

Alexa looked back and screamed as the monkeys were just about upon them. "It's no use," she cried. "This ship's moving slower than a turtle."

Jake thought for a minute about the sixth riddle. "**That's it!**" he exclaimed.

"What's it?" she asked.

"The answer to the riddle," he explained. "**TURTLES!**"

"Turtles?" they all questioned.

"Quackers!" agreed Pete.

" '**What paddles so green in the sea and eats its grass by night—that basks in the sand by the glow of the sun's light?**' " Jake repeated. "**TURTLES!**"

"It must be sea turtles, to be exact," thought Captain Snappy.

Jake immediately knew now they could get out of this mess by jumping through his magnifying glass, knowing the answer to the sixth riddle. "Where do we find sea turtles?" he inquired.

"That be The Great Tortoise Reef, off the coast of the island of Chelonia," Snappy explained. "But we be havin' no way of gettin' thar without Fred powering me ship!"

"Leave that to me!" Jake proclaimed, swinging his magnifying glass through the air.

Rex sprang over to him in protest, *"You're not seriously considering sending us on this floating wreckage through that glass, are you?"*

Jake nervously looked down at him as they both ducked another flying cannonball. "You got a better idea?" Jake wound up his arm and threw the magnifying glass like a major league pitcher out to sea, commanding, *"**Ethay Eatgray Ortoisetay Eefray!**"*

Far over the horizon, the magnifying glass shot a massive, blinding flash of light. The Bannana Brothers' ship pulled back, afraid of being destroyed from the wind that was ripping over the ocean's waves, tossing both ships about. It was almost as if Jake and the magnifying glass were one. It knew exactly what he wanted it to do and expanded large enough for the ship to jump through.

Rex looked back at the Escargot as it crashed against the violent waves of the sea. *"What is that floating around their ship?"* he curiously asked.

"It looks like...dolphins?" Jake stammered in awe.

"Is that a pizza box?" Rex spouted. *"I just don't believe*

this," he hissed. "*I haven't had a thing to eat, thanks to that stupid pig eating my grilled 'kraut and flounder sandwich. I can't eat my fishy crackers because they give me, as you well know—gas! And those slimy monkeys are getting a bunch of pizzas delivered by a school of dolphins. That is so unfair!*"

"Stop your whining, you knucklehead," Jake scolded, looking at the mushy mess around the deck. "If you're that hungry, go eat some of that mashed-up watermelon."

"*What do I look like—a dog?*" Rex meowed. He then ordered Penelope to turn the ship around so they could grab the pizza boxes off the dolphins' backs.

"She'll do no such thing!" Jake snapped back at him in anger. "Penelope," he yelled out through the howling wind, "turn the ship into the vortex."

"Aye—aye! Inspector, Inspector!" she announced.

"Hold on!" Jake yelled out.

Everyone quickly grabbed any ropes, belts, or rags they could find and started tying themselves down to anything that would keep them from flying off the ship. "Is this going to work?" Alexa asked as she secured Sandy in her backpack and grabbed onto Jake in fear.

"I certainly hope so!" he said with some hesitation, unsure of the outcome of their dilemma.

Rex jumped into Jake's arms screaming, "*We're doomed! Doomed, I tell ya!*"

Izzie, still all tied up in vines, went flying across the ship. Penelope snatched her up by her beak and held onto the crazy, cake-poisoning cook. Dangling far above the crew, Izziedura Smythe bellowed out into the sea, "Isn't anyone ever going to untie me!"

"**NO!**" they all shouted out in protest, entering the vortex.

Echoing into the magnifying glass, Mrs. Smythe cried out, "Why me—why do these things keep happening to me?—**Drat!**"

CHAPTER ELEVEN

Follow The Turtleback Road

The Krusty Katfish violently shook to and fro as it was drawn into the spiraling, turbulent wind of the magnifying glass. Everyone held their breaths, praying the ship would not fall apart as it swirled and spiraled out of control. Crates, supplies, and what was left of Izzie's precious watermelons went flying about. Twisting and turning, they screamed for their young lives. Faster and faster they sailed on through, holding on to the shaking and shuttering, dilapidated ship. Suddenly, a final blast of light exploded from the glass as the Krusty Katfish was cast out of the magnifying glass to the waiting dark and ominous waters on the other side.

The ocean was mysteriously calm with the dark-grey sky blanketed in a sea of fog. Dazed and wet, the ship's tiny toddler crew started untying themselves from the ropes, belts, and rags that saved their cursed, little pirate lives.

Alexa quickly searched her backpack, looking for her guinea pig. "Sandy," she called out in a panic, unable to find her.

"Help! HHH—H—Help!" Sandy cried out in terror.

Alexa ran frantically around the ship towards her crying voice. Finally, she saw Rex standing on a crate with Sandy sandwiched between two wedges of watermelon, about to be gobbled up.

"Rexal Moustachio!" Alexa yelled at him, snatching Sandy from his paws. "We don't go eating members of the family—now do we?"

"Why not?" he smirked, laughing himself silly. *"Jake said to go eat some watermelon off the deck. I was just adding a bit of protein to balance out my meal!"*

"Because!" she scolded, "it's not polite."

"Well, who said anything about being polite? I was just teaching her a lesson for eating my grilled 'kraut and flounder sandwich," he spouted, chomping on a piece of slightly-used watermelon. *"I wasn't really going to eat her!"*

"Not funny!" Alexa grumbled. "And I'm not too sure about that, either!"

Sandy shook in Alexa's hands after her unappetizing ordeal. "I miss my purple crayon!" she sighed.

"Don't worry, sweetie," Alexa consoled, stroking Sandy's short brown fur. "We'll find it."

"I hope so," Sandy declared. "Because when we ddd—d—do, I'm going to whack that cat over his big, ugly head with it for shoving me between those two slices of watermelon. I'm still bruised from the seeds."

As Jake commanded his magnifying glass to come to him, he asked, "Did we make it?"

Captain Snappy smelled the musty air and uttered, "That we did, Inspector. Tis be The Great Tortoise Reef."

"If the Bannana Brothers figured out the sixth sandstone's riddle, how long will it take them to get here?" Jake asked him.

"With a 578-seahorse-powered engine," Snappy grunted, "those ruthless monkeys could be here in under a wee twenty minutes or so."

"Then we need to hurry!" Jake urged.

Izzie was still dangling from Penelope's beak high above

the ship's holey deck, still yelling to get someone to untie her from the vines still holding her captive. "What about me?"

"We'll deal with you later," Jake yelled up to Penelope. "But for now, we have to get to..." He interrupted himself, looking curiously out into the foggy air, searching for the island of Chelonia and the turtles. But he could see absolutely nothing out there. "Where are all the sea turtles and the island?"

Suddenly, the ocean rumbled. Their eyes grew wide, looking at an enormous wave forming out to sea that was headed directly towards them.

"That doesn't look good!" Alexa screamed in fright.

"*Ya think?*" Rex uttered, covering his furry face with his watermelon-soaked paws in fear of what was to come next.

The salt from the sea foamed in a bubbly froth as the wave folded over itself. One by one, the deepest of diving, leatherback sea turtles came flying out of the foamy water. They were each six feet long with bright, olive-green, oval shells that were speckled with flecks of yellow. They swam around in a gigantic circle, flapping their giant flippers as the wave poured into its center. Except for the rushing water in the center of the circle the turtles were swimming around, the ocean was still as calm as could be. Then, unexpectedly, from the center of the circle, a water ball bigger than the ship blasted out of the ocean, shooting into the sky. There was an eerie silence when, suddenly, the sea turtles started to sing from their hawk-like beaks a weird clicking song, "*Nuck—nick. Nuck—nock. Nuck—nick.*" Over and over they chanted this repetitious sound. "*Nuck—nick. Nuck—nock. Nuck—nick.*" Without reason, they stopped, and it started to rain, but only over the circle of these strange sea creatures. Then, out of nowhere, the island of Chelonia erupted from the sea. The turtles then lined themselves up in a road-like pattern, popping their shells up from the water, leading from the Krusty Katfish directly to the island.

"Come on you guys, hurry!" Jake exclaimed as he jumped overboard and started running down the turtles' backs.

Alexa grabbed Sandy, leaping over the side of the Krusty Katfish, following her brother. "Aren't they cute, Sandy?" she asked. "The turtles made a road in the ocean in order for us to get to the island!"

"Hurry, Lexy, hurry!" shouted Jake. "The Bannana Brothers will be here any minute, and we need to find the seventh sandstone!"

"*Wait for me!*" Rex yelled out, springing into the air from the ship's deck.

"Come on, Pete," grumbled Captain Snappy, jumping off his ship, too.

"Quackers!" echoed Pete, flapping his wings all the way down.

"But what about me?" bellowed Izzie, swinging back and forth from Penelope's beak.

"Hold on ta her, Penelope!" ordered Snappy. "After we be findin' the seventh sandstone of the Seven Sea Gods, we be needin' her to find that missin' third stone. And you'd be good to be givin' Fred some ginger ale or somethin' to calm his bellyache. We be goin' to need him up and runnin' if we be gettin' outta' here alive!"

"Aye-aye, skipper, skipper!" mumbled Penelope, almost dropping Mrs. Smythe into the sea.

"And ya better know where that third stone tis be,

woman," warned the captain, dashing down the turtles' backs, "or ye be walkin' the plank to your end!"

"You are the rudest man I've ever worked for!" Izzie uttered out to sea as she swung from Penelope, twisting to get loose. "Let go of me you, overgrown turkey!"

Penelope batted her long, slightly-clumped, fake, black eyelashes at Mrs. Smythe and mumbled annoyingly, "I'm an ostrich, not a turkey, you silly little girl, girl!"

They all hopped, skipped, jumped, and ran down the turtles to the island, hoping the sea creatures wouldn't swim off, dunking them into the ocean.

"*Ya know,*" Rex snickered, "*if we find a tin man, a scarecrow, and a cowardly lion along the way, I am so out of here!*"

"Not to mention a wizard!" added Alexa with a big, bright smile as she skipped along.

"You are our cowardly lion!" echoed Jake ahead.

"*I resemble that remark!*" yelled back Rex.

"For once, you got that right!" shouted Jake through the misty fog.

The palm trees swayed in the gentle breeze as they arrived on land. Jake scoped out the surroundings with his magnifying glass, trying to figure out the best direction to start looking for the seventh and final sandstone to complete the puzzled map that would hopefully lead to the location of Earth's End.

"Where should we look first?" Alexa asked.

"*Why don't we ask the one-eyed, psychic duck-parrot?*" Rex smirked, licking some leftover watermelon from his whiskers.

"That sounds like a good idea!" announced Jake as he

wiped the fog off his magnifying glass with his shirttail.

"Quackers!" Pete clucked, pointing his wing towards a field of prickly pineapple plants.

They all followed Captain Snappy with Pete perched on his little right shoulder leading the way. The field was filled with wild pineapples and the most beautiful, multicolored tropical flowers the children had ever seen. Alexa picked the biggest of the red and yellow ones, placing them in her hair, and then plucked a teeny-tiny one, doing the same to Sandy. Suddenly, they heard a low-pitched hum that was getting louder and louder.

"What is that weird sound?" Jake inquired as he searched the smoky, colored sky in all directions.

Alexa also looked up into the sky, looking for what was to come. "It's getting louder and closer!" she warned.

"Ya know," smirked Rex, *"if I didn't know better, I would guess that was an incoming squadron of planes making that sound. But that's crazy—**right?**"*

Jake's eyes flew wide open, panicking at the scary sight before him. "Close enough!" he shrieked. "**Run!**"

"**Ahhhhhhhhh!**" screamed Alexa and Sandy.

In awe and fright, they all looked up to see countless vibrant-colored hummingbirds swarming upon them. There were thousands and thousands of them flapping their wings eighty times a minute, making that unusual humming noise. Some were flying backwards, others were flying up and down, while even more were hovering right over their heads, poking at them with their sharp bills as they ran for their lives.

Scurrying through the dense, tropical forest, Rex cried out, *"Are these bees going to sting us?"*

"They're not bees, you knucklehead," shouted back Jake. "They're hummingbirds! And they don't look like happy ones, either!"

"*Do they bite?*"

"I certainly hope not!" Alexa exclaimed as she tried to swoosh one of them away from her as she ran faster and faster.

"WWW—W—Why are they chasing us?" Sandy cried out, ducking from one particularly annoying bird hovering over Alexa's Inspector Girl backpack.

Jake was huffing and puffing as he raced across the island, trying to ditch the swarm of birds. "Hummingbirds are attracted to flowering plants, especially the red and yellow ones. They feed off the nectar."

"Then why they be chasin' us?" spouted Snappy, holding on tightly to Pete.

Jake looked back and noticed the two enormous red and yellow flowers sticking out of Alexa's hair. "Lexy—the flowers!"

"What flowers?"

"The ones in your hair!" he explained.

"These?" she questioned, pointing to them in a panic.

"Yes, those," he yelled back. "They must want them. Get rid of them."

Alexa didn't understand why the hummingbirds wanted the peculiar flowers. There were hundreds of the same flowers spread throughout the island. "And they're not even pink!" she protested. "I could see if they were pink, but, really—all this fuss over red and yellow. I mean these really aren't the prettiest of colors anyway."

"Would you stop giving us a color lesson and dump the

flowers already," Jake demanded of his sister as he ran and ran.

Alexa grabbed the red one and threw it into the air behind her head as she, too, bolted through the tropical island. But the hummingbirds kept coming and coming.

"Well, I guess red is not their favorite color," Alexa declared as she grabbed the yellow one from her hair. She was just about to toss it behind her when she felt something hard in the center of the large yellow flower. Running breathlessly, she peeled back the petals and, to her surprise, found what she thought was a tiny, flat, ordinary rock. But looking at it more closely, Alexa quickly realized what she had found.

"What's the matter?" Jake shouted back.

Alexa ran faster and faster to reach her brother while the hummingbirds hovered around her, poking at her head. "Stop that!" she yelled to a bothersome, blue one. "Look, Jake," she stated as she opened up her hand. "Are you thinking what I'm thinking?"

Still running, Jake snatched up the rock and quickly examined it with his magnifying glass. "Great detective minds think alike, my dear Inspector Girl."

"How lucky was that?" she said, sprinting along.

"I'm beginning to think destiny has something to do with all this," Jake panted. "Not luck!"

"Quackers!" went Pete, confirming that stone was indeed the seventh piece to the puzzle.

Alexa was sure once she threw away the yellow flower the hummingbirds would stop chasing them, but they had no such luck. The swarm of mischievously annoying birds kept coming and coming.

"Why are they still chasing us?" Rex bellowed. *"You'd think they'd be afraid of a cat after all."*

"Quackers! Quackers! Quackers!" agreed Pete.

"Arrrrr, me think you be correct, me fine, feathered friend!" mumbled Snappy, darting headlong into the forest.

Swatting an annoying purple bird with his magnifying glass, Jake asked, "Right about what?"

"These be no ordinary birds," the captain explained. "These be the protectors of the seventh stone, sent by the Seven Sea Gods to guard the secret of the whereabouts of **Earth's End!**"

A crack of lightning exploded suddenly over the island as a thunderous rumble shook everything around them. Shocked, the hummingbirds started to fly backwards in retreat, too frightened of getting zapped by the lightning. But they were only distracted for a moment, and the squadrons of colorful birds quickly regrouped in hot pursuit of the seventh stone.

"What are we going to do, Jake?" called out Alexa. "They're not going to let us get off this island with that stone, let alone alive."

Jake reminded her that when Captain Snappy mentioned Earth's End, the lightning frightened the hummingbirds into retreating. "A little Inspector Moustachio homemade lightning should do the trick," he explained as he held up his magnifying glass, waving it into the air as they continued to run. "Everyone get in front of me and head back to the ship," he ordered.

"But, Jake..." called out Alexa, fearful for her brother's life.

"No buts!" he declared, tossing Alexa the stone. "I'll be

right behind you—hurry."

"Don't hurt them, Jake!" she exclaimed. "They're just doing their job."

"I won't!" he shouted out.

They all scurried back to the ship along the turtleback road. A densely thick fog rolled in from the sea, making it difficult for the children to clearly see what was ahead. Jake was trailing right behind them. The hummingbirds were going wild, flying in all different directions, trying to protect the Seven Sea Gods' secret. Jake raised the magnifying glass and commanded, ***"Ightninglay oltsbay awayway!"***

With his command, little specks of lightning flew back behind him. Jake scared the birds just enough for Alexa, Snappy, Pete, Rex, and Sandy to make their way to the Krusty Katfish. Stumpy and Spikey quickly lowered a tattered rope ladder down to the group as they climbed frantically back onto the ship.

Jake kept sprinting with all his might along the turtles' backs. He shot just enough bolts of lightning from the glass to frazzle the annoying birds so he, too, could make his escape off the island.

"Hurry, Jake, hurry!" Alexa and Rex cried out from atop the ship.

"RRR—R—Run, Jake!" chutted Sandy. She shook in a panic, hoping he'd be safe and sound. As she looked down at the turtleback road, she saw something through the fog that looked just like her big, purple crayon floating between the sea turtles. "MMM—M—My crayon!" she screamed, jumping over the side. "My purple crayon!"

"Sandy!" screeched Alexa. "What are you doing?"

"My crayon—my crayon!" she shouted back. "I think I

see my purple crayon!" Sandy hopped from one turtle shell to another, frantically trying to find her long-lost crayon.

Jake saw Sandy scampering towards him and ordered her to go back. But unable to see her clearly as the fog got denser and denser, he never realized she was getting closer and closer to him instead.

Suddenly, out of nowhere, a crack of thunder sounded from above. The wind blew fiercely through the fog.

"Jake, I can't see what's happening through this heavy fog; is that Jezebel?" Alexa asked, afraid of his answer.

Jake looked up and sighed as he stood there shaking like a leaf. "No, something worse!"

Jake could hear the clanking of boots as they stomped along the backs of the sea turtles. As the silhouette got closer, he could see through the fog that it was, indeed, what he had feared. The evil Baron Von Snodgrass was back to seek his revenge.

Jake was trying to gain his balance on the turtleback road as the sea creatures started to separate and swim away. Snodgrass was firmly perched on two of the turtles' shells, blocking Jake's way halfway between the ship and the island. His yellow, linen duster coat flapped violently in the cyclone of wind emanating from his magnifying glass, which hovered high in the sky directly behind his head.

The hummingbirds started swooping down the turtle path, making their way towards the ship and the seventh stone, which Alexa had safely hidden in her Inspector Girl backpack. The stone joined the rest of the pieces to the puzzle except for the missing third sandstone, of course. Snodgrass became pestered by the colorful flock as they swarmed about him. He raised his hand up towards his glass and shouted in

a deep dark voice, "*Egonebay!*"

A shockwave poured out from his magnifying glass. Within a split second— '*Poof*, the hummingbirds vanished into thin air.

"You evil, evil man!" Jake exclaimed in anger. "What did those helpless birds ever do to you?"

Snodgrass sighed, rolling his eyes back in utter contempt. "Oh, don't get yourself in a tizzy, dear boy; I just sent them someplace else. At least I think I did!—Oh well!"

Jake quickly contemplated his next move. He thought to himself it wouldn't be that hard to fight Snodgrass. After all, he wasn't holding his magnifying glass. Jake very slowly raised his own magnifying glass, planning to blast the evil baron into oblivion.

"Ah...ah...ah, my young Moustachio," he snarled, realizing Jake's intension. "I wouldn't do that!"

"Why not?" objected Jake, ever-so-bravely.

"Because, dear boy, even though my magnifying glass is still floating in mid air, don't be foolish enough to think I can't command it to do my bidding. And as you can clearly see, it is aimed directly at that pathetic excuse for a ship. One wrong move from you and I will blast that floating junk pile and everyone on it to smithereens."

"How do you know I won't blast you away before you're able to command your glass," Jake threatened back.

Snodgrass stared long and hard at Jake, belting out a maniacal snicker. His wicked laughter echoed into the heavens. "Ah, young, foolish Moustachio. I've had a lifetime to figure out how to work my magnifying glass. Even you, the chosen one, couldn't possibly have learned the complexities of the glass in such a short period of time!"

Jake glared, just as coldly, back at Snodgrass's evil, pitch-black eyes. "You wanna bet?"

Snodgrass took a glance back at the Krusty Katfish as he heard Alexa and Rex calling out for Jake. "Oh, my," he snickered again, "that wouldn't be your precious little sister and that annoying feline guardian of yours—now would it? Pity, I would hate to see them go—'***Poof*** when I destroy that ship!"

"Leave them alone!" Jake demanded.

"Well—" Snodgrass sighed, "maybe this time I will spare their dreary lives as a favor to you, but you're going to have to return the favor by giving up something near and dear to your heart, dear boy!"

Holding very tightly on the cherry wood handle of his beloved grandfather's magnifying glass, Jake shouted out across the turtles, "You'll never get my magnifying glass!"

Snodgrass had an evil grin spreading across his ***M***-scarred face as he chuckled, "My dear boy, your magnifying glass will be mine all in good time. But for now**...I'll settle for the journal!**"

A devilish grin appeared on Jake's face as he cleverly questioned, "**What journal?**"

Snodgrass became enraged and angrily demanded. "You know very well what journal I'm talking about. You and your annoying friends stole that book from me at Comanche Canyon."

Knowing he had the fake book that Penelope had given him, Jake reached into his pants pocket and pulled out the book that resembled the one belonging to his grandfather

"Oh, you mean **this** book?" he smirked, dangling it over the water.

"Give it to me, you fool!" Snodgrass ordered. "You have no idea what you're dealing with."

"This belonged to my Grandpa, and you will never get your boney hands it!"

Alexa still couldn't see very clearly through the fog. She called out to see if Jake was all right. But he didn't answer. Snodgrass looked up at his magnifying glass and back to the ship and threatened, "Then your sister and everyone else on that ship will be destroyed."

Jake stared at his arch nemesis with utter disdain and warned, "If you touch one perfectly-combed, strawberry-blonde hair on my sister's head, I will blast this book into a billion pieces."

"If you knew what was in there, you wouldn't dare," Snodgrass screamed into the heavens.

"Try me!" Jake shouted back. "No one messes with my family or my sister's hair!"

Snodgrass became infuriated at Jake's boldness. He started ranting and raving at the thought of not getting his way. Meanwhile, more of the sea turtles were swimming away from the path they had made from the ship to the island. Jake and the evil Baron were starting to have a hard time balancing themselves on the few turtles that were left to stand on.

Jake held the book high up into the sky, aiming his magnifying glass towards it. "I guess you would call this checkmate, then," he sneered.

Barely able to stand, Snodgrass knew this was a no-win situation. He decided it was time to make his exit and deal with Jake and the book at a more opportune time. "Tell me, young Moustachio, have you ever read the book—***Nine Lives to Live?***"

"**NO!**" Jake stated in a firm voice.

"There's an old proverb in it," Snodgrass began to recite. "**Time is a luxury only fools can afford to waste!**" He then made an about–face, snarling in discontent at having to leave the book behind. "Don't be a fool, dear boy...till we meet again!"

Jake took a deep sigh of relief as he watched the Baron slowly walk back on the remaining turtles towards his own magnifying glass, which was still suspended in mid air.

The fog grew even denser as Snodgrass inched ever-so–carefully, watching each step he took in order to avoid a dunking into the ocean. He then mysteriously disappeared into the fog and out of Jake's site. While making his escape, the Baron noticed that big, purple crayon teetering on the shell of one of the turtles below. He bent over, picked it up with his long bony fingers, examined it so, and then threw it out to sea. Sandy was shaking as she hid in the water, holding on to the tail of that very same turtle, mourning for the second time the loss of her favorite crayon. Snodgrass proceeded to make his way down the remaining turtles' backs when he heard an unusual chuttering sound by his shiny, black boot. Looking down he leered, "**Now what do we have here?**" Sandy was frozen in fear, not able to utter a sound to save herself. He scooped her right up and belted out a sinister array of laughter as he jumped into his magnifying glass, disappearing with Sandy into thin air.

As the fog got sucked into Snodgrass's magnifying glass, Alexa could see clearly the sea turtles starting to swim away,

"Run, Jake—run!" she screamed out in fear.

With the turtles returning to the depths of the sea, Jake quickly shoved the book into his back pocket and the magnifying glass between his teeth. Running as fast as he could back to the ship, he jumped off the last turtle's back, making a flying leap onto the rope ladder of the ship just as the sea creature swam away. Spikey and Stumpy hoisted him up with all their tiny might and plopped him on the deck.

"Are you O.K., Jake?" Alexa asked with a sigh, relieved to have her brother back.

"*Who was that out there with you?*" Rex questioned.

"**Snodgrass!**" Jake explained, putting his magnifying glass back into his other pocket.

Rex was in a fearful panic as he darted about the ship looking out to sea for the Baron. "*Where is he?*"

"Gone!" Jake exclaimed.

"What do you mean gone?" Alexa questioned, searching Jake for any signs of Sandy.

"*Yeah, he would never give up that easily!*" Rex declared.

Jake explained that Snodgrass had come to reclaim Grandpa's secret book and that he was going to destroy the ship and everyone on it if Jake didn't give it up. "But I threatened to destroy the book if he hurt anyone on this ship," he continued, pulling the book out and waving it in the air. "With the sea turtles starting to swim away and Snodgrass never getting this book from me, he had no choice but to retreat."

Mrs. Smythe, still dangling from Penelope's beak, became enraged, knowing that Snodgrass was double-crossing her by going after the book on his own. She now knew that he would leave her behind once the curse was broken if she didn't get that book before he did. Izzie was more determined than ever to snatch it up and use it as a bargaining chip so the Baron would be forced to get her off the ship. If the book was in her possession, Snodgrass would have no choice but to do her bidding. "You weren't really going to destroy that book," she bellowed from above, "now—were you?"

Jake glared up at her with suspicion as to why she was so interested in Grandpa Buck's brown, leather book. "Why do you care what happens to my book?"

Not wanting to reveal her secret, Mrs. Smythe tried to cover up her self-serving interests by saying nervously, "Well—it is always a waste to destroy a good book, my dear. Do you know how many trees a year are cut down to make them? One should always recycle," she explained. "Go Green! You know, if you're done reading it, I would be happy to take it off your hands!"

"No thanks," Jake suspiciously smirked back. "I'm not done with it just yet!"

Captain Snappy patted Jake on the back and declared in his gravelly voice, "Ye saved me ship—me boy, from that dastardly Baron. Now everyone raise ye swords and give a proper Krusty Katfish thank ya ta the Inspector," he ordered.

"Hip, Hip, Hurray!" they all shouted out to the sea. "Hip, Hip, Hurray!"

"What are you fools thanking him for?" Izziedura Smythe screamed from above their heads. "Those slimy, stupid monkeys are still coming after us, Jezebel is still destroying the worlds, he still hasn't solved that ridiculous sandstone

puzzle yet, and we're still cursed into being a bunch of—
TODDLERS!"

"Well, she has a point!" Rex whispered to Jake.

"Thanks for your undying support," Jake sighed back to Rex.

"Don't mention it!" Rex snickered, patting Jake on the back with his paw. *"Glad I could help!"*

Alexa, meanwhile, was feverishly searching through Jake's shirt and pants pockets for Sandy.

"Lexy," he squirmed from the tickling, "what are you doing?"

"Where's Sandy?" she questioned, pulling his shirttail up. "Sandy—come out, come out from wherever you are!"

Jake flung his arms widely into the air, swooshing his sister off him. "What are you talking about?" he said. "I told Sandy to go back to the ship. And what was she doing running back down those turtles' backs—anyway?"

Alexa got an alarmed look across her face. "She thought she saw her purple crayon in the water," she nervously explained to her brother. "What do you mean you told her to come back to the ship? She never came back here. I thought she was with you."

Jake, too, got an alarmed look across his face. "I don't have her!" he confessed. "I thought she was with you!"

"I don't have her!" she exclaimed, rushing to the edge of the ship.

"Oh—no!" cried Jake, trying to figure out how to break the awful news to his sister.

"Don't say oh—no!" shouted Alexa, searching the water. She then ran frantically around the ship, screaming and screaming Sandy's name as her brother and Rex ran after her. "Jake, she's still out there. We have to save her!"

"We will, Lexy—" he vowed. "I promise!"

Alexa turned to her brother with tears cascading down her cheeks. "What do you mean, we will? Where is she?"

Jake started to stutter as he told her the dreadful news, "Wh—Wh—When he walked back down the turtles' backs, I saw him bend over and—and—pick something up. It must have been **S—Sandy!**"

Alexa started to shake and shudder as she gasped in fear. "Who bent down and picked her up?" she asked, afraid of his answer.

Jake just stood there motionless with a droopy face. He took a long, deep breath and declared unwillingly, **"SNODGRASS— that's who!"**

Alexa's face turned cherry-red. She let out the loudest, highest-pitched scream ever heard. The tiny pirates hid for their lives. Penelope, startled from the sound, dropped Izzie right on her butt.

Jake gave his sister a comforting hug as he whispered into her ear not to worry. "Snodgrass wants Grandpa's book. He'll be back, and I'll stop at nothing to bring Sandy back to you—I promise."

"*Snodgrass has pig breath?*" Rex gleefully yelled out. "*Wow—this is almost as good as the time I fed that stupid dog next door four-day-old jelly doughnuts and he got sick to his stomach—what a moron! Ya'd think he'd know not to eat them.*"

Jake's eyes nearly popped out of his head. "You did that?" he snapped in anger. "I got blamed for that and wasn't able to play *Sphynx-3* on my Gamebox for a week! And don't get overly happy about Sandy, you knucklehead. We're getting her back, and you're going to help."

"*Oh—all right,*" Rex scowled. "*But I'll be doing it for Alexa, not that stupid, grilled 'kraut and flounder sandwich-stealing pig!*"

"Thank you, Rexy Cat," Alexa sighed, wiping away her tears with Sandy's pink and purple flowered blanky.

"But first," declared Jake, "we need to solve that puzzle and get the heck outta' here before the Bannana Brothers find us!"

"*So, let me get this straight...*" Rex announced. "*We have to find the third, missing, sandstone, put all the sandstones together to figure out the puzzle, and get out of here before those idiotic, slimy monkeys get us. Then, we have to make our way to you-know-where, find Jezebel's conch shell, and trap her in it, which will release the Bannana Brothers' crazy mother. Then, that will reverse the curse, which will turn all these teeny-weeny pirates back into adults, rescuing all the ships that have been buried at Shipwreck Bottom. And in turn, save the world while trying to get pig breath back from Snodgrass?*"

"Precisely!" uttered Jake. "And we'll start with that nasty, little girl and that third missing stone."

Rex scurried right behind Alexa and Jake as they ran to find Izzie, moaning, "*Even I'm tired of saying this, but it's true—we're doomed!*"

CHAPTER TWELVE
To Earth's End!

Izziedura Smythe was rolling back and forth across the deck, still tied up in the vines the Bannana Brothers had trapped her in. "Someone untie me this instant!" she shrieked over and over.

"Only after you tell us where the third sandstone is," Jake firmly demanded.

"I have no idea what you're talking about!" she exclaimed, lying as usual.

Captain Snappy had just about enough of the poisoning cake, pie, and pastry cook. "Dump her overboard, me buckos," he ordered. "The sharks look like they can be usin' a snack about now.

The teeny-weeny lot of pirates started to carry her to the edge of the ship and her impending doom when she shrieked, "***Wait*—I'll tell you what you want to know!**" she confessed.

Captain Snappy, curious as to what she might say, shouted out to his crew, "Belay that order!"

Spikey and Stumpy, worried Izzie might rat them out, disobeyed the captain's orders and continued to carry her to the edge of the ship. Staring at Spikey's hooked hand, Jake started to remember the fresh wooden-paneled notch on the wall in Captain Snappy's quarters and quickly realized that the two toothless, pint-sized pirates must have been in on stealing the third sandstone of Sethena together, after all—***But why?***

"Just a blueberry-cotton-candy-pickin'-minute, you two," Jake yelled out to the pirates. "Why are you in such a rush to get rid of her?"

As Mrs. Smythe was just about to be dumped overboard into the shark-infested waters, she blurted out, **"These two! They stole the third sandstone—I can prove it!"**

"We be doin' no such thing!" argued Spikey.

"She be wrong in accusin' us, Captain," added Stumpy. "It be her who be takin' off with thar stone!"

Izzie became outraged as she squirmed her way out of their short arms, dropping hard onto the deck. "Why, you lying pieces of squid!" she uttered to the traitorous pirates. "Untie me this instant, and I'll prove they stole the stone," she swore to Jake.

Jake and Snappy quickly unraveled her from the vines and lifted her up from the deck. "Keep talking—" Jake ordered.

Izzie explained that when they were docked at Pirate's Point, she was busy baking her world-famous, overly-frosted crab cakes when she saw Spikey and Stumpy lurking down below. She saw them sneak up to the deck, cut open a watermelon, and hide something inside it.

Stumpy and Spikey laughed themselves silly, confident they got rid of the evidence by hiding the third stone in one of the watermelons and then shooting it over to the Bannana Brothers' ship.

"So you two were the ones that locked poor Pete in the chest," Jake declared.

"Quackers!" scolded Pete to them.

"That freshly-made notch down the wall must have been

made from your hooked hand," accused Jake, pointing to Spikey.

"But why, Jake?" asked Alexa. "Why would they want to stop us from finding Jezebel's conch shell?"

"*Yeah,*" added Rex. "*Without the curse being broken, those two morons will be stuck being toddlers, and then go—'**Poof**' into thin air when the ship sinks to the bottom of Shipwreck Bottom. That's crazy!*"

Stumpy and Spikey, not being very smart, just started to realize what they had done to themselves. Making a deal with the Bannana Brothers and giving them the third stone might not have been the brightest of ideas after all.

Captain Snappy just stood there snarling at them. "You greedy, stupid fools. You be not realizin' what you be doin'."

"I don't think they fully understood the curse," Jake said, staring at their sad, little, toothless faces. "How much did they offer you?"

"Offer?" questioned Snappy.

"You don't think those two were smart enough to do this on their own—do you?" Jake proclaimed.

In an outrage the captain grabbed a sword and placed it right under both of the mutinous pirates' chins. "Ye be tellin' us the truth, or ye be meetin' your end—here and now!"

"They don't have to," smirked Jake. "I think I may have just figured this all out. Spikey and Stumpy were paid off by the Bannana Brothers to help them sneak on board the ship at Pirate's Point to rob it!"

"Arrrrr, you double-crossing scoundrels," Snappy grunted, pushing the blade of the sword further against their necks. "What'd those monkeys pay ye to betray me, a couple thousand clams—arrrr!"

"They not only helped the brothers rob the ship, they also must have led them down to your cabin to search for the stones," Jake added.

"*How else would the monkeys know where the sandstones were hidden?*" Rex exclaimed.

"That must have been when Pete left the cabin to get some salt water taffy," thought Alexa.

"Right you are, my smart sister," smiled Jake. "Spikey and Stumpy took the opportunity to sneak the monkeys below when Pete left."

"*So Spikey and Stumpy must have stolen Captain Snappy's extra set of keys, then!*" Rex said.

"That be why I couldn't find me keys!" Snappy declared, tightening his grip on his sword.

"Right," confirmed Jake. "Stumpy and Spikey unlocked the chest, and my bet is the monkeys went wild ransacking the room, throwing everything about as they searched the chest for the last sandstone that you found."

"*That explains why the cabin was such a mess!*" Rex declared.

"That was the fourth stone with the riddle to the fifth piece to the puzzle they were looking for!" explained Alexa.

"Right again," agreed Jake. "The monkeys didn't need to actually steal all the sandstones. They didn't care about solving the puzzle and reading the map. Tony and his brothers just needed to find the last sandstone Captain Snappy and Pete found, which was number four, read the riddle, figure it out, and find the next stone, number five, before Snappy and Pete did, therefore, breaking the chain to solve the puzzled map and preventing anyone else from finding Jezebel's shell."

"And releasing their mother!" added Alexa

"*Yeah,*" thought Rex. "*Stopping us or anyone else from finding the fifth sandstone makes it impossible to find the sixth and seventh stones, therefore, preventing anyone from solving the puzzle and releasing the monkeys' mother from the conch shell she's trapped in!*"

"And that be keepin' Jezebel out of her shell, roaming the seas forever—arrrr!" grumbled the captain with Pete quacking in agreement.

"Keeping the Bannanas' mother trapped in that shell," Jake explained, "allows Jezebel to destroy the world."

"*Not to mention Tony gets to be the boss of the family!*" snickered Rex.

"And since sea monkeys can survive on land and in the sea, Tony and his wise-guys couldn't care less if Jezebel floods the world and destroys us all!" Jake shouted out to the crew.

"But then what happened?" wondered Alexa.

"My guess is that once the Bannanas read the riddle on the fourth stone, they high-monkey-tailed it off the ship so as not to get caught. That was about the time Pete came waddling back to the cabin with his salt water taffy."

"Quackers!" Pete quacked out his love for salt water taffy.

Jake continued to explain that when Pete entered the cabin, Spikey and Stumpy must have been cleaning up the mess the monkeys made. Afraid of getting caught, they most likely panicked, throwing everything they could back into the chest, including Pete. "But they left something out of the chest by mistake after they locked it with Snappy's extra set of keys!"

"That had to be the third sandstone of Sethena!" whispered Alexa.

"Pete said it was dark in the cabin when he returned," recalled Jake. "One would have to suspect that you must have dropped the keys on the floor because that's where I found them," he accused the stone-stealing pirates.

"*But Snappy said he had two sets of keys,*" Rex asked. "*Where's the other set?*"

Izzie stumbled over to a small, tin box nailed to the bottom of the mast and pulled out the spare set of keys. "I saw that old fool hide them here weeks ago. He just forgot where he hid them!"

Captain Snappy toddled over to her and yelled, "Well, why didn't ya tell me they be thar, woman, when I be lookin' for 'em?"

"Because you are the rudest man I've ever worked for!" she uttered in anger as she snatched his sword, swinging it madly in the air at him. "If it wasn't for you and my being on this stupid, decrepit ship, I never would have been cursed with the rest of you fools after all. Look at me, just look at me. I'm still a five-year-old, little girl! And I hate you—That's why!"

Snappy grabbed back his sword and pointed it right under her little chin. "It be the grandest day of me life when I see the last of you—woman!"

"Mine, too!" she snarled back. "Mine, too!"

Ignoring them, Jake continued to explain that Spikey probably made that scratch on the wall with his hooked hand as he bent down in the dark searching for the keys.

"But you, instead, stumbled upon the third stone that didn't get put back into the chest," he said, pointing to Spikey. "Realizing without the keys to unlock the chest, you couldn't possibly put the stone back. And with Pete causing such a commotion quacking away locked inside the treasure chest, you two decided to run from the scene of the crime and keep the stone for your greedy selves."

"Arrrrr," grunted the captain at them. "What ya be thinkin'? Ye be goin' to sell the stone for a high bounty?"

"Spikey and Stumpy must have thought they were going to be rich," Jake explained to them, walking about the deck. "You never realized that you were sealing your own fate by hiding that stone, preventing us from completing the puzzle and breaking the curse."

Jake glared directly at them and pronounced, "Without us finishing this case, you two will vanish into thin air like every other pirate before you— *'Poof'!*"

"And the ship will sink to the deepest depths of Shipwreck Bottom," warned Alexa.

"Not to mention that crazy sea witch turning the planet into one gigantic bathtub!" added Rex.

Stumpy and Spikey were now panicking, realizing what they had done. "But we be shootin' all the watermelons at the monkeys' ship!" cried out Stumpy in fear for his cursed, little life.

"Yeah!" cried out Spikey. "The stone be long gone by now."

Jake, being the great detective he was, looked over at Izzie who had a wickedly-familiar smile blossoming across her young but slightly-less-than-pretty face. "But I suspect you knew all along how to break the curse," he said accusingly to her. "I'm not exactly sure how you did because only Captain Snappy and Pete knew that when the Seven Sea Gods' sandstones were put together they formed a puzzled map."

Izzie just stood there grimacing away, knowing Jake was on to her.

"Arrrrr—she be snooping around me ship watching me every move for weeks now!" sneered the captain. "That's how she be knowin' about the bloody curse and how the stones be workin'!"

"My detective skills are telling me that you know exactly where that third stone is—don't you, Izzie?" Jake asked her.

A half-crooked grin grew across Mrs. Smythe's face.

"The third stone didn't get shot over to the Bannana Brothers' ship—now did it, Izzie?" he smirked back at her.

"Well, I must admit—" she shrieked as she walked over to an oversized water barrel. Izzie then started to lift it up with all her teeny-weeny might. "There is absolutely no way I am going to spend the rest of my life as a five-year-old girl—let alone go—'*Poof*' into thin air with these idiots!" She raised the barrel all the way up as the crew gasped in disbelief, unveiling the watermelon with the third stone hidden inside it that she, herself, snatched to hide after Spikey and Stumpy snuck away from the pile of watermelons.

"Are you ever wrong?" Rex leered at Jake.

"Well, my dear pussycat—*No!*" he said.

"And that's how I know we're going to get my Sandy back!" Alexa exclaimed with a satisfied smile, "because Jake said so!"

Rex grumbled under his whiskers, "*I'm counting the minutes!*"

Jake quickly grabbed the third stone and bolted down the hatch to Captain Snappy's cabin. Alexa, with the remaining stones safely inside her Inspector Girl backpack, ran right behind her brother with Rex and Pete hot on their trail.

"Hurry," Jake cautioned, "we don't have much time. Those slimy monkeys will be here any minute."

Captain Snappy ordered Penelope to throw Stumpy and Spikey into the brig. "I'll be dealin' with the likes of ya traitors later," he barked. He then ran to his engine room, pulled up the door, and ordered Fred, who was feeling much better after gulping down a dozen or so ginger ales, to rev himself up for their escape. Snappy then ran to join the others while Izzie tried to sneak down behind him. "What do ya think ye be doin'—woman?" he snapped at her.

Pushing past him in the hallway she bargained, "I'm very good with puzzles you know! Besides, if you get hungry, I can always whip up a snack!"

"Will it be havin' sugar and frostin' in it?" he grumbled.

"But of course!" she muttered as they stumbled into his cabin.

"Arrrrr!" the captain frowned in disgust at her inedible baking.

Jake and Alexa had already dumped all the seven sandstones of the Seven Sea Gods—Tethias, Herus, Eos, Sethena, Rhus, Endoseidon, and Aryas—across the table. They were all different shapes and sizes with riddles written on the back of each one. The puzzle-solving group quickly started moving the pieces around, trying to get them to fit into something that might resemble a map.

"No, that's not right," snapped Jake at Rex, who was insisting he was right.

"How about this?" asked Alexa as she replaced the stone of Herus with the stone of Rhus.

"Quackers!" complained Pete that it didn't look right.

Glaring down at the unsolved puzzle with one eye and keeping the other on Jake's secret book sticking out of his back pocket, Izzie asked, "Why don't you put them in alphabetical order, like a librarian would do with books?"

Jake shrugged his shoulders, thinking her guess was as good as anyone else's. But having done that, there still was no readable map forming to Earth's End.

"This is hopeless," Rex whined. *"We're never going to figure this out. And those wise-guy monkeys will be here any second to fit us with cement shoes and feed us to the sharks. We're doomed, I tell ya—doomed!"*

"Oh, stop being so overly dramatic, you crazy fur ball—we'll get it!" scolded Jake. "At least I hope so," he mumbled under his breath. Jake started repeating Earth's End over and over and over again in his head as he stared long and hard at the sandstones.

"What you be thinkin', me boy?" Snappy wondered.

"Dad always says, '*when things look complicated*'..." said Jake.

"...'*think simple!*'" finished Alexa.

"It can't be that simple?" Jake thought as he picked up the stone of Eos, placing it first in line. "Can it?" He then plopped the stone of Aryas right next to Eos.

"It fits, Jake!" exclaimed Alexa in awe of her brother's detective skills.

A clever smile appeared across his face as he grabbed the stone of the sea god Rhus, fitting it right into Aryas.

"Quackers!" shouted Pete, encouraging him on.

Captain Snappy's eyes lit up as the map started to appear with each properly fitted piece to the puzzle. "Keep goin', me boy—keep goin'!"

Jake then snatched up the stone of Tethias, then Herus, placing them in order like train cars right in a row.

"They fit!" blurted out Rex with a sigh of relief. *"We may not be doomed after all!"*

Jake placed the third stone of Sethena right next to Herus'. *"**EARTHS**,"* he whispered to the group. *"**E**os, **A**ryas, **R**hus, **T**ethias, **H**erus, and **S**ethena!"*

They all gasped in disbelief. The first letter from all the names of the Seven Seas Gods' sandstones spelled the word ***"Earth's."***

Jake's smile beamed brighter than the candle lights in the room as he dropped the final and biggest of the stones last in line. "Endoseidon!" he announced to the group.

"He be the ruler of all the sea gods," whispered Snappy to the group.

*"**End**oseidon stands for **End!**"* Jake proclaimed.

*"**Earth's End!**"* they all repeated softly together as if someone could overhear their new-found secret.

*"**Uh-oh!**"* sighed Rex. *"Not again!"*

The rickety sea vessel rocked back and forth as a massive array of lightning shot across the sky with a crack of thunder so loud it nearly tore apart the ship. Jake quickly dove across the table, spreading his body over the stones to protect the completed puzzled map from scattering as the thunderous roar continued to rumble from above. They all screamed for their lives as the Krusty Katfish was tossed about in the violent sea that raged from beneath the hull of the dilapidated ship.

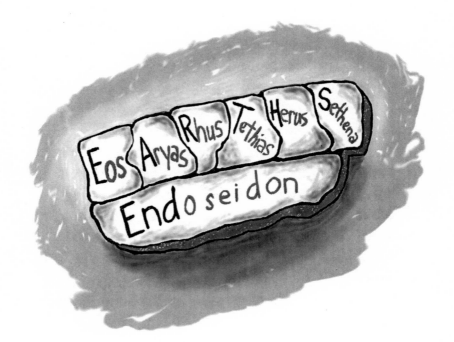

"What's happening, Jake?" yelled out Alexa as she barely held onto a chain dangling from the wall.

"I don't knooooow!" he exclaimed, burrowing his nails into the sides of the table he was trying to cling to.

"It be a tidal wave!" shrieked the captain as the ship was starting to be lifted out of the sea. "It's got ahold of me ship!"

"Quackers!" agreed Pete. "Quackers!"

The ship was scooped up by the gigantic wave as it was thrust across the Seven Seas, headed for a mysterious, treacherous, unknown part of the world.

"*I'm too young and handsome to die!*" blubbered Rex.

"So we've heard over and over again!" shouted out Jake.

Flopping around the room as he was tossed about, the pesky cat cried out, "*Plus, I'm not even sure how many of my nine lives I have left!*"

"This is the worst job I've ever had!" shrieked Mrs. Smythe.

"*I think we've heard that over and over again, too!*" murmured Rex.

"This is all—your fault!" she yelled over to Captain Snappy, hanging on for her life.

"Well, if we be goin' to be gobbled up by the sea, woman," he barked back, "at least I be seein' the last of you and your bloody frosted cakes!"

"You are the rudest man I've ever worked for!" she scorned.

"Ahhhhhhhhh!!!!!!!!" they all shouted in terror.

The ship was riding the crest of the wave like a gigantic surf board, swerving and swaying violently about.

"*We're doomed!*" yelled out Rex. "*Doomed, I tell ya!*"

"Tell us something we don't knooooooooow!" screamed Alexa.

The large, antique, brass compass could barely hang on the wall. The arrowed needle on it spun around and around, not able to get a fix on the location of the ship as it was thrown from one end of the world to the other.

"Ahhhhhhhh!" they all screamed as the ship was catapulted across the seas. Suddenly, the tidal wave broke into the ocean, dumping the ship into its new location with an enormous splash that rippled for miles and miles.

"Where are we?" moaned Rex, dizzy from all the spinning about of the ship.

"I'm not sure," whispered Jake as he stared at the compass's needle as it came to an eerie rest, not at magnetic north but at true north. Jake shuttered in fear while examining the compass for any cracks with his magnifying glass. He knew that there was only one place on the planet that a compass's needle would point true north, but the thought of being there was too scary to even think of.

Snappy stumbled dazed and confused, mumbling under his breath to Pete, who was quacking away in a tizzy.

"Jake, I'm scared," cried Alexa as she watched Snappy spread his nautical maps across the table in a crazy frenzy.

"You be right to be scared, lassie!" he barked, examining and comparing the sandstone map to his nautical maps so he could get a fix on their location.

"Why?" screeched Izzie in complete hysteria.

Snappy kept dashing from the table to the compass, back and forth as he plotted the position of his ship. He kept mumbling their position, staring eagerly at the sandstone map: 32 degrees north by 64 degrees west...32 degrees north by 64 degrees west. "It can't be!" he uttered in dismay.

"What can't be?" Jake asked back, now scared himself.

"Earth's End!" he whispered to them. But this time there was neither a rumble nor a spout of lightning from the above—just an eerie silence.

"What are you babbling about—you old fool," stammered Izzie.

Alexa looked out the tiny port window in the cabin and asked, "Is this *Earth's End?*"

"Not exactly," Snappy answered as he stared down, trying to make heads or tails of the sandstone puzzle.

"What do you mean—not exactly?" groaned Rex.

Jake examined the puzzle and Snappy's maps with his magnifying glass. He once again confirmed that the compass was pointing true north. He shook as he tried to hold his magnifying glass steady, but his fear of the truth made that impossible. "According to the puzzle, this is not—*Earth's End*. It's the...*ENTRANCE!*"

"And where would that be?" Rex asked hesitantly.

"The Devil's Triangle," Snappy grumbled. "Dead center of the worlds, to be exact!"

They all gasped in fear, **"The Devil's Triangle!"**

"Isn't this where planes, ships, and people have been known to mysteriously disappear, never to be seen or heard from again?" Alexa asked, shaking in her sneakers.

"Why would the Seven Sea Gods put the entrance to Earth's End here?" Rex questioned, prancing around the room in a nervous snit.

"It actually makes perfect sense," declared Jake. "Remember when we came back from Comanche Canyon and we wanted to hide all those unraveled toilet paper rolls?"

"Yeah?" mumbled Alexa with a curious look across her face, not sure where her brother was going with this.

"We hid the toilet paper rolls in my closet," he declared. "Why?"

"*Ya got me!*" exclaimed Rex. "*I was busy doing my business in my litter box—boy, did I have to go!*"

"Who are you kidding, you pesky pet? You were just hiding so you didn't have to help us clean up the bathroom," Jake scolded.

Alexa remembered that they hid the toilet paper rolls in Jake's closet because it was such a stinky mess. She explained that no one would ever think of going in there. Way too scary, thus making it the perfect hiding place for the toilet paper rolls. "Oh, I get it," she declared. "The Devil's Triangle is like Jake's closet. The best place to hide something is where no one would ever go looking for it!"

"Right you are, Inspector Girl!" Jake shouted out. "There's not a person in the universe who would deliberately travel into The Devil's Triangle. By placing the entrance to Earth's End here, the Seven Sea Gods knew they would be protecting their secret hiding place for the mystical conch shells."

Rex had an uneasy look spreading under his slightly bent whiskers.

"What's the matter, Rexy Cat?" Alexa asked as she tried to straighten out his whiskers.

"*Is it my imagination, or are we moving backwards?*" Rex asked.

Captain Snappy and Pete ran to the porthole and, indeed,

saw that they were sailing backwards. "Come on!" he shouted, bolting out the door to the top deck of his ship.

"Quackers!" quacked Pete, waddling in a panic right behind him.

They all dashed out of the cabin, worried about what they would find on deck. Mrs. Smythe lingered behind Jake, trying to make an attempt to snatch the book.

Alexa noticed the nasty girl glaring at the tattered, brown, leather book sticking haphazardly out of Jake's back pocket. "What do you think you're doing?" she snapped.

Wide-eyed and startled, Izzie tried to hide her sneakiness as Alexa pushed her on her way and up the stairs. "Well— how utterly rude," she complained. "I was just going to push that book into his pocket so it wouldn't fall out, you know! Excuse me for trying to help!"

"I'll take care of my brother," Alexa advised, giving her a knowing look. She then shoved the mysterious, brown, leather book deeper into Jake's pocket as she warned him again to be more careful with it.

"*You know she's up to something!*" Rex whispered.

"I know!" Jake stammered. "I know!"

"I miss my Sandy!" Alexa sighed.

"Don't worry—I'll get her back!" her brother promised.

"*Well, don't rush on my account,*" mumbled Rex.

Hearing a suspicious, crunchy food rolling around and around Rex's mouth, Jake clamored, "What are you eating?"

"*Nothing!*" he mumbled as pizza fishy crackers came spewing out of his mouth.

"Rexal Moustachio," Jake yelled out, "did you go and eat any of those pizza fishy crackers?"

"I'm starving," he grumbled. *"This is the worst food-eating mystery ever! There's nothing but cakes, pies, and mushy, left-over watermelon chunks lying around!"*

"Naughty, naughty, Rexy Cat," Alexa scolded. "You know pizza fishy crackers give you gas!"

A wide grin sprang from beneath his whiskery nose, *"And now...everyone else will know that, too!"* he meowed in mischievously satisfied delight.

"Eeeeeew!" the children shrieked.

Upon arriving on deck, they found the entire pint-sized pirate crew and Penelope drenched from the tidal wave.

"What be happenin' on me ship?" Snappy barked to his crew.

Exhausted from the events, Penelope swung around still hanging on the tip of the boom, bopping the captain right on the head. Her long, thick, fake eyelashes stuck shut over her enormously large, emerald-green eyes. "Big wave," she squawked as her eyes popped out from under her lashes. "Bigger than big—***BIG! BIG!***" The soaked, blue-gray feathers that adorned her neck quickly blew dry from the gusty wind that was kicking up out to sea. Jezebel was on her way after them. She started to blow closer and closer to the ship, trying to prevent them from completing their mission of finding that conch shell.

"Jezebel!" Snappy snarled, pointing out to the west. "Thar she blows. She be not takin' me ship!"

Alexa looked out the south end of the ship and saw something equally treacherous, the Escargot. "Ahhhhh!" she cried, pointing to the Bannana Brothers' ship. "Jake— we're in bigger trouble. It's the monkeys!"

"The tidal wave must have taken them with us!" he

215

shouted against the wind.

Rex's whiskers trembled alarmingly. "*Why are we moving backwards in a circle? Does anyone care that we are moving backwards in a circle?*" he babbled on and on in a panic. "*This can't be good! Does anyone think this is good?*"

Jake snatched a pair of binoculars off a pole and climbed up the mast into the crow's nest to get a better look out to sea.

"Be careful, Jake," his sister warned.

"What do you see? What do you see?" interrogated Izzie, fearful Snodgrass would arrive before she got her greedy hands on that book.

Both the Escargot and the Krusty Katfish were trapped within a massive whirlpool, spinning around and around backwards. Jake's eyes nearly fell out of his head as he saw that they were being spun closer and closer to a black hole in the center of the whirlpool. He scurried down the pole, screaming to everyone that they needed to get out of there before they get flushed down the black hole.

"Ahhhhhh!" screamed Penelope, Alexa, Izzie, Rex, Pete, Snappy, and the rest of the crew as they scurried about the ship in an unruly panic.

Alexa ran to her brother, pleading with him to use his magnifying glass to get them out of there. "Good idea!" he shouted. He then raised it high into the heavens and commanded, "***Outway omfray isthay aceplay!***" But nothing happened.

"Is it broken?" she questioned, worry reflecting from her crystal clear, blue eyes.

Jake repeated his command again and again, but nothing happened. "The weird electromagnetic force within the triangle must be interfering with my magnifying glass!" he said as panic slowly overtook him.

"**What?**" cried Rex. "*Are you telling me you can't get us outta' here? Check the batteries in that thing!*"

Jake just shook his head, uttering in complete exasperation, "There are no batteries in the magnifying glass—you pest!"

Rex collapsed on the deck bellowing, "*I'm too handsome to die!*"

"**What?**" Izzie uttered. "You can't get us out of here? I should have gotten off this floating wreck the moment I got on!" She ran right up to Snappy and screamed, "If it wasn't for you and being on this stupid, decrepit ship, I never would have been cursed in the first place. Now we're being flushed down a gigantic toilet, and I'm **still** a five-year-old, little girl!"

Upon hearing that, Rex scurried up the mast to take a look at the dark entrance into the ominous abyss for himself. "*She's right,*" he moaned frantically. "*We're all being flushed down that hole like a dead goldfish! And I can't swim!*"

"What do you mean you can't swim, you crazy fur brain," Jake inquired. "We've all taken swimming lessons with Ms. Leeza—even Sandy! Where were you?"

"*Ah—visiting those cute felines next door?*"

In the meantime, both ships were getting closer and closer to the black hole as the skies roared from Jezebel's anger.

"I'll deal with you later!" Jake scolded his flirtatious

pussycat. "But for now—" he warned. "Hold on!"

Suddenly, each ship was engulfed in a gigantic, glass-like bubble as the newly-formed spheres plunged one by one into the awaiting abyss. Penelope, Alexa, Izzie, Jake, Pete, Snappy, and the rest of the crew let out a horrific scream as Rex uttered an echoing cry, *"We're Dooooooooooooooooomed!"*

CHAPTER THIRTEEN
Triple Trouble

The rush of the ocean's water flushed them to the ends of the Earth. Screaming as they swirled around and around and around in the frothy salt water, both ships plummeted to the depths of the sea.

"*Help!*" cried Rex, clinging to a torn piece of the Krusty Katfish's white, linen sail. "*I can't breathe. We're going to drown!*"

"Stop hyperventilating, you fur brain," Jake moaned, as he, too, held tightly onto his sister as they both dangled from another end of the sail.

"We're encased in some sort of protective air bubble," Alexa shouted out through the tumultuous sounds of the rushing water.

"Wooow!" they all exclaimed as the spheres bounced out of control down the abyss. Twisting and turning, the spheres dropped violently until they made one final turn, knocking into each other. They then shot out from the darkness like two silver balls at the start of a wild and crazy game of pinball. The imprisoned Krusty Katfish and the Escargot looked like two ships in bottles as they came to rest next to each other at the bottom of the sea.

Dazed and confused, everyone tried to regain his or her balance as the spheres slowly stopped rolling. Catching their breath, they all realized that they had arrived, finally, at **Earth's End**.

"*Oh, I think I'm going to be seasick!*" moaned Rex as he

pressed his nose up against the glass of the sphere, staring directly at the Escargot. There was an ocean of water between the protected ships. Rex did a double-take, rubbing his eyes with his paws, not quite believing what he was looking at. There they were—Tony, Savannah, Little Johnny, and the other Little Johnny all tied up to a gigantic barrel with a dozen or so bananas shoved into their mouths, keeping them quiet. *"Well, looky over there,"* he chuckled. *"It's a barrel of monkeys!"*

Jake and Alexa ran over to see what he was laughing at as the rest of the crew scuttled close behind.

"Who do you think did that?" Alexa pondered in stunned curiosity.

"I'm not sure," Jake answered, "but my detective skills are telling me it can't be good."

"Well, it's obvious someone out there must like us," screeched Izzie, "by tying up those slimy, green, hairy monkeys and that pink ape."

"Don't be too sure, woman," warned Snappy. "Sometimes tis enemies of ye enemy be **your** enemy!"

"Quackers!" agreed Pete.

*"**What?**"* snapped Rex. *"Ya know, I haven't understood a word you two have said since this case started."*

Jake got an embarrassed look across his face as he scolded his less-than-polite cat. "What he means, you pest, is that whoever tied up the Bannana Brothers might be more trouble for us than they are!"

*"**Oh!**"* snipped quickly Rex. He then thought and thought about who would be worse than those wise-guy monkeys. *"**Ohhhhhhhhhhhhhhhhh!**"* he sighed as he began to worry.

"I miss Sandy," Alexa moaned under her breath as she applied some strawberry lip gloss to her overly dry lips.

Jake assured her he would get her back safe and sound. "Is it me, or is it just a little too quiet down here?"

"Tis be the calm before the storm, me boy!" grumbled Snappy under his breath. "Jezebel, she be breathin' down the backs of our necks any minute now!"

"Quackers!" whispered Pete in agreement.

Jake, remembering his magnifying glass did not work in The Devil's Triangle, sighed, "That's what I was afraid of."

Suddenly, a vacuuming force sucked all the water out from around the two spheres. The stranded group gasped in disbelief as a newly-formed ceiling of water hung high above their heads. Then a high-pitched, ringing sound filled the spheres, causing them to pop like bubbles, one by one. Each ship dropped to the ocean floor with a thud. As the children looked down below, they could see spread far and wide across the abyssal plain nothing but conch shells. Not just ordinary conch shells—the most beautiful, mystical conch shells ever seen. They had spirally-constructed shells with long eye stalks and the most colorful ring-marked eyes. Each one had its own glow to it as if it had its own story to tell from inside. Their polished pearl-like surfaces varied in color from the pinkest of shades to the orangest.

As they all stood there frozen in fear, wondering how long the ceiling of water would hold before drowning them, Rex bellowed, *"You're not thinking of leaving this ship, are you? That crazy witch will be flying down that abyss any minute!"*

"The cat be right thar, Inspector," informed Captain Snappy.

Jake looked across the ship to the Bannana Brothers, who were screaming a muffled "***Help***" beneath the dozen bright-yellow bananas stuffed into their grammatically-impaired mouths. "Well," he said, "the monkeys are all tied up, and we did come here to solve a case, after all. Let's find that pink and white, zebra-striped shell, get that sea witch back into it, reverse the curse, save the world, and call it a day!"

Alexa got a worried look on her pretty face. "We'll find Sandy before we call it a day—right?"

"*Are you loony?*" Rex grumbled. "*You want to go looking for that crazy, evil, awful, maniacal, mean, bad, nasty Snodgrass just to save that stupid pig!*"

"**You flatter me, dear boy!**" echoed a familiar, dreaded voice from the other ship.

"*Uh-oh!*" sighed Rex as his tail puffed up.

Slithering up onto the deck of the Escargot was none other than the Baron. His wicked laughter bounced endlessly under the water ceiling above. His long, yellow, linen coat waved in the approaching stormy winds of Jezebel like the wings of a bat about to attack its prey. His evil, dark, deep-set eyes were slightly covered by the rim of his odd, flat-brimmed hat. A half-crooked smile sprang from underneath his tiny black moustache, spreading his jagged ***M***-shaped scar further across his cheek.

The Bannana Brothers were crying out for help, trying to escape from the barrel that Snodgrass had them tied to.

"You know," Snodgrass chuckled across the ships, "I was going to make myself a banana split sundae, but I seemed to have run out of bananas after stuffing them all into these ill-speaking, annoying monkeys' mouths. Oh, the way they speak, it hurts my delicate ears so. Did you know that these two have the same name, Little Johnny and Little Johnny?" he said as he shoved more bananas into the twins' over-stuffed, helpless mouths. "Who names their children the same name? It's so unoriginal," he bellowed, slithering towards the edge of the ship. "Don't you think so, young Moustachio?"

Jake stared him down, showing no emotion as he contemplated the predicament they were in.

"What's with the grim face, dear boy?" Snodgrass asked, gesturing to the barrel of tied-up monkeys. "I did you a favor getting rid of these ridiculous, slimy, green, hairy creatures, not to mention the pink ape with that hideous coconut swimsuit. Now, now—it wouldn't be polite not to thank me!"

"Where's my guinea pig, you meany?" Alexa exploded from across the ship.

"Oh—don't you worry, my dear," he explained. "She's down below looking for some stupid purple crayon she lost, all safe and sound for now. Give me that book, and you can have the pig and the monkeys, for all I care!"

"Come and get it!" Jake challenged him.

"*Are you out of your mind?*" scolded Rex. "*He'll blast us into smithereens!*"

"**YEAH!!!!!**" chimed in Alexa.

Jake explained that the odds of Snodgrass's magnifying glass working in The Devil's Triangle were slim to none if Jake's didn't work. This was a perfect opportunity for Rex and Alexa to sneak aboard the Escargot to save Sandy while

Jake kept Snodgrass busy.

"And if you're wrong about his magnifying glass?" quivered Rex.

"Then, my good pussycat, we really will be doomed!" Jake sighed.

"That's what I was afraid of," he whimpered.

Snappy toddled over to Jake and whispered into his ear that they didn't have much time left before Jezebel came storming down the abyss. "We best be findin' that shell before me ship vanishes to Shipwreck Bottom and me crew go— '***Poof*** inta thin air!"

"I can't let anything happen to Sandy!" Jake exclaimed. "I promised my sister. Take your crew and start looking for the shell. Once you find it, you can trap Jezebel and reverse the curse yourself."

"I may be findin' the shell, but I be not trappin' the sea witch meself, me boy!" Snappy declared.

"Why not?" Jake asked.

"Well, what do ye be thinkin' I called ye for?" Snappy barked. "I ain't be havin' the powers to be stoppin' that wicked sea witch—you do!"

"I do?" Jake asked.

"He does?" repeated Rex and Alexa.

"Ye bloody do!" announced the captain.

Jake lost sight of the Baron as he disappeared from the deck of the monkeys' ship. Trying not to panic, he instructed Snappy to search for the shell while he took care of Snodgrass. Once he found it, Jake promised he would re-trap Jezebel and reverse the curse of Shipwreck Bottom.

"But don't let any other sea witches or warlocks out of any more conch shells," Jake warned the captain. "We have enough trouble as it is!"

"You be gettin' that thar right, me boy!" Snappy exclaimed. "The swells from Jezebel are more than the seas can take—arrrrr!"

Everyone ran off on their own missions. Snappy and his pint-sized pirates jumped overboard, looking for the pink and white, zebra-striped, shell while Penelope kept her perfectly long, fake, black, eye-lashed eyes on the abyss for any signs of Jezebel. Rex and Alexa started making their way to the other side of the ship so they could sneak onto the Escargot unnoticed to find Sandy.

As Alexa looked back at her brave brother preparing to do battle again with that evil Baron, she noticed something strange. Izzie was lingering around Jake. "Why do you suppose she's not running away in fear of Snodgrass?" Alexa asked Rex.

Rex looked back at the annoying little girl slinking behind Jake. *"I'm telling you, she is up to no good!"* he declared. *"I think she wants the book!"*

"I'm beginning to think you're right!"

"But why?"

Alexa became very determined to find out what Izzie was up to. She grabbed a fuzzy, pink hair scrunchy from her backpack and pulled her hair into a tight pony tail, ready for a fight of her own. "You take my backpack and go find Sandy," she ordered. "I'm staying behind to take care of Izzie. No one messes with my brother!"

With a grimace forming under his whiskers, Rex uttered, *"Why do I have to go and save pig breath?"*

"You want to deal with Izzie?" Alexa proposed.

"*Ahhh—nope!*" Rex muttered. "*She's a crazy, little thing!*"

"Then scoot!" she commanded.

As Alexa tried to figure out the mystery behind Izzie's infatuation with Grandpa Moustachio's secret, brown, leather book, Rex jumped over to the Escargot and prowled around, trying to sniff out Sandy with his best pussycat curiosity and sense of smell.

"*Here piggy, piggy,*" he called out, sniffing all around. "*Is that pizza I smell?*" he asked himself as the aroma pulled him down below towards the galley. The tied-up monkeys were mumbling under the bunches of squashed bananas stuffed into their mouths, trying to tell Rex not to go down below, but he was paying absolutely no attention to those green, slimy, hairy clods. Rex thought he really should continue searching for Sandy, but he could not resist the prospect of finding some of the left-over pizza the Bannana Brothers had ordered from Dolphino's Pizzeria. He knew the pizza, when combined with the pizza fishy cracker he ate earlier, would end up explosively bad, but he didn't care. Rex just had to find that mouth-watering, smelling pizza pie.

The air now completely smelled like a pizza parlor, drawing him into the ship's kitchen. He slowly pushed open the door, hesitated for a moment, then crept inside.

"*Well, well, well,*" said a familiar voice. "*Look what the cat dragged in!*"

Rex's big, round, golden eyes lit up in shock. He hissed angrily at the unexpected surprise as he stared deadly into the cold eyes of his arch enemy—**Tobias**. Instead of Rex's rusty, golden fur, Tobias had an ash-grey coat and a devilish-looking tuft of black fur, resembling a goatee, dangling under his fuzzy, white, grimacing chin.

"*Care to join me for a midday snack,*" Tobias snarled, holding up a slice of pizza with Sandy plopped on top. "*I just love pizza smothered in guinea pig! Don't you, old chum?*"

"HHH—H—Help!" gulped Sandy in fear as she tried to pull away from the gooey, melted mozzarella cheese she was stuck on.

"*Tobias!*" Rex hissed in anger. "*Put the pig down!*"

Tobias just snickered, licking his whiskers. "*What's the matter, dear boy? Lost your appetite for rodent?*" The evil, grey-haired cat laughed, dangling the guinea pigged slice of pizza high in the air, mouth opened wide. "*You used to eat anything that had a heart beat and crawled. What's the matter Rex—have you gone soft?*"

Sandy started to slide off the cheese, getting closer and closer to Tobias's opened mouth and her end. "RRR—R—Rex?" she begged helplessly.

Rex started to think now would be as good a time as any to get rid of pig breath. But his conscience got the best of him. "*No one eats my family members,*" he declared, "*except for me—of course! Put her down, Tobias!*"

"*Make me!*" Tobias purred, licking Sandy, who was now dangling from a string of cheese.

"*With pleasure!*" Rex meowed.

Tobias flung the slice of pizza across the room, while Sandy hung from the stringy mozzarella cheese for dear life. "**CCC—C—Cat Fight!!!!!!!**" she nervously screamed out, soaring through the air.

Rex and Tobias pounced on each other, fighting like a bunch of alley cats. Kicking and clawing, they rolled out into the lower hallway.

"*Well, well, well,*" hissed Tobias, "*you still got a lot of fight left in ya, old boy!*"

"*Who are you calling old?*" Rex snarled back, making a flying leap onto Tobias's back. "*You're the same age as me!*"

"GGG—G—Get him, Rex. Get him!" Sandy cheered on as she followed the brawl around the ship.

"*Tell me, old chum—how many lives have you used up?*" Tobias questioned as he grabbed Rex by the tail and started spinning him around and around and around. "*I myself have only used up three!*"

"*Four, five, maybe six,*" Rex yelled out while spinning around and around, "*but who's counting!*"

"*Naughty, naughty—losing count, dear boy,*" Tobias ranted about as he clawed Rex in the head. "*We only get nine lives—you fool! Maybe I should just kill you now and see if you come back to life!*"

"*Ohhhh—I'll come back to life all right, you maniacal guardian of all that is evil and bad,*" hissed Rex. "*And I'll keep coming back until I've finished you once and for all!*" Rex then grabbed Tobias's back leg as they rolled and rolled around entangled in a rusty-golden, ash-grey ball of fur.

"*Not if you're on your last life you won't, old chum!*" declared Tobias, pouncing on Rex's tail.

Rex flipped over on top of Tobias and spewed, "*So kind of you to worry about me—but I have plenty of lives left in me, I assure you!*"

"GGG—G—Get him, Rex!" urged Sandy, jumping around them, trying not to get squashed.

"*After all these years you haven't changed a bit,*" meowed Tobias. "*Still the foolish noble cat, guardian of all*

*that is pure and good! Tell me, does the new keeper of your
magnifying glass know who you really are?"*

Both cats stood there bruised and drenched in sweat,
glaring into each other's determined eyes. Rex didn't utter a
word as his heart beat ever–so–heavily.

"*I didn't think so!*" uttered the evil cat. "*Meow!*" he
screeched as Rex chased him up the stairs to the top deck of
the Escargot.

Snodgrass was just about to jump ship when he glared
back in delight, watching the guardian of his magnifying
glass fighting with the guardian of Jake's.

Alexa was frantically trying to figure out what Izzie was up
to when she saw the two cats rolling around on deck past the
barrel of tied-up sea monkeys. As she saw her lost guinea pig
running after Rex, she exclaimed with relief, "Sandy, thank
heavens you're all right!"

"CCC—C—Can't talk now!" chutted Sandy breathlessly. "I
gotta help Rex!"

Meanwhile, Snodgrass leaped from the Escargot onto the
Krusty Katfish with his magnifying glass swinging in the air,
ready to blast Jake into smithereens.

"Ready to relinquish the journal, young Moustachio?" he
exclaimed in a mad tirade.

"Not a chance, you crazy maniac!" Jake exploded.

Snodgrass aimed his magnifying glass directly at Jake
and bellowed, "Then the pig, your sister, that annoying
feline, and **you** will pay for your foolishness!"

Jake, praying that Snodgrass's magnifying glass wouldn't
work in The Devil's Triangle, proclaimed, "Take your best
shot!"

Snodgrass became enraged at Jake's lack of fear

and commanded his magnifying glass, **"Otay ouryay endway!"** He waited and waited and waited, but nothing happened. Snodgrass then held his glass under his long, slender nose, examining every inch of it. He blew the dust off it with a puzzled look, waved it high into the stormy sky, and ordered again, **"Otay ouryay endway!"**

Jake started laughing himself silly. "What's the matter—lose your powers? Maybe you should check the batteries!"

Snodgrass's eyes widened with anger as he tried to make sense of the situation. "Tell me, young Moustachio, why aren't you swirling your magnifying glass at me? You could finish me off right here, right now, and be done with me for all of eternity." Snodgrass scanned the area, deep in thought, as his scar crinkled in a newly-formed grin. "Ahhhhh—I see," he echoed beneath the ocean. "The magnifying glasses don't work down here! Fascinating turn of events! Wouldn't you say so—young one?"

"Fascinating!" Jake smirked back, watching his arch nemesis staring at a set of pirate swords hanging from the boom of the ship.

Izziedura Smythe was standing directly behind Jake, smiling to Snodgrass over Jake's head. "Did you get the book, my dear?" he asked of her.

"Not yet!" she sighed in a huff, glaring directly at the book in Jake's back pocket.

Snodgrass sprang over to the swords, grabbing one as he ordered, "Well—what are you waiting for?"

"Look out, Jake!" Alexa screamed, tossing him a sword from across the ship.

Jake didn't waste a second grabbing it. He and the Baron

became embroiled in a fierce sword fight, swashbuckling all over the ship.

"Well, well, well—Moustachio, you're quite the swordsman," ranted Snodgrass between the steel clashing on steel of their weapons. "Why, I think you might even be better than your grandfather—*Is!*"

"What do you mean—*Is?*" yelled out Jake as they dueled back and forth, forth and back across the deck.

"*CLANG-CLANG*," echoed the clashing of the cold metal of their swords under the ocean's waves.

Snodgrass jumped up onto a barrel and swung across the ship from the ropes draped off the sails. "That's one mystery, young Moustachio, you're going to have to solve for yourself!" he manically laughed. Snodgrass went flying through the air with Jake in hot pursuit.

Izzie looked up as Jake flew over her head. The brown, leather, book unexpectantly popped out of his pocket and plummeted to the dilapidated deck below. "Got ya!" she screamed out in delight.

"**I don't think so!**" yelled out Alexa as she pounced on Izzie, trying to pry the book out of her grubby, little toddler hands. The two little girls went rolling and rolling on the deck as they fought for possession of Grandpa Moustachio's mysterious, brown, leather book.

Penelope, dazed and confused, didn't know where to look and what to do as Jezebel made her ominous entrance into the abyss. Jake and Snodgrass were chasing each other across the boom. Rex and Tobias were still cat fighting over on the Escargot, while Alexa and the soon-to-be-revealed Mrs. Smythe were rolling on deck, each unwilling to give up that book.

"Sea witch! Sea witch!" Penelope squawked in overwhelming fright. "Big trouble, trouble. Bigger than big—BIG! BIG!"

The force of Jezebel's furious hurricane winds interrupted the battles as they all were tossed about like leaves fluttering in a storm. "Woooooooow!" they all shouted.

"Time's a wasting, wasting," snapped Penelope, grabbing Jake by her beak and tossing him overboard.

Alexa ran to the edge of the ship, screaming out Jake's name.

"Come on, Lexy. We have to stop Jezebel!" he shouted through the gale-force winds.

"But Jake—what about the book?" she yelled out. "I can't find it!"

"We'll find it later!" he echoed, running through the conch shells towards Snappy and his pint-sized crew.

Penelope scooped up Alexa and flung her overboard. Alexa ran as fast as she could to catch up with her brother. Knowing they didn't have the book, Snodgrass and Mrs. Smythe both scurried about the ship, fighting the blustering winds, searching for Grandpa Moustachio's mysterious journal.

Finally, Izzie saw it wedged between two crates. "**Got you!**" she uttered again in delight.

Snodgrass's eyes illuminated upon seeing her fondling the brown, leather casing. "**Give it to me!**" he ordered.

"Not until Moustachio reverses the curse and you get me off this blasted ship!" she bellowed back at him.

As they watched the events unfolding overboard, Snodgrass uttered reluctantly, as he caressed the jagged

M-shaped scar on his face, "Very well, my dear. Very, very well!"

Jake, Alexa, and the entire teeny-tiny pirate crew scoured through thousands of conch shells, searching for the pink and white, zebra-striped shell to trap Jezebel in.

"Hurry, guys! Hurry!" exclaimed Jake as he scrutinized a large, rose-colored shell with his magnifying glass.

"Is that it, Jake?" pondered Alexa, diving into a large pile of her own, tossing out pink-looking seashells one by one.

"Nope!" he muttered, tossing it back into the pile. "It has no stripes."

"The bloody shell has to be here somewhere!" shouted Captain Snappy through the tumultuous winds of the storm. He then ordered his men and Pete to search another pile. Jake and his sister ran over to a new pile of their own, hoping to find that one shell that would save the world.

Jake plunged headfirst into the new pile while Alexa's eyes were fixed on the events unfolding above her head. Shocked, she stared motionless at the ceiling of water hovering over her as the entrance to the abyss blew wide open.

"**Jake!**" she cried out as her eyes grew wider and wider in fear. "**Jake!**"

"**What?**" he echoed from below.

"**Jez—Jez—Jezebel!!!!!!!!**" she screamed.

Popping his head out from under the pile, he squealed frantically, "**Uh—oh!**"

There she was, the most wicked-looking creature ever to roam the Seven Seas—Jezebel, the sea witch. She was monstrous in size, with long, slimy, green, suction-cupped octopus tentacles for hair that wildly blew in her own wind.

Swarming toward the children, one of her tentacles reached out, trying to nab them.

"**Run, Lexy! Run!**" ordered Jake as he grabbed her hand, dragging her across the shelled ocean floor.

"**YOU WILL NOT ESCAPE ME!**" she exploded.

Jake and Alexa ran as fast as they could back to the ship with Jezebel relentlessly chasing them through the abyss. Suddenly, Jake tripped on a large shell as they both went tumbling to the ground. Jezebel had stormed right on top of them, about to unleash her wrath. With their faces buried deep into the shells, they both looked down and focused on a peculiar-looking, large shell with the pinkest and whitest zebra-striped pattern spread across it.

"Are you thinking what I'm thinking?" Alexa asked her brother with a shred of hope beaming from her crystal blue eyes.

"There's only one way to find out!" he exclaimed as he grabbed the shell and flipped around on his back.

Sandy ran to the edge of the Escargot to see what all the commotion was about as Rex and Tobias, mesmerized by the sight, stopped their cat fighting long enough to join her. The maniacal Baron and the poisoning Mrs. Smythe, with smirks emerging on their faces, slithered to the edge of the Krusty Katfish to watch with much happiness as Jake and Alexa were about to be destroyed by the evil sea witch.

"This is going to be a good day, after all!" gloated Mrs. Smythe, clutching ever-so-tightly onto Grandpa Moustachio's secret book.

"Watch and learn, my dear," instructed Snodgrass. "**Watch and learn!**"

They all watched as Jake held firmly on to the large, pink and white, zebra-striped conch shell, directing the opening up towards Jezebel. It glowed in his hand as it drew power from deep within him.

"Give me that book, you annoying woman!" Snodgrass ordered, noticing Jake struggling to control the shell.

"Why do you want this book, anyway? I thought you wanted the other magnifying glass," she asked, dangling it temptingly in front of his pointy nose. "What secrets lie within these pages?" she pondered, flipping through them. "With those annoying children about to be destroyed, you will finally have the other magnifying glass once and for all!"

"It's not that simple, my dear," he sighed, scowling at Jake, not powerful enough to stop Jezebel on his own.

"I don't understand?" she asked confused. "Delbert told that annoying sleuth that he who possesses both magnifying glasses will be able to unlock the mysteries of the universe. With the boy out of the way, that will be you!"

An angry grimace sprouted beneath the Baron's thin, black moustache. "Delbert keeps things from young Moustachio. It is not — '**He**' who possesses both magnifying glasses, but— '**They**'!"

"I still don't understand," she uttered.

They both glared out to the ocean's bottom as Jake tried to desperately get Jezebel zapped back into the mystical conch shell alone.

"Just as I thought," snarled Snodgrass. "Young Moustachio doesn't have enough powers alone to ruin my plans, after all."

"What plans?" she spouted in glee.

"My plans to rule the universe—you foolish lemon tart!" he scolded.

"Ooooh, that sounds delicious! Can I help?" she asked, hoping to rule the universe, too.

"Help me find the other magnifying glass, my dear, and you can have anything your poisoning heart desires!" he promised.

"But the other magnifying glass is right down there in Moustachio's pocket. In a few moments there won't be anything left of those annoying children, and then we can rule the universe—I mean **you** can—of course!"

"That's only one of the two magnifying glasses now belonging to the Moustachio family, you dried-up crumb," he whispered into her inviting ear. "We would still need to find the other one!"

"But you have your own magnifying glass. Isn't that the other one?"

"That's what I've led everyone to believe," he explained. "The glass that I possess, shall we say, is—*Evil*. It alone will never be able to unlock the mysteries of the universe."

"Where's the other one?" she greedily asked him.

Snodgrass gazed down at Grandpa Moustachio's journal that Mrs. Smythe's teeny-weeny toddler hands were clutching so tightly.

"You mean—?" she mumbled.

"That's right, my dear—" he snarled back at her. "The secret to the whereabouts of the other magnifying glass lies buried somewhere within that book!"

"How utterly scrumptious!" she dangerously giggled.

The echoes of Jake's cry for help from his sister radiated

against the ocean's floor.

"But we need to find that other magnifying glass before they do," Snodgrass declared, staring hatefully at the children.

"What do we care about them for?" questioned Mrs. Smythe. "That crazy witch will have them for supper any minute now. And **we** have the book!"

"The girl!" Snodgrass shouted in a deep voice. "Watch the *girl!*"

Alexa bravely joined her brother in grabbing on to the pink and white, zebra-striped conch shell, holding it firmly in her hands. A glow emanated around them as her undiscovered, inner powers joined with Jake's.

"Don't let go, Lex!" shouted out Jake as the shell rumbled in their hands.

"I won't!" she shouted back.

Snodgrass sniveled in anger as he watched the events draw to an unfortunate conclusion. "You see, my dear, the girl possesses the same powers as her troublesome brother. They are both the chosen ones. They just don't know it yet. If they find out that there is a magnifying glass in the universe meant for her, and find it before we do, she will become the keeper of *that* glass. And my plans to rule the universe will be—**ruined!**"

"What do you want me to do?" the poisoning baker groveled.

"The moment we leave The Devil's Triangle, my magnifying glass should work. You give me that book, and we vanish from this awful place," he snarled.

"But what about the Moustachios?" Mrs. Smythe inquired.

"First, we find the other magnifying glass, and then we'll destroy those meddling children."

"And the cat?" she asked, giggling with the thought of destroying Rex.

"As you wish," the Baron granted, caressing his scar. "We'll destroy the cat, too!"

Mrs. Smythe got a worried look on her face as she blurted out, "But only after the curse is reversed—right? I'm not traveling to the ends of the universe as a five-year-old, little girl. Being a child once was enough for a lifetime—agreed?"

"Very well, my dear," Snodgrass agreed. "Very well."

CHAPTER FOURTEEN

The Curse Tis Be Broken!

The wicked sea witch was putting up quite a fight as her long, slimy, hair-like tentacles started wrapping around Jake's and Alexa's legs.

"**YOU WILL NEVER TRAP ME!**" she howled through the hurricane winds.

Jake and Alexa held tightly on to the pink and white, zebra-striped conch shell and, unknowingly, combined all their powers into capturing Jezebel.

"Wanna bet?" yelled out Jake.

"Hold on to her, me boy!" echoed Captain Snappy through Jezebel's raging storm. "You be almost catchin' the likes of her."

"Quackers!" agreed Pete, flapping around.

"Ahhhh," Alexa screamed as one of the tentacles started to grab her arm. "I think it would be easier to reel in a great white shark than this gooey witch."

"Don't let go, Lexy," Jake shouted. "We almost have her!"

"I don't know how much longer I can hold her, Jake," Alexa proclaimed. "Let go of me, you wicked monster! Where's a good witch when you need one?"

"One strong pull should do it," he declared. "We almost have her!"

Suddenly, an enormous blast of energy came surging through the children's hands. The energy wave engulfed the witch as she screamed "**NO!**"——They had her.

"In you go!" shouted out Jake with a satisfied grin. With that said, Jezebel was sucked right into the mystical, pink and white, zebra-striped conch shell, trapped for all eternity once again. Jezebel's hurricane vanished off the face of Earth's End, leaving calm waters across the seven seas. Jake and Alexa sighed a deep breath of relief from their victory and smiled at each other, having conquered the storm.

Jake was still holding onto the shell as it started to rumble in his hands.

"What's happening?" Alexa squealed.

"I'm not sure," he questioned.

Suddenly, the shell flew out of his hands and hit the ground as a flash of light exploded from it. There, in front of their eyes, appeared the ugliest of sea creatures, none other than the wise-guy Bannana Brothers' mother, the notorious Ma Bannana.

She was just as hairy, green, and slimy as her sons. Her webbed hands swung in the misty sea air as she yelled for them. "Where are those good-for-nothin' monkeys of mine?" she clamored, stomping her dragon-like tail, which poked through the back of her water lily-patterned sundress. The scaly, flapping gills on the side of her neck flapped open in anger as she looked around the abyss for her sons. "How dare they leave me trapped in that smelly conch shell after all I've done for them!"

Jake, Alexa, Captain Snappy, and his still pint-sized crew just stood there speechless as the madcap monkeys' ma searched high and low for her sons. "Where are they?" she demanded.

Jake and Alexa, without saying a word, pointed over to the monkeys' ship. Ma Bannana patted them both on their heads with her slimy, webbed hand and said, "Thanks—I owe youse two!" She then ran off to find her good-for-nothing sons.

"Eeeeeew—my hair will never be the same!" Alexa winced.

"I wouldn't want to be those monkeys when she gets ahold of them," Jake laughed.

Suddenly, Jake saw a droplet of water fall on his sister's head as they both looked up at the suspended ocean's ceiling over them.

"Uhhh—ohhh!" he moaned out in a panic as it started to rain from above.

"The waters, they be collapsin' above us!" declared the captain, ordering everyone back to the ship.

"We're going to drown!" Alexa cried out in fright as she and the others ran for their lives.

"Quackers!" echoed Pete, flapping his wings wildly in fear, flying back to the ship.

"Hurry, everyone, hurry!" ordered Jake. "The abyss is flooding with water!"

Earth's Ends shook and rumbled as the ocean's ceiling poured in around them. Everyone ran as fast as he or she could ahead of the rushing water, making a hurdling leap aboard the Krusty Katfish. Alexa's frantic voice echoed as she yelled at Rex and Sandy to leap over from the Escargot to the Krusty Katfish. Tobias quickly followed them aboard, jumping right into the arms of his evil master, Snodgrass, who was hiding in the back of the ship unnoticed with Mrs. Smythe. Jake scanned the other ship as he watched Ma Bannana anxiously untying her boys and Savannah.

Everyone took cover as they witnessed the unthinkable.

An enormous tidal wave was about to engulf both the ships.

"Ahhhhhhh!" they all called out.

"*We're doomed,*" cried Rex. "*Doomed, I tell ya!*"

Just as the wave was about to crush them, both ships were once again enclosed in a gigantic, glass-like bubble.

Penelope's big, emerald-green eyes flew wide open in a panic as she saw what was approaching the bow of the ship. Her long, flowing, fake, black eyelashes fluttered in the wind as she shouted, "Hold on, on!" With an incredible force, the tidal wave smashed violently into the spheres. The rush of the water sent both glass balls rolling wildly against the ocean's floor. The mystical conch shells went swirling around and around and around. Trapped, both ships and their passengers went spinning out of control within the bubbles that imprisoned them.

"*I think I'm going to be sick!*" uttered Rex.

"From the sss—s—spinning?" questioned Sandy as they got tossed about.

"*No!*" moaned Rex. "*Watching all those stupid monkeys rolling around in all that mashed-up watermelon—yuck!*"

Suddenly, the spheres were shot right out of the abyss as they went soaring through The Devil's Triangle out to sea.

With their faces plastered against the glass bubble, everyone let out a horrific scream as the spheres shot through the sky then plummeted down to the awaiting waters below. **Crash** went both glass bubbles into the water. Within seconds of the balls landing, the bubbles popped, dumping the ships back into the sea.

"*Oh—I'm so, so dizzy,*" Rex moaned, flopping all around the deck, trying to get his balance.

"I second that!" complained Mrs. Smythe. Dazed and

confused, she rolled on top of the evil Baron as they both tried to get up unnoticed across the ship from the children. He quickly shoved her off of himself as he anxiously contemplated their escape.

Rex was stammering about the ship, still trying to steady himself. *"I'd cough up my lunch but I can't—because someone ate all my grilled 'kraut and flounder sandwich!"* he groaned.

"Are you still complaining about that after all we've been through?" Jake scolded as he helped Alexa up.

"Yeah, Rexy Cat!" added Alexa, herself still dazed and dizzy from the ride.

"Look at the pretty purple-ppp—p—pink polka dots in the sky!" Sandy chutted away. "They remind me of my crayon. I mmm—m—miss my purple crayon!"

"What polka dots?" they all exclaimed in awe, staring out into the purpley-pink-drenched sky.

"Tis not be polka dots," warned Captain Snappy with a worried scowl across his face. "Tis be flyin' jellyfish!"

Flying Jellyfish!" they uttered in horror.

"And they're hovering over us because?" pondered Jake nervously as he examined their long, electric tentacles dangling from their squishy bodies with his magnifying glass.

Perplexed, Captain Snappy scratched his toddler head, not able to answer Jake's question. Pete also shook his beak, clueless.

"Look at the pretty ggg—g—glow!" murmured Sandy, climbing back into Alexa's Inspector Girl backpack so she could nibble away at the last of the Clunky Chunky Bars.

Alexa's eyes grew wider as the glow emanating from the

jellyfish got brighter and brighter. "J—Jake," she stuttered, "those things only glow brighter when they're about to..."

"**Sting!**" screamed Jake, grabbing his sister and Rex, diving into a pile of fish nets for cover.

The swarm of flying jellyfish started zapping electric shocks at each of the unexpecting, teeny-weeny, cursed crew. A hazy, pinkish cloud swirled around each of them as they were transformed from the cursed toddlers they were back into the dirty, swashbuckling, toothless, adult pirates they were meant to be.

Captain Snappy, standing tall and proud, started jumping for joy at the turn of events. "You did it, me boy!" he exclaimed. "You be breakin' the curse of Shipwreck Bottom. Me crew is back to its old, grungy self!"

"*I think grungy is a bit kind,*" snickered Rex, "*don't you? After all—they're downright* **ugly!**"

"Rexy Cat, be kind," scolded Alexa. "They are pirates, you know! Pirates who need a good bubble bath but, needless to say, just pirates."

Staring at the crazy ship's cook, Izziedura Smythe, Rex chuckled, "*What's with her?*"

Baffled himself, Jake uttered, "I haven't got a clue!"

In fear for her selfish self, trying not to get zapped, Mrs. Smythe, still a little girl, went running madly about the ship while being chased by the biggest of all the jellyfish. "Get away from me, you gooey blob!" she bellowed. "Get away from me!" Suddenly, the jellyfish wrapped its tentacles tightly around the annoying little girl, stinging her from head to toe. As with the other crew members, a pink cloud blanketed her, transforming her from the nasty, five-year-old girl back into the equally nasty, cake and pie-poisoning cook she was when she boarded the ship.

Upon gazing at her upside-down, downside-up, pineapple cake apron, Jake, Alexa, and Rex finally realized who the mean, little girl was.

"**Ahhhhhhhhh!**" they screamed in horror.

"That be exactly what I be sayin' the first time I laid me eyes on her, too!" grunted Captain Snappy. "She be uglier than me crew!"

"How dare you—" she snapped back, throwing a hatchet at the captain's head, barely missing him by an inch. "You are the rudest man I've ever worked for! If it wasn't for you and being on this stupid, decrepit ship, I never would have been cursed with the rest of you fools in the first place!"

"Calm yourself, my dear," sneered Snodgrass at her as he went slithering about the ship, petting Tobias lovingly in his arms. "One could say this is fate colliding with destiny. Wouldn't you agree, young Moustachio?"

Jake just stood there grasping his magnifying glass, hoping it would work upon Snodgrass's next move. "The greatest gift in life," Jake leered back at him, "is the power to believe. And if all this is fate colliding with destiny, it will be you who will lose in the end!"

"Maybe so, young Moustachio! But not before the most cataclysmic of events unfold." Snodgrass then threw his magnifying glass up to the sky and commanded, "*Eavelay isthay orldway!*" A burst of energy exploded as the force of its wind howled across the sea. "Remember, Moustachio," the Baron yelled through the wind, "Time is a luxury only fools can afford to waste! Don't be a fool like your grandfather!" And with that said, Snodgrass, Mrs. Smythe, and Tobias vanished into the vortex of Snodgrass's evil magnifying glass with Tobias's hiss lingering in the salty air.

"I can't believe that snotty little girl was Mrs. Smythe," Alexa stammered, shaking her head in disbelief. "And right here under our noses the whole time!"

"*I thought something smelled fishy about her all along,*" Rex proclaimed.

"And what's with that cat?" Jake asked. "Where the heck did he come from?"

Sandy popped her little head out from Alexa's backpack, her mumbling mouth overly-stuffed with chocolate. She tried to explain all about Tobias and being held captive on the Bannana Brothers' ship by the Baron when Rex, in all the confusion, grabbed her, smothered his paws over her mouth, cutting her off from telling the truth. "*Hey pig breath, orgetfay aboutway atthay atcay andway atwhay entway onway, onway atthay ipshay! Got it?*" he whispered away from the children.

"WWW—W—What?" she chutted back.

"*The ship—the cat, you stupid rodent!*" he grumbled, licking chocolate from his paws. "*Keep it to yourself.*"

"What ship? What ccc—c—cat?" she murmured, licking the last bit of the Clunky Chunky Bar from her frazzled, puffy cheeks.

A mischievous grin sprang from under Rex's whiskers, knowing the identity of Tobias would be kept secret from the children for now. "*You know,*" Rex chuckled, giving her a snuggly hug, "*it's times like this I appreciate that your pea-sized brain can't remember anything. Maybe I won't put you between two pieces of bread, smother you in mustard, and eat you after all!*"

Dazed and confused, Sandy spouted out, "I miss my

purple crayon!"

"*Oh, brother!*" sighed Rex, dropping her to the rotten, wood deck below.

Suddenly, a watermelon came crashing onto the Krusty Katfish from the Escargot. Crazed and mad, Tony Bannana was firing upon them.

Captain Snappy ran to the edge of his ship screaming at the slimy, no-good monkey. "What ya be thinkin' on doin', ya crazy monkey?" he bellowed.

"Nobody makes a fool outta' Tony Bannana and lives!" he screamed, shooting another watermelon cannonball at the ship.

"Yeah—nobody makes a fool outta' Tony and lives!" repeated Little Johnny and Little Johnny as they fired up another cannon.

"Tis be war!" scorned the Captain, ordering his men to fire back.

"Yeah—that's right!" screeched Savannah. "Nobody makes a monkey outta' my husband."

"**HUSBAND!**" yelled out Ma Bannana in a fury, leaping right over to Tony. She grabbed him by his big, green, hairy ear and scolded, "Tony, youse didn't go marryin' that ugly, pink ape—did ya?"

"But Ma!"

"Don't 'but Ma' me," she scolded. "That ape is the ugliest sea creature that ever swung from a coconut tree. Do you have any idea what your children are goin' ta look like?"

"Who youse callin' ugly?" Savannah screamed at her new mother-in-law.

Ma Bannana got right into Savannah's face, bellowing, "You did this! My Tony would have never left me in that conch shell to rot for all of eternity if it wasn't for you!"

With all the yelling and name calling coming from the Escargot, the Bannanas forgot all about the Krusty Katfish. Jake and Alexa just stood there laughing themselves silly, seeing Tony Bannana being yelled at by his mommy and his wife.

"Well, Inspector Girl," he declared, "I guess this would be as good time as any to sail out of here!"

"I would have to agree with you on that, Inspector," she giggled back.

Captain Snappy was shaking his head as he held the hatch open to the engine room.

"What's the matter?" Alexa questioned.

"Tis Fred," he stammered as they all looked down at the overly-tired one-seahorse-powered engine. "We be not goin' anywhere in the shape he be in!"

"Quackers!" agreed Pete.

"What do we do, Jake?" Alexa asked. "We can't leave them stranded here!"

Jake thought for a minute and came up with a solution. "Do you think the ship can hold together for another jump?" he asked the captain.

"She be a little weary, but me thinks she be strong enough to make one more go of it through thar magnifying glass, laddie."

"*Are you crazy?*" Rex protested. "*You're not seriously considering sending this floating wreck through that glass again—are you? Forget about them. Let's just go home.*"

"We can't leave the ship drifting out here alone," argued back Jake. "So unless you have a better idea, you knucklehead, we're taking her in!"

"*We're doomed! Doomed, I tell ya!*" Rex moaned out into the ocean air.

Jake wound up his arm and threw his magnifying glass once again out to sea, commanding, "***Iratespay Ointpay!***" The magnifying glass shot a massive blinding flash of light into the sky as it grew larger and larger. The Escargot pulled back, afraid of being destroyed from the wind that was ripping through the ocean's waves, tossing both ships about.

Remembering the last time the ship jumped into the glass, the crew ransacked the ship for any nautical rope they could find and started tying themselves down to anything that would hold them from flying off the ship.

"Can we do this again?" Alexa asked, nervously scooping up Sandy and plopping her safely into her backpack.

"I certainly hope so!" Jake announced through the wind with some hesitation trembling in his voice.

Rex jumped into his arms, screaming they were doomed, as Penelope blurted out, "*Here we go again, again!*"

The Krusty Katfish violently shook to and fro as it was pulled into the spiraling, turbulent wind of the magnifying glass. Everyone held their breaths, praying the ship would not fall apart this time as it swirled and spiraled out of control through the gigantic vortex. Twisting and turning, they screamed for their lives. Faster and faster they sailed on through, holding on to the shaking and shuttering, dilapidated ship. Suddenly, a blast of light exploded from the glass as the Krusty Katfish went shooting out of the magnifying glass to the waiting, friendly waters of Pirate's Point.

CHAPTER FIFTEEN
Whack The Frog!

As far as their eyes could see, the ocean was filled once again with ships sailing the Seven Seas. With the curse of Shipwreck Bottom broken, all the sunken ships returned to their voyages with their crews reappearing one by one.

"Ya did it, me boy," cheered Snappy.

"No...we did it!" Jake shouted out, smiling as widely as could be.

Captain Snappy gave them a warm and slightly-grungy hug, bellowing happily, "Ye broke the curse, trapped that wicked sea witch, got rid of all those slimy monkeys, and filled the ocean with happy pirates and thar ships once again. Me ship and me crew and the likes of us and every other pirate on the Seven Seas is indebted to ya for all of eternity. Now everyone raise ye swords and give a proper Krusty Katfish 'thank ya' ta the one and only Inspector Moustachio and his swashbucklin' crew," he ordered.

"Hip, Hip, Hurray!" they all shouted out to the sea. "Hip, Hip, Hurray!"

Captain Snappy ordered Penelope to turn what was left of the tattered sails into the wind so they could dock the ship back at Pirate's Point. "Aye-aye, Cap'n, Cap'n!" she squawked jubilantly.

The dilapidated Krusty Katfish barely made its way back to the pier.

"Let's get off this floating hunk-a-junk before it finally sinks!" snickered Rex.

"Rexy Cat," scolded Alexa, "be nice!"

"Yeah, Rex," added Jake. "The ship held up pretty well, all things considered."

"Ya got that right!" grunted Snappy. "Tis be a fine ship. A little paint, some spit, and lumber, and she'll be as good as new!"

"Quackers!" agreed Pete, flapping his duck wings wildly in the wind.

Penelope dropped the anchor as the ship bumped against the dock of the marina. "All ashore that's going ashore, ashore!" she ordered, stretching her blue-grey neck out long enough to scoop up the children and their mystery-solving pets with her beak. She then plopped them one by one onto the boardwalk. "Get a move on, on. Times a wasting, wasting!"

"Hey!" yelled Jake as she clunked him on the head. "Stop that! We weren't ready to leave! "

Fluttering her long eyelashes in his face, she uttered, "Yes, you were, were!"

"No, we weren't, weren't—I mean weren't!" Jake yelled back.

"You broke the curse, trapped that wicked sea witch, got rid of all those slimy monkeys, and filled the ocean with happy pirates and their ships once again, again. What else were you planning to do today, today——save the universe or something, something? Besides, the boardwalk is closing any minute now, now!"

"*Is it me, or is she just the rudest turkey on the planet?*" Rex hissed.

"Turkey? Turkey?" she squawked, clunking him on

the head. "I'm an ostrich, you foolish feline, not a turkey, turkey!"

"Turkey smirkey!" he laughed. *"You've seen one stupid bird, you've seen them all!"*

Penelope became extremely impatient as she nudged them further down the boardwalk.

"Take care of ye selves!" shouted out Captain Snappy from above. "You be always welcome aboard the Krusty Katfish!"

The children waved goodbye as they happily ran back down the boardwalk. "Well, Inspector," exclaimed Alexa, "I think we've done all that we could do that we've done today!"

Jake smiled giving his sister a hug. "I would have to agree with you there, Inspector Girl."

"Well—I for one think we deserve a treat!" Rex proclaimed, tail held high, prancing along. *"How about a codfish sandwich or some liver chunks?"*

"Eeeeew!" the children winced.

"LLL—L—Let's play a game!" chutted Sandy.

"Much better idea than eating liver chunks!" laughed Jake.

They all scampered anxiously down the boardwalk, looking for a game to play.

"I still can't believe that annoying, little girl was Mrs. Smythe hiding all along on that ship," spouted Alexa, "and right under our noses, too."

"I know," added Jake, beaming with pride. "And she and Snodgrass really wanted Grandpa's book."

"Oh—no!!!!!!" cried out Alexa in a panic. "Snodgrass and Mrs. Smythe escaped with Grandpa's book!"

"No, they didn't," Jake smirked.

"What do you mean? The book fell out of your pocket when you were dueling with the Baron, and they swiped it," she recalled.

"That wasn't the book," he confidently explained. "When I was searching for another crayon for Sandy in your backpack after she lost her purple one..."

"I mmm—m—miss my purple crayon," Sandy interrupted with a sigh.

"I decided it would be safer to switch Grandpa's book with the one Penelope gave me," Jake continued. "That way, if Snodgrass got his evil hands on it, he would have the wrong book! Good idea—wasn't it?"

Alexa's crystal-clear, blue eyes nearly popped out of her head.

"What's wrong?" Jake asked.

"I...I...I," she stuttered, "I had the same idea and switched the books, myself."

"**WHAT?**" he cried. "**WHEN?**"

Alexa explained that when they all went tumbling out of the magnifying glass onto Moneke Island, the book fell out of Jake's pocket onto the ground. She grabbed it and was about to scold him for being careless when she got the idea to switch that book with what she thought was the fake one in her backpack.

"Oh—no!" he cried out. "You handed me back Grandpa's book, and now that maniacal Snodgrass and that crazy, poisoning cook have it in their clutches!"

"I'm sorry. I didn't know," sighed Alexa. "It's all my fault!"

"No, it's not," comforted Jake with a sad sigh of his own,

"It's my fault for not letting you in on my plan."

Rex just stood there grinning happily.

"What's so funny, you knucklehead?"

"Funny you should ask what's so funny," laughed Rex. *"Critter Detective has once again saved the day!"*

"How so?" questioned Jake, raising his left eyebrow in curiosity.

"Well," Rex started to explain, *"just when those stupid monkeys were firing on us and the watermelons went flying everywhere, I found the book just lying there on the deck. You know you really need to be more careful with that thing!"*

"And?" shouted out Jake.

"I was just about to yell out that I found the book when I thought to myself it would be safer if I hid it in Alexa's Inspector Girl backpack. So, without anyone noticing, I switched the real book for the fake one that Jake won on the boardwalk. Brilliant, wasn't it?"

Jake and Alexa immediately ransacked the backpack for the book. Empty Clunky Chunky Bar wrappers went flying everywhere.

"You mean this is Grandpa Moustachio's **real** book?" Jake asked of Rex.

"But of course!" he exclaimed with a smile bursting from under his wide whiskers. *"You switched the books once. Alexa switched them back, and then I switched them back again."*

"Rexy Cat," Alexa shouted out, giving him a huge hug, "I love you!"

"Me, too!" declared Jake as he hugged Rex, sandwiching their cat between them.

"*I can't breathe,*" Rex groaned. "*You're squeezing me too hard; enough of the pussycat sandwich!*" As the children let go of their cat, he looked down at all the empty Clunky Chunky Bar wrappers. Sandy started to slinker away. "*Hey, pig breath, you didn't eat all those Clunky Chunky Bars, did you?*"

"Ummmmmm?" chutted Sandy nervously.

"Sandy," scolded Alexa, "a girl has to watch her figure!"

"WWW—W—Well," she stuttered, "I ggg—g—got hungry!"

"*HUNGRY?*" Rex yelled out as he searched Alexa's backpack for his pizza fishy crackers, only to find an empty bag. "*You ate my grilled 'kraut and flounder sandwich, all my pizza fishy crackers, the coconut snowballs Mrs. Panosh gave us, and you left us not a crumb of an entire box of Clunky Chunky Bars—YOU PIG!*"

"Who you calling a pig, you common alley cat?" she squealed "I am a princess guinea pig from Peru!"

"*I don't think you lost your purple crayon after all,*" he hissed. "*I think you—ATE IT!*"

"I did nnn—n—not," Sandy spewed in protest. "Mrs. Smythe threw it down the drain after she was arguing with that evil man! Ooops—now why did that pop into my head just now?"

"**Snodgrass?**" the children shouted out, confused and surprised.

"I...I...I think?" Sandy said, shaking in confusion. "You know I have a hard ttt—t—time remembering stuff."

With a scowl across his face, Rex uttered in contempt, "You mean to tell us that when you went looking for that stupid purple crayon, you stumbled upon Snodgrass and found out that that nasty toddler was Mrs. Smythe, and it just slipped your mind?"

"**Well!!!!**" chutted Sandy. "I tried to tell you, but by the time I got back on ddd—d—deck, I forgot."

"*Why don't you get some sauerkraut, smother yourself in it, slide between two pieces of bread, so I can finish you off, once and for all, and put myself out of my misery!*" he groaned. "*I should have left you on those stupid monkeys' ship, after all!*"

"Rexy Cat, shame on you," Alexa scolded.

"Yeah, Rex," added Jake. "If it wasn't for Sandy writing down the phone number of our mysterious secretary in her notebook before Pete ate the card, we never would have had the numbers."

"*What good is having three numbers from a ten-digit phone number?*" snarled Rex. "*It's not like she solved that mystery!*"

"Maybe not," declared Alexa as she gave Sandy a much-deserved, snuggly hug, "but getting those three numbers are going to help us solve the mystery to the identity of the unknown woman who is posing as our secretary. Well, at least eventually!"

"Inspector Girl's got ya there, Rex!" Jake exclaimed.

"*Oh, brother!*" he moaned.

Alexa looked over at Jake, who had a worried look sprouting upon his face. "What's wrong, Jake?" she asked.

"Well, I know we have the mystery of the unknown woman to solve, but I'm beginning to think there's something else."

"What do you mean—Jake?"

"Do you remember me telling you back at Comanche

Canyon that Snodgrass said that I was more trouble than Grandpa—*Is?*"

"Yeah!" they all answered.

"Well, when he and I were sword fighting, he said that I might be a better swordsman than Grandpa—*Is!*"

"I don't understand!" Rex spouted out.

"He keeps saying—*Is*, as if Grandpa is still here," Jake declared, somewhat confused himself.

Alexa, looking puzzled herself, added, "But that can't be!"

"*He's just messing with your head,*" declared Rex as they strolled further down the boardwalk.

"I don't know, Rex," Jake declared. "This may be another mystery we may just have to solve, too!" Jake looked off into the distance. His eyes grew wide with excitement at the game that lay ahead. "But for now, my mystery-solving family, I think there are some frogs with our names on them."

"**Frogger!**" Alexa screamed out with delight as they dashed over to the lime-green booth with the gigantic frog billboard.

"And the sign says, fff—f—free!" Sandy exploded in delight.

As they reached the game, they each grabbed a bucket of rubbery frogs. "I just love this game. All you have to do is catapult a rubber frog onto one of those revolving lily pads, and you win a prize!" Alexa exclaimed.

"Right you are missy, missy!" squawked Penelope, mysteriously appearing from the back of the billboard as it swung around.

"*Not you again,*" muttered Rex in disgust.

After clunking him on the head, she announced in a snit, "Of course it's me, you foolish feline, feline. Who were you expecting, a turkey, turkey?"

Rex tried to swat her back for clunking him on his head. "*Stop that!*" he hissed.

You know, I have to do everything around here, here!" the overworked ostrich continued. "Now grab your frogs and your mallets, and let's get whacking away, away. It's almost time to close the boardwalk, you know, know!"

Everyone grabbed a mallet and placed one rubber frog onto the tiny catapult. Alexa never noticed Sandy crawling along across her frog when she whacked the mallet really hard, sending Sandy and the frog catapulting through the air.

"WWW—W—Weeeee!" chutted the guinea pig, soaring across the lily pads.

"Sandy!" they all shouted.

Alexa's frog plopped right into the water as Sandy landed right on a lily pad. "That's a win, right?" she called out in excitement.

Penelope raised her big, old eyebrows as she batted her clumpy, fake eyelashes. "Certainly not, not!" she squawked.

"What do you mean—not a win?" Jake protested. "She made a direct hit!"

Penelope stretched her long, feathered neck out and clunked him right on his red haired head. "Does this look like a game of leaping guinea pigs to you, you? You don't win a prize unless you get a frog on the lily pad, pad!" She then snatched Sandy right up and dropped her onto the counter. "Now, let's try this again—shall we, we?"

Once again everyone grabbed a mallet and started whacking frogs everywhere. Frogs went flying to the right, then to the left. But never did a frog reach a lily pad. The buckets were near empty when Jake grabbed the last one and made one final whack. Soaring across the water went the most raggedy, rubber frog of the bunch. They all gasped in hope as it just barely made it onto a yellow lily pad.

"Yes!" he screamed in delight.

Penelope had a questioning look in her big, emerald-green eyes. "Well, I don't know, know."

"What do you mean, you don't know, know—you stupid bird?" Rex grumbled in objection.

"Yeah, Penelope," declared Alexa firmly. "The frog is on the lily pad!"

"Well, the back right leg is touching the water, you know, know!" she complained.

"WHAT?" they all screamed.

Penelope took a big gulp of the salty sea air and sighed, "Oh, all right, right. If you promise to take a couple of bags of that slightly–used, blueberry cotton candy you fell into and ruined, I'll call that a win, win."

"Eeeeew!" they moaned.

"Well, deal or no deal, deal?" Penelope yapped.

Having no intention of ever eating the slightly-used and dirty, blueberry cotton candy, the children and their pets reluctantly agreed.

Alexa, wide-eyed in anticipation, asked the wheeling and dealing bird what the prize would be. Penelope dove headlong behind the counter and started throwing stuffed animals wildly into the air with her beak.

"No, that's not it, it!" she muttered, throwing more stuffed animals and tiny toys around the booth. "Ah—ha, here it is, is!"

"What iii—i—is it?" Sandy asked in a hush-hush voice. "Is it a purple crayon?"

"*Don't be ridiculous,*" laughed Rex. "*That would be the lamest prize ever!*"

Penelope proceeded to pull out a slender, aged manila envelope with a red, **M**-embossed, wax seal stamped on the face. "Here's your prize, prize!" she announced, plopping it down on the counter.

They all looked at her like she was crazy. "*I changed my mind,*" Rex smirked in disbelief. "*That is the lamest prize ever!*"

Pointing across the booth, Jake sighed, "I really wanted the grey shark over there."

In protest, Penelope yet again clunked Jake right on his sore, red head with her beak.

"Ouch—!" he screamed in pain. "What did you do that for?"

"What's that matter, matter?" she asked. "Do you already have a slender, aged manila envelope with a red, **M**-embossed, wax seal stamped on its face, face?"

"Well, actually..." Alexa said, rummaging through her Inspector Girl backpack, "...no!"

"So why don't you want this one, one?"

Jake stretched his neck out over the empty frog bucket and looked Penelope right in her clumped, eye-lashed eyes, ready to claim his shark, and answered, "Because I want the shark!"

"No, you don't, don't!" she squawked.

"Yes, he does, does!" argued Alexa.

"No, you don't, don't!" squawked Penelope again.

Jake grabbed the envelope with the red, *M*-embossed, wax seal stamped on its face to examine it with his magnifying glass. "So why do I need this?"

"Because! Because!" she exclaimed.

"Because why?" he questioned, glaring at it through his magnifying glass like a world-class detective.

"Just because, because!" Penelope declared.

"That's stupid. We don't need your stinkin' letter!" shouted out Rex. *"We want the stuffed shark."*

"YYY—Y—Yeah, the shark!" added in Sandy as she made room for it in the backpack.

Penelope got right down into Jake's face. He could still smell the left-over, blueberry cotton candy on her breath. Her fake eyelashes brushed up and down his face with each blink she made. "You know when fate collides with destiny, cataclysmic events can happen, happen."

Jake crinkled his forehead and blurted, "So I've been told!"

"You never know when an envelope like this might come in handy, handy." Penelope suggested. "What's it going to be, Inspector—the useless shark over there or this potentially life-altering envelope with the red seal, seal?"

Jake remembered how the second book Penelope gave him came in handy and decided to take the letter instead of the shark. As he started to open it, Penelope let out an alarming squawk and clunked him on the head several times. Jake threw his arms up in protest, swooshing her out of the way. "What did you do that for?"

"What do you mean, what did I do that for, for?" she

blurted out. "Why did you try to open up the letter, letter?"

Jake was furious, still rubbing the bump on his head. "What do you mean, why did I try to open up the letter? It's a letter, isn't it? Aren't you supposed to open it up?"

"Not this letter, letter!" she explained in a snit.

"Why not?" asked Alexa. "All letters have to be opened up eventually."

"They do, do?" Penelope cried out. "Why—yes, I guess they do, do! But this is a very special letter. Only to be opened when you know it is time to open it!"

"*That's crazy!*" Rex argued in confusion. "*How do you know that now isn't the time to open it?*"

"Because it's not, not!" the crazy ostrich exclaimed. "Is it, Inspector, Inspector?" Penelope then tried to blink her left eye at Jake, but the glue from her false eyelashes made her eyelids stick once again together.

"I—I—I guess not," he stuttered.

Penelope explained that when the time was right, he would feel it in his heart, and then, and only then, should the letter ever be opened. "Then you'll wait, Inspector, Inspector?" she asked. "After all, the greatest gift in life is your power to believe. Now isn't it, it?"

"I'll wait," Jake confirmed.

"Promise? Promise?" the ostrich squawked.

"I promise!"

"Wise choice, Inspector, Inspector!" she winced, pulling her eyelids apart. "A very wise choice, indeed, indeed! Now hurry, hurry! The boardwalk's closing, closing. Time to go home, home!"

CHAPTER SIXTEEN

The Calm After The Storm

Jake stashed the letter deep into the pages of Grandpa Moustachio's secret book, and then hid it inside Alexa's Inspector Girl backpack.

"Boardwalk's closed, closed!" blurted out Penelope as she flipped around behind the Frogger sign. "Don't forget the blueberry cotton candy, candy!" she echoed, disappearing from their sight. "Oh, and one more thing—if you're going to jump back through that magnifying glass, would you mind doing it away from my stands, stands? You make an awful mess of things, you know, know!"

"That is one annoying turkey!" Rex exclaimed.

"I heard that, that!" squawked the ostrich.

"Time to go?" suggested Jake with a big grin as he handed Sandy the bags of blueberry cotton candy to pack away.

"What are we ever going to do with all this?" asked Alexa as she zipped up her backpack with Sandy all safe and sound, snuggled into all that pillowy cotton candy.

"*Eat it?*" suggested Rex. "*I'm sure that stupid pig won't have a problem doing that!*"

"I hhh—h—heard that!" mumbled Sandy, nibbling on some of the used cotton candy.

"Eeeeew!" the children screamed.

"*We're animals—we eat anything!*" stated Rex.

"Eat what you want, you crazy fur ball," announced Jake, "Just as long as we don't have to smell ya afterwards."

"*Hey, it's not my fault pizza fishy crackers give me gas,*" declared Rex as they started walking down the boardwalk. *"I have a delicate stomach. Speaking of delicate stomachs, I'm going to need to use that gigantic litter box in front of your grandmother's house any minute now!"*

"Rexy Cat," scolded Alexa, "that's not a litter box!"

"It's the beach, you pinhead," explained Jake.

A smirk of discontent grew under Rex's twitching whiskers as he declared, *"If it looks like a litter box, smells like a litter box, and feels like a litter box—it's a litter box!"*

"You're hopeless," Jake groaned, grabbing his magnifying glass from his back pocket. He then threw it into the sky and commanded, ***"Andmasgray ottagecay!"***

And with that said, the magnifying glass grew larger and larger as it exploded, ready for the crime-stopping, mystery-solving foursome to jump back home. One by one they jumped into the ominous whirlpool to Grandma Moustachio's cottage, which awaited them. They shot tumultuously through the gigantic flow of air, endlessly twisting and turning inside the magnifying glass. Rex's scream of *'my litter box awaits,'* echoed as the children laughed through time, sliding faster and faster with every bend and turn. They body-surfed once again through the tidal waves of sparkly stars that flew past their wide open eyes until the magnifying glass erupted, thrusting them out one by one.

Rex roared like a lion, ***"Meow!"*** bolting out the back door, heading directly down the deck to the sandy beach.

"It's not a litter box, you confused cat!" grumbled Jake in the dark as he commanded his magnifying glass to return to his hand. "It's a beach!"

Just as Grandma came tottering in from the kitchen with

the matches to light the candles, the lights that the storm blew out mysteriously came back on. Looking around the messy room at all the Go Fish cards, pillows, seashells, and fishy crackers scattered about, she exclaimed in horror, "What in the world happened? It looks like the hurricane blew right through here!"

While Alexa unzipped her backpack to grab Sandy, who was covered head to toe in blueberry cotton candy, she stuttered, elbowing her brother, "I—It was quite a storm, Grandma. Wasn't it—Jake?"

Jake, not wanting his grandmother to know that the mess actually came from jumping through the magnifying glass, stuttered back, "A—Ah, yeah, th—that was some—some storm!"

"Well, it had to be to blow the back door right open and make such a mess of things!" exclaimed Grandma in a curious tone. She then waddled over to the TV and turned on the weather channel to get a storm update.

"*Hurricane Jezebel has mysteriously blown out to sea and disappeared off the face of the Earth,*" announced the weatherman.

Alexa gasped in disbelief. "Did we do that?" she whispered into her brother's ear.

As he caressed his magnifying glass, he whispered back, "I do believe we did!"

They both stood there, uncontrollably giggling, having trapped the wicked sea witch, stopping her fast and furious storm from destroying the world.

"What's so funny—you two?" Grandma asked. "You look like a cat that ate a canary."

"Nothing—!" they exclaimed, still giggling.

Grandma and the children started to clean up the mess as Sandy nibbled away at an unclaimed fishy cracker in the corner near Grandma's conch shell that had fallen off the mantle in all the ruckus.

"Oh—no!" cried Grandma, scurrying over to the shell. "My beautiful conch shell that Grandpa gave me. I hope it's not broken." She quickly scooped it up and examined every inch of it for any cracks or missing pieces. She shook it repeatedly to see if anything rattled inside.

"**Nooooooo!!!!!**" the children screamed out in protest.

"**Whaaaaaat????**" Grandma screeched in a startled panic, clutching the cherished shell for dear life.

"Don't shake it!" demanded Jake.

"Yeah, Grandma," added Alexa, "never ever shake a conch shell that hard!"

"Why not?" she unbelievingly asked as she checked her shell for any damage from the fall.

"There might be a wicked sea witch..." explained Alexa.

"...Or warlock in there," added Jake, "that may escape and destroy the world or the universe."

Grandma Moustachio just stood there looking at the two very determined and serious faces of her grandchildren. Suddenly, she started bursting out in laughter as she placed her prized conch shell unharmed back safely on the mantle.

"You two had me going there for a minute," she said with a tickle still in her voice. Imagine that, wicked sea witches and warlocks trapped in conch shells. You two have your Grandpa Buck's wild imagination. He was always saying such crazy stuff like that to me! Life was never dull with him around, and I have a funny feeling things are going to get a whole lot more exciting with you two—too! Where's Rex, by

269

the way?"

The children explained that he had run out the back door looking for a litter box.

"Crazy cat!" she exclaimed. "His litter box is in the bathroom, not out on the beach."

"That's what we tried to tell him!" proclaimed Alexa.

"Well, it looks like the sun is coming back out," said Grandma. "Why don't we go outside and clean up the deck?"

They all skedaddled back outside into the calm after the storm. Jake lagged behind, picking up the last of the Go Fish cards. He then placed the deck filled with lobsters, sea turtles, walruses, goldfish, octopuses, and dolphins on the dining room table. Looking up at the painting of the mysterious, majestic ship hanging now crookedly on the wall, he went to adjust it ever-so-straight once again. As he moved it a little to the right and then again a little to the left, he noticed some tiny writing on the corner of the ship. He grabbed his magnifying glass, scanned the words one by one and, to his surprise, read the name of the ship—***The Lady Lilac***.

His eyebrows rose in question, not sure exactly what this all meant. But he knew as he ran out the back door that he, his sister, and their crazy mystery-solving pets were somehow involved in something that was bigger than them. A comforting feeling blanketed him at the thought of eventually solving the mysteries of the magnifying glass, Grandpa's journal, the unknown secretary, and that unopened letter.

As he headed down the deck towards the dunes, Grandma was sitting there in her favorite, white, wicker lounge chair with the blue and white-striped cushion, snuggling Sandy in the warmth of the sun. "I think you'd better go help your sister," she giggled. "It looks like Rex is once again tangled up in some kite string."

Shaking his head in disbelief, Jake sighed in exasperation, "That crazy fur ball will never learn!" He jumped over the dunes, down to the beach and ran after his sister and their pesky pet along the edge of the water. Startled by an unexpected wave, he looked down and saw something odd rolling in and out of the surf. He bent down and grabbed the object and brushed off the wet sand. In utter amazement, he was holding none-other than Sandy's gigantic, purple crayon.

Mesmerized by the turn of events, Jake just stood there clutching Sandy's most prized possession, staring out into the open sea. A warm mysterious breeze that smelled like lilacs blew in from beyond. As he took a sniff of the fragrant air, an enormous smile spread widely across his cheeks. He thought to himself about his beloved grandpa, Captain Snappy, the evil Baron, and the poisoning Mrs. Smythe. He thought about the swashbuckling world far out to sea, and he went running happily down the beach, eagerly anticipating the many misadventures that were yet to be!

THE END?

Coming Soon!

The Secret of the Pharaoh's Feline

The inherited destiny of the Moustachio children and the fate of the universe are becoming apparent to Jake and Alexa as they and their mystery-solving pets are swirled into a sand-blasting, spooky mystery on All Hallows Eve!

Secrets are revealed, and lies are told on the other side of their grandpa's mystical magnifying glass as they are called upon by Mimi Pashmeanie, the exquisitely exotic owner of the Perrrfect Petz cat litter company. The Moustachios are drawn into the mystery of Mimi's missing canary, Diamond, who vanished from her secret factory hidden under the Great Pyramids of Egypt.

Awaiting our young detectives beneath the Seventh Wonder of the Worlds is a collection of the most spine-tingling, scary suspects ever to walk King Khufu's tomb.

Lurking behind every corner of this ancient ruin is the evil Baron Von Snodgrass. With the help of his pernicious pet cat, Tobias, and the wickedly-poisoning cook, Mrs. Smythe, Snodgrass sets his menacing plan to destroy the Moustachios and rule the universe by unleashing the most maniacal force known to mankind!

There are only two children on Halloween who can find the missing canary, Diamond, solve the secret of King Khufu's cat, unravel the mystery of their own destiny, and save the universe from its impending doom. *Inspector Moustachio* and *Inspector Girl* are their names, and solving mysteries is their specialty!

Join Inspector Jake Moustachio, his sister, Alexa (a.k.a. Inspector Girl), her precious pet guinea pig, Sandy, and the one and only Rex the cat in their next spooky misadventure...

IF YOU ENJOYED

THE CURSE OF SHIPWRECK BOTTOM

BE SURE TO READ

BOOK ONE
The Case of Stolen Time
ISBN 9780979087899

BOOK TWO
The Mystery at Comanche Canyon
ISBN 9780979087882

AND DISCOVER THE REST
OF THE MISADVENTURES!

Look for
The Misadventures of Inspector Moustachio
series at your local bookstores and libraries, or order online.

Published By
Community
PRESS

239 Windbrooke Lane, Virginia Beach VA 23462

About the Author

Wayne Madsen

Wayne Madsen is a dad from New Jersey. In 2007, he was nationally recognized as a **Reading is Fundamental (RIF)** booklist pick author for the first book in *The Misadventures of Inspector Moustachio* series.

Book one, **The Case of Stolen Time**, book two, **The Mystery of Comanche Canyon**, and book three, **The Curse of Shipwreck Bottom**, have become must-reads on school and library reading lists.

The Misadventures of Inspector Moustachio series is also a celebrated winner of the distinguished **iParenting Media Award**, a **Disney Interactive Group Media Property**.

Wayne's inspiration for writing comes from the real-life antics and misadventures of his children, Jake and Alexa. Adding in the escapades of the Madsen's crazy pets, Wayne has created an amazing universe of unforgettable characters who have become favorites on family bookshelves everywhere.

Wayne has just completed the fourth book in *The Misadventures of Inspector Moustachio* series, **The Secret of the Pharaoh's Feline**. He is currently working on book five, **The Mishap with the Mad Scientist**.

Printed in the United States
207647BV00006B/15/P

Pigs, Piggies and Piglets

Edited by
Susan Fortunato and
Giema Tsakuginow

LONGMEADOW PRESS

We gratefully acknowledge the following artists and representatives for letting us use their work: Mike Wepplo, Gay Bumgarner, Scott Anderson, Debra E. Arnold, Scott Pollack, William Akunevicz, Jr., Jerry Howard, Cynthia Watts Clarke, Bryant Haynes, Lisa Palombo, The Den of Antiquities, Stockworks, Eileen Moss Representative, Positive Images, The Image Bank, and Artworks.

HOG WILD ③

Cover design by Barbara Cohen Aronica and Jan Halper Scaglia
Interior design by Barbara Cohen Aronica

ISBN: 0-681-41573-8
Printed in Singapore
First Edition
0 9 8 7 6 5 4 3 2 1

To Chris & Graham

"The time has come," the Walrus said,
  "To talk of many things:
Of shoes—of ships—and sealing wax
  of cabbages—and kings—
And why the sea is boiling hot—
  And whether pigs have wings."

> —*Lewis Carroll,*
> *Through the Looking Glass,*
> *1871*

■ 9 ■

Pro-Pigganda

Pigs Are Not Stupid

It is well documented, although still not well received, that a pig's intelligence is far more comparable to that of a dolphin than of a horse or a cow.

Pigs Are Not Dirty

The image of the pig wallowing in mud has probably done more to hold the pig back from becoming a premiere household pet than any other misconception. But wallowing serves an important purpose. It protects the skin from sun and insects. A pig's skin is very delicate, much like our own, and pigs have very few sweat glands, so it is vital that they keep themselves protected and cool in the hot sun.

Pigs Are Not Greedy

When trained, a pig is just a loyal and well mannered as a cocker spaniel. The writer Milan Kundera wrote in his novel *The Unbearable Lightness of Being* about a pig, Mefisto, and his relationship with a man, Tomas.

> *The collective farm chairman became a truly close friend. He had a wife, four children, and a pig he raised like a dog. The pig's name was Mefisto, and he was the pride and the main attraction of the village. He would answer his master's call and was always clean and pink; he paraded about on his hoofs like a heavy-thighed woman in high heels.*

Some, like the Roman poet Horace, were early advocates of the pig's virtues. In fact,   he was so won over by the virtues of the pig that he described himself as "a shining pig from the herd of Epicurus."

There exists perhaps in all creation no animal which has less justice and more injustice shown him than the pig.

—*Sir Francis Bond Head*

Myth Piggies

The pig always inspires passion. An unlikely hero, it
lacks the strength of the ox and the grace of the horse,
and he is certainly too cute and pink to present a
convincing threat. Yet the pig's place in mythology and
legend is almost universal. Maybe it is the duality of
pigs that makes them so appealing to the collective
imagination.

The paradise of my fancy is one where pigs have wings.

—*G.K. Chesterton*

Ancient Greek Pigs

In ancient Greece the sow symbolized fertility and was
an important part of religious ceremonies and tradition.
Demeter, the goddess of corn, was often represented as
a sow. Even the Eleusinian mysteries, which were
celebrated by both the Greeks and the Romans, and are
still shrouded in secrecy, had the sow playing a major
role. The Romans also identified the pig with the
goddess Maia, calling the pig *maialis*, or the one dear
to the heart of Maia.

The Swine Who Would Be Swine

Perhaps the most famous Greek legend of the pig is in the *Odyssey*. Ulysses had just witnessed all but one of his ships destroyed by the Laestrygones when his ship came to the island of Aiaie and he sent a party of his men to explore. He didn't realize that the island was run by a beautiful witch named Circe who turned all men who dared come onto her island into beasts. When she saw Ulysses's men, she turned them into swine, but kept their human minds so they would be aware of this state.

One of Ulysses's men managed to escape and tell him the fate of his companions. Ulysses started out alone for Circe's house, but on his way he encountered Hermes. Hermes gave Ulysses an herb that would stop Circe's magic, so that later, when Circe used her magic and Ulysses was able to resist, Circe fell in love with him and agreed to release all of his men.

Some versions of the story, however, have Ulysses's men convincing him not to restore them to men at all, but to let them remain pigs. This is the version we pig lovers like to hear.

Pigs see the wind.

—Wiltshire saying

You Lucky Pig

Legend has it that Buddha, upon leaving the Earth, summoned all the animals to him. The pig was the last of twelve to appear. Persons born in a Year of the Pig can consider themselves to have the qualities of a pig—patience and a balanced disposition.

According to the Chinese horoscope, 1995 will be a Year of the Pig.

Watch Out for the P–I–G!

Some cultures won't even say the **P** word. The Scotch called them "the short-legged ones," "the grunting animal," or the "grunters." In the Talmud the pig is referred to as *davaraher*, the Hebrew phrase for "another thing," and observant Jews are not supposed to mention the pig. To this day, some fisherman in Nova Scotia are so frightened of this curse that they would bring their boat into the dock if anyone on board mentioned a pig.

Good Luck to you
on St Patrick's Day.

Good Fortune
on St Patrick's Day.

Pig Pals

To market, to market, to buy a fat pig,
Home again, home again, jiggety-pig.

We have been cheering on the pig since we were old
enough to turn the pages of The Three Little Pigs, so
it should come as no surprise that some of the most
influential political, spiritual, and literary figures were
also porcinophiles. Reading about the pig's role in
history, how can you help but wonder what the dog's
résumé would look like in comparison?

Hollywood Hogs

Porky Pig
Piggly Wiggly
Miss Piggy

Arnold the Pig

A generation of Americans cannot conceive of a
week passing in their youth without the melodious strains of
Green Acres. For many of us, our relationship with the three
little pigs was eclipsed by our bond with Arnold Ziffel, the
TV-watching adopted pig son of a living and
supportive Hooterville family. Arnold was
truly a pig's pig.

A person who has an affection for pigs is called a porcinophile.

The Most Expensive Pig

Glacier, a Duroc boar was sold to Wilbert and Myron Meinhart of Hudson, Iowa for $42,500 February 24, 1979.

Famous Friends of Pigs

Some of the more famous porcinophiles:

James Dean
Thomas à Becket
James Taylor
Sir Walter Scott
Michael Korda

The Saint-Pig Connection

St. Anthony

The most important pig lover of all was St. Anthony, the first
Christian monk. As a young man, St. Anthony began to
practice an acetic life. During his years of solitary prayer and
meditation, he was often tested by Satan, who once came to
him in the form of a grunting, thrashing pig. St. Anthony did
not slay the pig, who tore at him with his horns and teeth.
Instead, he prevailed with his calm faith. Then a wondrous
light enveloped him, driving the demon away, leaving him in
the company of a humble, innocent pig.

In years to come, European monks would select certain pigs to
be spared from slaughter. They would tie bells around the
pig's necks and go out seeking alms with the pigs at their side.
The pigs became known as "tantony" pigs in honor of
St. Anthony the patron saint of pigs.

Several other saints have been aided in their holy ascents by our portly friends. Here is a list of how pigs have assisted them:

Saint	*Pig Connection*
St. Brannoc	Sow and piglet led him to future church site
St. Kentigern	Pig tilled the land where his church was built
St. Malo	The Saint healed pig and got land for his church from the pig's grateful owner
St. Oswald	Pig moved church construction to site where Saint died

This little piggy went to
   market;
This little pig stayed home;
This little pig had roast beef;
This little pig had none;
And this little pig cried, Wee,
   wee, wee!
All the way home.

Askel Gedee of Denmark was the proud owner of the largest litter of
piglets in the world: 34, born June 25–26, 1961.

The Hail Piggy Play

During the English Civil War the royalist army was laying siege to the city of Gloucester. The city was near collapse until, in a last desperate gambit, the last remaining pig was sent squealing along the perimeter of the city. The king, imagining a multitude of pigs, and ample stores for the city to continue holding out, withdrew his army.

Sébastien Le Prestre, Comte de Vauban
(1633–1707), Piggy Banker

How many pigs would a pregnant sow parent, grandparent, and great-grandparent in a ten–year period? This question and many more were answered by this French nobleman and military engineer who calculated that a pregnant sow and her children would increase the pig population by 6,434,338 in a mere decade. This led Vauban to conclude that if you could buy one animal with which to make your fortune, it should be a pig.

The gestation period for a pig is three months, three weeks and three days.

Pigpourri

Truffles

In a world of processed cheese and indoor grills, it's good to remember that some of the best things in life are inconvenient. The pig, in his relentless pursuit of his favorite fungi, reminds us of this as often as he can.

These rare mushrooms grow at the base of certain oak trees and can be harvested between November and March. The pig has traditionally been used to find the elusive truffles. He is so fond of them and his sense of smell so developed that he can root out their scent. Unfortunately for their human companions, the pigs, having found their prize are loath to surrender their delicacies, even for the going rate of about $300 a pound.

The most prized truffles come from the Perigord region of France. They are a deep black, in comparison with the Italian "white" truffle, which is really dark brown or beige.

"P Stands for Pig"

P stands for Pig, as I remarked before,
A second cousin to the Huge Wild Boar
But pigs are civilised, while Huge Wild Boars
Live savagely, at random, out of doors,
And in their coarse contempt of dainty foods,
Subsist on truffles, which they find in woods.
Not so the cultivated Pig who feels
The need of several courses at his meals,
But wrongly thinks it does not matter whether
He takes them one by one or all together.
Hence, Pigs devour, from lack of self respect,
what Epicures would certainly reject.

MORAL:
Learn from the Pig to take whatever Fate
Or Elder Persons heap upon your plate.

Hilaire Belloc, A Bad Child's Book of Beasts, 1940

Pig-tionary

Shoat—A young pig

Pig—A small domestic animal

Hog—A pig that weighs over 120 pounds

Boar—An adult male

Sow—An adult female

Swine—Pigs, hogs, boars, and sows.

Mud Baths in Bath

In 863 B.C. the city of Bath was founded on the site where Baldred was cured of leprosy. Baldred's father, the king of the Britons, had sent him to study in Greece, but while there he was struck with leprosy. He returned to England, but was only fit to be a swineherd because of his disease. He noticed that the pigs wallowed in the mud, and their skin problems seemed to be minimized.

The mud bath was born, and Baldred's leprosy was cured.

The sow came in with the saddle
The little pig rocked the cradle,
The dish jumped up on the table
To see the pot swallow the ladle.

There was an old man of Messina
Whose daughter was named Opsibeena;
She wore a small wig,
and rode out on a pig,
To the perfect delight of Messina.

Edward Lear, More Nonsense, 1872

Pigs may whistle,
   but they ha'e an
      ill mouth for't.

—Scottish proverb

PALUMBO

In the Hindu religion, the boar represents the third incarnation of Vishnu. In a thousand-year battle to save the world from evil, the boar, Varaha, dived down to the bottom of the ocean and saved the earth. In Indian art, he is shown balancing the world on his tusks.

Piggy Poet

W.B. Yeats, perhaps the greatest modern poet, was also the father of pig poetry publishing poems such as the "Valley of the Black Pig" and "Swine of the Gods."

How you say pig?

Language	Word for Pig
French	cochon
German	schwein
Italian	maiale
Spanish	puerco
Japanese	buta
Danish	gris
Turkish	domuz
Romanian	porc
Portugese	leito
Serbo-croatian	syinja

In Ireland it was considered good luck to have a pig driven into your house on the first of May, but bad luck the rest of the year.

Pig Places

Pigs is Pigs
—Ellis Parker Butler

If pigs is pigs, pig places are definitely the places for pig collectors and enthusiasts to be!

Where Pigs Stay
The Mansions
San Francisco, CA
(415) 929-9444

The Pig Store
Hog Wild !
7 Faneuil Hall Marketplace
Boston, MA 02109
(617) 523-PIGS

Pig Labels
Colorful Images
6711 Winchester Circle
Boulder, CO 80301

This company sells, by mail and fax, address labels that feature pig drawings and photographs. Prices from 300 labels for $4.95 to 144 labels for $6.95.